praise for Michael Guillebeau's **Emerald Coast: Free Money.**

"...edgy and fun, with raunchiness and innuendo. Characters are intensely inhabited...
— *Foreword Reviews*

praise for Michael Guillebeau's **MAD Librarian (2017 Foreword Review Indie Award for Humor Book of the Year)**

"Guillebeau blends humor and mystery perfectly in this comic thriller...Guillebeau keeps things light with frequent laugh-out-loud lines."
— *Publishers Weekly*

praise for Michael Guillebeau's **Josh Whoever (Library Journal Mystery Debut of the Month)**

". . . the collection of oddball minor characters and surprise twists deepen an already strong story. An engrossing debut. Mystery Debut of the Month."
— *Library Journal*

Emerald Coast: Free Money

Michael Guillebeau

Madison Press
Madison, Alabama

Published by Madison Press
Madison, Alabama
madisonpresspublishing@gmail.com

Book Layout © 2017 BookDesignTemplates.com
Cover Design by Donna Cunningham of Beaux Arts.
Author Photo by Randall Bachmeyer.
Rel02142019

Emerald Coast: Free Money by Michael Guillebeau. -- 1st ed.
ISBN: 978-0-9972055-4-1

dedication

To all the sunburned honest beach people, and particularly to the Beach Girl herself.

LIZZIE HAD NEVER in her life taken a thing that didn't belong to her, and this is where it got her: grouchy from being up too early, tired from staying up too late—and the wig itched like hell. It was just her luck to get stuck wearing a god-damned cheap, sweaty, platinum blonde wig while going out into the searing Florida Panhandle heat and back into freezing hotel rooms. Over and over, all day long, trying to save money working on minimum wage cleaning rooms at the Emerald Coast Beach Hilton.

She tapped on the door to room 415 twice.

"Housekeeping," she said in a clear, cheerful voice, the way the corporate trainer had told her.

There was no sound from the room. She stepped inside to the residue of a night of joy and margaritas and coconut oil—just like every other Florida hotel room. She peeled the gloves off her clammy hands and took the wig off to scratch her head. In the mirror, an angry young woman with a bright red mohawk and brown stubble on each side of her head stared back at her.

The mohawk had worked when she was in Los Angeles. There it was all about attitude and style. Lizzie Borden had been the future of rock and roll and she strutted out there, a cute, ballsy, fresh-faced little girl doing Florida blues rock with an L.A. edge to it. Both the crowds and the suits told her she was the new Janis Joplin.

Critics loved her first album. But then the record company was sold, and the new owner didn't love her. He pulled the album, kept the rights to Lizzie's music and her name, and told her she could buy it all back for a hundred thousand dollars.

So here she was, standing in front of a mirror in a dirty hotel room back in her hometown, trying to save up a hundred grand on minimum wage, pushing the cleaning cart around every day with a notebook tucked under the towels. She'd pull it out when new songs came to her, get the song down, and get the room cleaned fast. She couldn't afford to get fired.

The wig was the hotel's idea: No tattoos, no weird hair or piercings. The Hilton was a five-star hotel. So, she stopped shaving the sides of her head a couple of days ago.

To hell with it all, she thought. *I'm a maid now, not a singer. Get over it.*

As she finished the room, a line popped into her head. She started singing quietly, and then added a twist, a little downbeat blues riff with an angry vibe laid on top. Then she was jumping on the bed in front of the mirror, holding an invisible microphone, singing the song low to stay out of trouble, but singing it. Someday, she'd sing this one loud.

She hopped down and looked back in the mirror. The defiant red streak of hair burned straight and true through the brown bristles on the sides of her head.

"The hell with someday," she told the mirror. "I'm shaving the sides tonight. After all, I'm the queen of rock and roll."

She pulled the wig back on, smoothed the bed, and stepped out the door before pushing her cart to room 417.

The door was not quite closed. She knocked and called out the same robotic "Housekeeping." The unlatched door made her nervous, but she pushed in anyway.

The smell hit her as soon as she opened the door. The room looked unused, except for a closed suitcase and an open overnight bag on the dresser.

"Housekeeping?" she called out again, hoping someone would answer and she could leave the room for the afternoon girl.

No one answered. She propped the door open with the cart and looked down at the open bag. It was filled with neat stacks of crisp hundred-dollar bills in paper wrappers, more money than she had ever seen. She stared at it for a moment, and then pulled her eyes away.

She tiptoed to the foot of the bed and peeked into the bathroom where the smell seemed to be coming from. There was nothing there but tiny bottles of unopened shampoo and unused towels. Maybe she could back out carefully and not have to clean at all. Get this room for free.

On her way out, she tripped over something at the edge of the bed and jumped. There was a man in a suit lying on the floor in the narrow space beside the bed and the bathroom wall.

"Sir?" she whispered. She looked at his head, which was lying in a pool of black-red blood and featured a neat hole in the middle of his forehead.

"Sir?" Her voice cracked. Lizzie leaned over and checked his neck for a pulse, and jumped back when she found his skin was already cold. She stood rooted in place for a minute with her hand over her mouth and her brain churning.

Lizzie had never in her life taken a thing that didn't belong to her.

She took the money.

THE TWO DETECTIVES STUDYING the body were an odd pair: John Blackbeard, who stood closest to the victim, looked like the old Florida native he was: grizzled and old, short and scrawny, wearing the same dark suit that he wore every day. Brad Terry, tall and young, looking like an MTV producer's idea of a square-jawed detective in a white linen suit and pastel T-shirt, stood on tip-toes, peeking over Blackbeard's shoulder to see the body in room 417.

Blackbeard leaned over and said, "Huh." Terry shifted for a better view and saw the body of a heavy-set guy with thinning hair, an expensive suit with no tie, and a neat bloody hole in the middle of his forehead. His eyes were open and his mouth hung open, too. Looks surprised, thought Terry. Maybe he was.

"One shot to the head," Terry said. "No struggle. Pro."

Blackbeard squatted down and edged the jacket back with a pen, looking for a wallet.

A uniformed officer leaning against the room's doorway said, "That what you brought the kid for? Solve the crime for you?"

Blackbeard stood up and shot the uniform a tired, flat look.

"Brandon, this is my partner Terry. Terr, this is my cousin Brandon, cousin on my mother's side."

"You the new guy?" said Brandon, giving Terry a cool look, trying to establish the upper hand even though Terry was a detective and Brandon still a uniform.

"Been here over a year now," said Terry. "Longer than half the people in ECB, way people come and go down here. What I got to do to stop being the new guy?"

"Tell us what year you graduated from Bay High School, and who the homecoming queen was. Then tell us lies about how she used to take you down to the beach before there were any condos."

Terry stiffened and started to say something but Blackbeard stepped around him and motioned him to the body.

"See what you can find out," said Blackbeard.

Terry squatted, his quads a little sore from last night's workout, and fished out the wallet from inside the coat.

Flipped the wallet open. "Albert Vincent Keeper," he said. "Or so says the license." He straightened up to stretch his legs. "Credit cards. Plenty of money." He looked at Blackbeard. "Doesn't look like robbery."

Blackbeard frowned. "Don't get ahead of the facts." Then Blackbeard turned and looked around the room. "You ever see anything like this?"

Terry followed Blackbeard's eyes. "Class," he said.

"Too fancy for my tastes," said Blackbeard.

"Three times the size of any hotel room I've ever stayed in," said Terry. "Better furniture than I'll ever have. TV's so big you could probably show that football player from Alabama, the big kid, life size. Show him eating a quarterback for breakfast, spitting out the bones. I feel like jumping on the bed."

"Don't." Blackbeard scowled back at Brandon. "Who made the bed? I keep telling you uniforms, nobody touches anything 'til I get there."

Brandon held up his hands. "Hey, we got it. The room's the way Jerry, first guy in, found it. Nothing touched. Other than Jerry and the ME, and Eric the tech, no one's been in the room without gloves and those cute little paper booties you make us wear."

"So who made the bed?"

Brandon stiffened, flipped open his notebook. "Damned if I know. Maybe we should call a real detective who knows one end from the other. Look, call came in at 1:12 in the PM. Jerry got here at 1:15. Maid's name, the one who found the body and ran out screaming, is Evonda DeFuniak. Before you ask, don't know if she's related to folks up in DeFuniak Springs or not. She's downstairs, hoping y'all will solve the crime on the spot so you won't have to bother her with questions. Maybe she made the bed. Damned if I know.

"All I know to tell you real detectives is this: you got a white male with one shot through the forehead over there in front of you. Maybe he never slept in the bed. Again, damned if I know, call a detective. Manager says he checked in yesterday evening for a three-day stay he reserved a week ago. Registered as Albert Keeper, like your boy says. So far, no next of kin or occupation, but maybe you real detectives can figure that out."

Terry had had it with this guy's attitude and was going to say something, but Blackbeard turned back to him.

"So, what do you think?" Blackbeard said to Terry. Terry saw that Blackbeard was going to give him a chance to show off in front of the patrol officers standing in the door by making the initial assessment. He took a step back, to the foot of the bed.

"Shooter stood here." He raised his hand, pointed his finger like a gun. "No signs of a struggle. Doesn't look like robbery."

He looked at the dresser. "One suitcase, a small one. Doesn't look like it's even been opened."

He looked back at Keeper. "Bet we won't even get powder from the vic's hands. Happened too fast for him to even raise them up. So the vic trusted the shooter. Maybe a friend, maybe even a girl. Who knows? One shot to the head, close. Betting it's a twenty-two, as the slug's still in the head and there's no splatter on the wall behind. Pro's weapon, pro's style."

He looked at Blackbeard. "If I were back in Chicago, I'd say this was a mob hit."

Blackbeard smiled and shook his head. "Can't be. You know we don't have real criminals down here in Emerald Coast Beach, playground of the South. Just drunk college kids on spring break. Ask the chamber of commerce. No murders, just fun, fun, fun."

"Why I came here from Chicago," said Terry. "Saw a Girls Gone Wild video, looked like ECB was a fun place to be."

Blackbeard stared and waited for Terry's mind to get back to work.

Terry looked around. "If the shooter took anything, he didn't have to rummage around for it. No sign the shooter was here long, no glasses or food sitting out, bed not rumpled by one of them sitting on it. Only a guess, but I'd say in and out, pop him and walk away."

Blackbeard said, "Rumpled? I like that word. Sounds like you're writing your life story again." He turned to Brandon. "How come the maid didn't come 'til one? Mr. Hilton too lazy to clean his rooms in the morning like the Motel 6's that poor folks like me can afford to stay at?"

Brandon shrugged, still looking for a fight. He opened his mouth to say something but Blackbeard interrupted him. "Yeah, yeah, I got it. Damned if you know. Thanks for the help."

"You can be a pain, you know, Blackie," said Brandon.

"I want us to do our jobs. All of us." Blackbeard locked eyes with Brandon and held him with a flat, emotionless stare, like some kind of reptile, until Brandon broke it off and muttered something too quiet for them to hear.

"What's that?" said Terry. "Speak up when you're talking to Senior Detective Blackbeard."

Brandon looked up defiant. "I said, maybe the chief should hire some hotshot kid out of Chicago to come down and teach Blackie and us country boys how to handle homicides."

Blackbeard had turned back to the room, working the case, ignoring Brandon.

Terry took an aggressive step toward Brandon. "That's Detective Blackbeard, to you, on the job," he said. "Not Blackie. Don't care if you're one of his cousins or what. He's the senior officer on scene here, and deserves respect. Only thing he's ever done to piss you people off is solve homicides that some didn't want solved, and insist that ECBPD act like real cops instead of tourist babysitters."

"It's OK, partner," said Blackbeard. "I don't need defending."

Terry walked to the window, looking down at the floor to be sure he didn't step on anything important. He gazed out the window at the stretch of perfect white sand that ECB was famous for. It was October, and most of the tourists had gone home. Nothing but a few early snowbirds and late-season couples walking the white sand of the beach or standing waist-deep in the clear, blue-green water.

Emerald Coast Beach was a small town of ten thousand honest and dishonest citizens trying to make a living from the millions of tourists who vacationed there in the summer. Terry looked to the left and saw the pastel shops of the Pier Mall Shopping Center that he and Blackbeard had driven through, and thought how things can change in a heartbeat. Ten minutes ago, he had been finishing a plate of barbecued shrimp, complaining to Blackbeard about how calls always came in while they were eating.

It was an empty complaint, though. Serious calls were few and far between in a small beach town where a big crime was arresting a drunk college kid for running up and down the beach naked at two am yelling, "War Damn Eagle." Unlike Chicago, he spent more time down here chasing seafood and barbecue than chasing murderers. But then a call like this would come in and everything would change.

He looked back at Keeper's body, the man's last heartbeat gone in one terrible moment. Yeah, things change.

He heard Sarah, the medical examiner, talking to Blackbeard behind him. "I'd say he's been dead twelve or fourteen hours if I had to guess. Know more once I open him up."

Blackbeard turned to the tech, Eric, who was dusting for prints, and pointed to the do not disturb sign hanging on the outside of the door. "Hey, don't forget this."

Eric nodded back.

"And get pictures up and down the hallway, too. Probably nothing, but everything's nothing until it's something."

Eric shrugged and Terry knew where this would go. Blackbeard would demand that the techs take their time on every little detail. The tech boss would complain later about the overtime it took and Blackbeard's lieutenant would talk to Blackbeard about easing up. This was ECB, for Christ's sake, not a big city with a budget for big crimes. But nothing would change: Blackbeard got to be a pain in the butt because he and Terry were ECB's only homicide detectives and Blackbeard had always solved cases—when they had them.

"Next?" said Terry.

Blackbeard sighed. "We got the manager and the maid. Let's start with the manager, then work the security video when we're done with the two of them."

Terry struck a dramatic pose by the window and started to say something.

"Sweet Jesus Christ, no," said Blackbeard, looking at the pose.

"Got to have a line to set the scene."

Blackbeard stared. "We don't need one of your Captain America, lets-go-save-the-world lines like you always want to come up with. This ain't no TV show."

"Hey, a man's dead," said Terry. "We're on a mission for justice to protect the little guy. We need a line to set the tone. It's important to see your life as a story with a meaning and write your own script. Otherwise, you're just drifting along with no purpose, wondering what you're doing out here every day."

"So you think Keeper is the innocent little guy here?" said Blackbeard. "In a mob hit?"

"Big guy, little guy, bad guy, good guy, doesn't matter." Terry found his pose, jaw jutted out and eyes narrowed. "Everybody matters, or nobody matters."

Blackbeard looked like someone had served him a bowl of rancid sushi when he had ordered fried shrimp. "You ain't no Harry Bosch," he snapped. "Don't steal from Michael Connelly. Ain't right for a cop to steal."

"So what's our line then?" Terry asked.

"How about, do your job?" Blackbeard spun and stalked out the door with his head down. Terry scurried to catch up.

three

BLACKBEARD AND TERRY GOT NOTHING new
from the manager and asked him where they could find the
maid.

"Which one? You want the early maid, Elizabeth Gaffney,
or the late maid, Evonda DeFuniak?"

"One that found the body."

"That'd be Evonda, the late maid."

"How do I find her?"

The manager laughed, "Question is, how can you miss
her?"

He waved at a door.

"That way to the beach. If your eyes don't find her right
away, look for all my beach boys. Supposed to be out there
pushing drinks on paying customers, but for some reason
they think they need to check on a hotel maid every thirty
seconds." The manager's phone rang and he turned to answer
it. "You'll figure it out."

Blackbeard said, "Huh" and Terry looked at him and
smiled. They walked out through the lobby past a tired man
and woman trailed by what seemed like a dozen kids dragging
suitcases and pool toys to the registration desk. Terry stopped
for a minute, looked at them and tried to figure out their
story, then hurried to catch up with Blackbeard.

They stepped out onto the concrete patio and Blackbeard stopped to get his bearings. To their right was a large pool shaped like a figure eight with two islands, one of them with a waterfall and a swim up bar. Ahead and to the left was a tiki hut that rented beach chairs and sold tickets for parasail rides. Blackbeard took a step toward the guy in the hut to ask for directions but Terry caught his elbow and pointed toward the beach.

A line of blue Hilton beach umbrellas was planted in the sand along the waterline. Nearest to them, a couple of kids splashed in the flat blue-green water, and a woman with a floppy pink hat in a lounge chair read a Stephanie Plum book while keeping an eye on the kids. Up the beach, one lounge chair sat alone with no umbrella and a small, whitewashed wooden table on either side. Two college-aged boys jostled for attention on one side of the chair but the woman propped up in a chaise lounge, eyes closed with a pose that said she had found the perfect sun angle and wasn't going to change it for anyone, never opened her eyes.

Terry and Blackbeard trudged across the beach with the pure white Gulf sugar sand squishing into their dress shoes. Terry knew that people were staring at the two guys in jackets, but he was focused on the woman in the lone lounge chair. She was young and black, impossibly dark-skinned and long-legged, model-thin with big breasts, face up to the sun like a queen on a throne, maybe Cleopatra. Like Cleopatra looked—if Cleopatra ever wore a tiny white bikini with the top and bottom pushed down as far as the law would allow.

The college boys scattered like sea gulls as Blackbeard and Terry approached. The woman opened one bored eye and took in Blackbeard. The eye then turned to Terry. She opened both eyes and smiled at him.

"Well, well, well," she said. "The fuzz."

Terry smiled back. "I haven't heard that line since last night on TV."

"Must have been an old *Starsky & Hutch*." She stretched lazily, like a lioness, and looked at Terry. Terry looked to see if any of the bits of white cloth shifted enough, but they hadn't—quite. She caught him looking and gave him a smile that said, yeah, I can eat you up any time I want.

"Maybe *Miami Vice*," she said, "looking at those threads."

"Are you Evonda DeFuniak?" said Blackbeard.

"The one," she said to Blackbeard. Then she turned back to Terry and said with a big smile, "and only."

Blackbeard pointed at the drinks on the table, sweat dripping down their sides. "Are you old enough for these?"

"Maybe he could search me for my ID," she said, dangling a hand at Terry. But Terry had stopped smiling, following Blackbeard's lead and getting down to business.

"I haven't touched them." She turned back to Blackbeard. "The beach boys like to bring them to me. They always say one of the tourists ordered the drink and changed his mind. Funny how often that happens, even if nobody else is on the beach. If I drank a tenth of what they bring me, I'd stay plastered all day and couldn't work."

"I thought you finished your work for the day?"

"Not that work. Modeling. I do the maid thing for a few hours in the middle of the day, mostly so I can tan out here after I'm done." She gave Terry a smirk. "You think black girls don't tan? Dark-skinned exotics are in demand now. Got a shoot out in Rosemary Beach at sunset for a fake wedding for a line of formal shops. Fake bride might be blonde, but they want me in the shot to show how broad-minded and worldly she is."

Blackbeard finished writing her name in his notebook.

"Thank you, Miss DeFuniak," he said, keeping his eyes on the notebook. "Can you tell us about today, ma'am?"

She sighed and got down to business. "Like I told the officer, I walked into the room and screamed, and I ran out."

"I need you to start earlier, ma'am. Start when you got up this morning and came to work. We'll get to the room itself soon enough."

"Yes, sir. Well, my roommate Jenny woke me up early, about nine o'clock. Jenny doesn't like to sleep late, doesn't like anybody else to sleep when she's awake. I like to stay up; why I took this cleanup shift. Only work for a couple of hours and hit the beach." She looked at Terry and winked. "No tan lines."

While Terry was wondering what she meant by that, she went on with Blackbeard. Soon Terry felt like he was drowning in details. He wasn't sure why it was important to know whether her waffle had blueberries or those cute little M&Ms, but Evonda liked to talk and Blackbeard liked to take notes. Every time she started to wind down and leave even a minute out, Blackbeard prodded her for more details. Finally, they got to room 417.

"So this was the sixth room you had done so far today?" Blackbeard was counting the room numbers she had given him, making sure it added up.

"Yes, sir. There were only ten on my list today, so I thought, 'Half done.'"

"Then what?"

"I got to the door and saw the do not disturb sign on the door. I knocked twice, called out 'housekeeping,' waited, knocked again louder, called out again, louder. Used the pass-key. The smell got worse. Went to check the bathroom and saw the dead man lying on the floor by the bed like something out of a horror movie. I screamed like I was an extra in the movie. Turned and ran out the door. Left the cart behind and punched the elevator button like I was Mike Tyson. Waited about two seconds for the elevator before I took off running down the stairs. I didn't stop until I got down to the desk and Yolanda and Andrew got Mr. Peterson and they went back up. I didn't go with them."

"So what did you touch in the room?"

"Nothing. I swear I didn't touch anything at all."

"You must have touched the door handle."

"Well, of course I touched the door handle."

"OK, I'm sorry about being so picky, but I need to get every detail right. Let's walk through the room, carefully, step by step."

Evonda nodded her head and closed her eyes. "Got it. OK, pushed the door lever down, pushed the door open a crack. Said, 'housekeeping' and then pushed the door open the rest of the way. Bad smell then. Stepped into the room, right foot first."

The sun went behind a cloud and she frowned at the cloud.

"Took a couple of steps past the bed towards the bath. Probably didn't touch the dresser, 'cause if you get a finger-print on something, you have to clean it. This room looked unused. I was hoping to get out without much work. But end of the bed, there's a foot sticking out, one shiny black shoe. I looked past the bed and saw him. Then I screamed and ran like hell. I could have touched anything then. Oh wait, I know I touched the door from the inside to pull it open more. Does that help?"

It was getting hot on the beach. Terry felt the sweat creeping up through his white linen suit, turning his cool look into a sticky mess. He looked at Blackbeard, who had sweat on him too, but didn't seem to notice. He just stood there expressionless, as he always did with witnesses. Showing no emotion or interest, he could have been a robot-like census worker asking the required questions from the form on his notebook.

Terry smiled at Evonda but talked to Blackbeard. "You have found what is known as a kindred spirit, Blackbeard. No detail too small." He flashed his best Hollywood smile at Evonda, the one he used when he might want something from someone. He decided he did want something. "That's the most detailed description I have ever heard from a witness."

She smiled back at him and Terry wondered if she was flirting, or toying, with them.

"Thank you, sir," she said.

Terry thought, the smile's a good sign. The 'sir' was a little deflating, though. He thought of his next line, but Blackbeard closed his notebook and gave Terry a look.

"Well, I think we're done here, miss," he said. As he started to walk away Blackbeard added, "Oh, one more thing I need to get straight. Don't y'all usually clean up earlier? Why wasn't the room cleaned in the morning?"

"I'd be out of a job if we could get them all cleaned in the morning," she said. "Or at least I'd have to go back to morning shift. See, morning shift maid tries to clean them all early. But if the people are still in the room, or if the do not disturb sign is on the door, they leave it for me."

Blackbeard nodded and Terry handed her a business card. She touched it to her lips and locked eyes with him. He was about to ask her for her number when she looked at the card and frowned.

"Now see," she said. "I would have designed a card for you better than this, more style. I'd have your name bigger, show how important you are. Make the ECBPD logo small and tasteful." She laughed, still locked onto him. "You didn't know I was smart, too, did you? In high school, my design teacher said I had a future. Could have had a college scholarship, too, probably could still get one. But I decided then and there I was going to be a big-time model. Spend my life posing and partying."

Terry looked at her and his smile faded. He thought of the burned-out women he saw at night in the ECB bars, women who had owned the world when they were young and pretty and thought they could make it as models or actresses. But once time and alcohol had done their job they had nothing left. He looked at Evonda and didn't see the woman, but the girl Evonda's father probably saw: a cute little girl playing dress up in a woman's body who would have nothing to trade when the cuteness was gone.

Terry frowned and said, "You really ought to look into the community college, Miss DeFuniak. Give you something to carry you through when times get tough."

She laughed like she didn't believe him. "So I should call them, and not you, tonight, then? You don't like to party?"

"Call me when you've got a year of college under your belt."

He turned and walked away across the beach, slipping deeper into the sand and aging with every step.

"I DON'T WANT NOTHING that's not mine," Lizzie said, staring into the fire in the trash drum. "I'm an honest woman." Through the flames, she could still see the black overnight bag that was on top of the burning pine straw and trash. The bag was finally starting to curl and catch fire. Soon it would be gone, and she could tell herself it had never happened.

Of course, the money wasn't burning up. The money was still in the boathouse, in the hidden space in the wall she had found after Daddy died. It was hard for her to know why a man who made his living running crab traps needed a secret hidey spot, but she had found it after he died. While she never figured out why it was there, it was coming in handy now.

She poked the fire again and added a handful of pine straw. She could let it all burn down while she fixed some dinner and ate. Then she would take the burned-down embers somewhere out in the water and dump them where they couldn't be found.

What am I missing?

She felt like a character in an Edgar Allen Poe story, the one where the guy killed someone and buried the body under his house and then went crazy imagining he could hear the body's heart beating. When she was driving home from the

Hilton with the bag under her seat, every car looked like cops to her, except the one guy screaming at her on Highway 79 when she was doing forty-six and everyone else was doing seventy. It didn't matter. She did the speed limit plus one all the way home. Kept the wig on, too. This was not the day to have her car searched for drugs because some redneck cop didn't like her hair.

What am I missing? She hadn't touched anything in the hotel room; she'd gone over that a hundred times in her head. She had picked up the bag in her left hand and taken two steps to the door. Put the bag in the hiding place under the towels with her notebook. Reached back, took the do not disturb sign from the inside door handle and moved it to the outside so she had a reason for saying why she skipped the room. She didn't touch the inside handle or the door. Then she closed the door and wiped the outside handle with a dirty towel.

She didn't see anybody either way in the hall. She then moved on down the hall and did the rest of her rooms, seven minutes on each room today. Then she pushed the cart down to the laundry room and left it there while she walked, not ran, to the locker room next door. On the way she hummed a bright, happy Bangles song to show anybody who might be listening that nothing was wrong. She then took her big purse to the cart and put the moneybag and her notebook inside, and carried it all back to her locker.

Maybe that was the flaw. She didn't think anyone had seen her, and probably no one would care if they did, but maybe someone had seen her, and maybe they did care. *Maybe, maybe.*

Then she had emptied the laundry and taken the cart back. She had gone to the office, smiled and told Yolanda she was finished thirty minutes early. Yolanda frowned and told her to empty the trash in the lobby before she left. Maybe that was her mistake. She had never smiled at Yolanda in her life and never volunteered for anything at the Hilton. Yolanda knew if Lizzie really did finish early, she would have gone around the back for a smoke break. Lizzie didn't smoke, had never liked what it did to a singer's voice. But she had learned quickly that smoking was the only way to take a break here, so she'd gotten used to standing in the little alcove with a lit Cool in her hand.

Telling Yolanda she had finished early was going to get her into trouble. Yolanda would remember. She imagined the desk clerk sitting in an interrogation room right now, the room filled with cold metal with one bright light shining on Yolanda, who would be smoking a cigarette.

"One more thing, Detective Wonderful," she could hear Yolanda saying. "There was this girl, a real bad seed, liked to wear disguises to cover up her criminal haircut. She lied to me about where she was the morning of the crime, the morning she undoubtedly killed that poor innocent man. Lied to my face. And she had this horrible expression, an expression I'd never seen on her, like she was trying to smile, but that girl don't know how to smile. Least not to me."

Lizzie thought about it and then relaxed. Not a problem, she realized. Yolanda would never put that many words together to help out anyone, especially the police. The only two things Yolanda knew how to say were, "Damned if I know, I look like Miss Google to you?" and "Get the hell out of here and go to work."

But I better go over the whole thing again one more time just to be sure. Let's see. I picked up the bag in my left hand, took two steps to the door . . .

The trash fire had gone out while she was thinking. She stirred it to be sure there was nothing recognizable left and went down to the dock while the fire cooled down. At the end of the dock she pulled up the line, hand over hand on the slimy nylon cord until the metal crab trap came out of the water and she set it dripping and filled with chattering crabs on the dock. It was a good catch: four jimmies, male crabs, and one sookie, a female. That was enough for a good dinner tonight, better than canned tuna or even the bluefish filets from the freezer in the garage. She released the sookie crab back onto the dock to go make more crab babies.

"Shoo 'way, momma," she said. "Daddy told me girl crabs belong to the water and you ain't mine."

The small crab waved it's claws at her, not intimidated at all, warning the big soft-skinned land creature to stay back, stay back or I'll tear you up, don't want to hurt you, but I'll rip you up for my babies' dinner if you come near me. Lizzie smiled at the crab as it scuttled away and hit the water with a splash.

Lizzie thought, *that's an album cover some day. A momma crab, claws up for a fight, on a dock with a big people shadow over the crab, maybe Lizzie's head on the crab. Call the album,* Rip You Up. *Yeah.*

She gathered the jimmies one by one, grabbing them from the back to avoid the claws and stacking them together until she could hold them all in one hand, eight claws waving angrily in the air. She checked the bait and threw the trap back for tomorrow.

She took the crabs into the house, careful not to even look at the boathouse, with all the money inside. She put the crabs in the big steamer and poured half a bottle of stale beer in and turned on the burner so the crabs would steam while she fixed the grits.

When it was all done she stood at the kitchen counter picking out crab meat, making a little pile of the white sweet meat speckled with orange Old Bay seasoning on a clean chipped plate. A little piece of orange shell snapped off in her fingers and jumped onto her shirt, and she left it there. This was the prized shirt, one of her last memories of Daddy.

When the Alabama Crimson Tide played for the national championship in 2016, Daddy met Lizzie in Phoenix to see both the game and her, driving his old pickup truck cross-country because he didn't trust airline pilots. Lizzie's agent got them two tickets to the game, the only good thing that agent ever did for her, and they went to the stadium and screamed their lungs out while the Tide rolled to championship number sixteen. Later, Daddy bought them matching T-shirts outside the stadium. Crimson of course, with a big number sixteen. He cut the sleeves off of hers with his folding knife, and they went out and got drunk together with thirty thousand other Tide fans that night. It was the first and last time they ever got drunk together.

Well, that Daddy knew about. There were plenty of times Lizzie had come home in high school after a night of drinking beer and singing with the pickup band in Donnie's garage down the road and found Daddy passed out in his work boat. She'd get a blanket from the house and push him around to make him comfortable. But you couldn't really count that as being drunk together.

This was her lucky concert shirt, back in LA. She washed it carefully and saved it for the really big gigs. And she wore it when she came home for a visit, standing in this same kitchen with Daddy. Once, she got a bite of egg on the shirt and stood at the sink washing it out and explaining to Daddy why the shirt was important.

Daddy laughed and said, "Clothes are for wearing. It's not yours 'til you've got a stain on it you can talk about." And he picked up the Tabasco bottle and started shaking red sauce on her like he was a kid with a water gun until she threw a half-full bottle of beer at his head but he could tell she was laughing and they were both laughing, the shirt a mess, but better now. No matter how many times she washed it after that it smelled of sweat and hot sauce. It smelled like her music, and it smelled like her.

She took the plate with crabmeat and fresh tomatoes and grits pink with hot sauce into the studio in the garage. She stood at the mic stand, eating bites when she could, singing the Stones' "Paint it Black," with the background track turned up so loud she had to scream to be heard above it. It was her warm-up song for writing, her I'm-mad-and-con-fused-and-don't-care-why song that would lead her to her own angry songs.

But not today. This time it led her to a quiet song, a song that would never make it to a CD. A song for Daddy. If Lizzie had known how to cry, she would have cried writing it. If her audience had ever heard it, they would have cried listening to it. But she hadn't cried in all her adult life, and an audience would never hear it, so there were no tears.

But there was a revelation: she knew what to do about the money. She would go see Captain Dave.

If she could do it soon enough.

She thought she heard a noise and went to the window and looked out. There. She heard it again, coming from the boathouse. She heard it now, as clear and loud and plain as anything that was real.

Bump-bump, bump-bump. The beating heart of the money called out to her, accusing her. "Bump-bump, bump-bump," said the money. "I don't belong to you."

BLACKBEARD AND TERRY SAT inside the video cave at the Hilton while a Hilton technician ran the video starting ten minutes before Keeper checked in. Terry had a laptop computer open in his lap and Blackbeard was holding a printout of the registration log from last night.

"There, hold it," Terry said to the tech. He stopped the video and the image froze on the eight by four array of LCD screens on the wall, each showing a different part of the hotel at the same time. Terry pointed at one.

"Family coming out of a room. Looks like seventh floor, right?"

"Yeah," said the technician.

"Any guess on the room number?"

"710-720 block. Call it 714."

Terry typed that into his netbook.

"Really," said the technician, "you don't need to write all this down. We'll give you the discs for all the video."

"It'll take days to go through all that carefully. I want this now," said Blackbeard. "Tonight and tomorrow, we're going to interview anybody who might have been in the halls, see what they saw. I particularly want to see if we can find anybody on the video we can't identify."

The technician sighed. He was on overtime already. Actually, unpaid overtime. Terry nodded him to continue and the technician sighed again, hit a button, and they all went back to watching mostly empty hallways at four times real time.

"You're a fraud," said Blackbeard, keeping his eyes on the screen but talking to Terry. "You come on like James Bond, but you got the insides of a little old lady."

"Where'd that come from?"

"Back there, the beach, Miss Hootchy-Kootchy."

Terry took his eyes off the screens and looked at Blackbeard.

"Miss Hootchy-Kootchy? What, you been reading again? Damon Runyon, maybe one of your contemporaries from the thirties? Hootchy-Kootchy?"

"You know who I mean. She was ready for you."

And I was ready for her, thought Terry.

"Too young," he said.

Blackbeard snorted. "What about that redheaded girl hung around with you for a couple of weeks in the summer? That one couldn't been much more than twenty."

Twenty-two, thought Terry. But Alicia, the redhead, was an old twenty-two. She was on her way to a first job with a big bio-med company in the fall. ECB and Terry were only a memorable summer fling along the way for her. Both of them knew what it was, treasured it, and let it go when it was time.

But Terry didn't want to get into that.

"What you do, Blackbeard, is live vicariously"—he dragged that word out as long as he could, trying hard to learn

to speak Southern now that he was living down here—
"through me. You sit there in the Backwoods Church of God
next to BeaAndra, wishing you were me lying on the beach
with some imaginary blonde."

Blackbeard smiled but kept his eyes on the screens. "It's
Front Creek Pentecostal," he said. "And Brother Bob does
get a mite dry sometimes."

"Coming up on time," said Terry, looking back at the
screens.

The clock ticked past eleven. Three minutes later a
heavyset man waddled up to the registration desk.

"Keeper," said Terry, typing.

"Yeah. With two suitcases."

"Huh," said Terry. "Pause that here, will you?" He fiddled
with his netbook.

"We need to go back upstairs when we're done here and
double-check. I believe we only had one," said Blackbeard.

"Yeah," said Terry. "I got Eric's photos loaded onto my
computer before he left. Yeah . . . here it is." He squinted at
the screen. "You're right. One suitcase on the dresser. Empty
space next to it, toward the door. Know what that means?
Something important enough in that bag to kill for. Find the
bag, find the killer."

"Maybe. I'm just a poor country cop. I ain't smart enough
to believe anything until all the facts is in." He paused, still
focused on Keeper's face, looking at probably the last picture
of the man while he was alive. "Bullet in the head and a missing bag are one heck of a pair of facts, though."

"Strong language for you."

"BeaAndra will probably make me wash my mouth out with soap when I get home." He looked at his watch. "Hope that's all she'll do. I've already missed revival tonight." He jerked his chin at the technician. "Mind making us a couple of prints of this frame?"

"Sure."

As the printer whirred behind them, Terry leaned over to the technician.

"So which screen should he pop up on next?"

"What floor did you say his room was on?"

"Four."

The technician made a noise and said, "What you saw is what you got. No cameras on four."

"None?" said Terry.

"None." The technician shrugged. "Budgets. Only have cameras working on one out of three floors. Supposed to add more next year. Spread the cost out."

Blackbeard said, "Let's roll on."

Keeper checked in, just another tired businessman looking for a room at the end of the day. He took his key and walked out of the frame toward the elevators. A minute later a young couple came to the registration desk. They were laughing and looked a little drunk, or maybe a little in love and unconcerned about whether the clerk knew it. The clerk waited patiently while the woman, country-girl heavy but still pretty, bent the man over the counter with a long kiss. They broke, laughed, and got a room.

"Who's that?" said Terry. He motioned to the technician to pause.

Blackbeard flipped through the log. "Registered as Mr. and Mrs. Dan Caughlan of Troy, Alabama. We'll check them out when we get to the station tomorrow."

Terry typed on the laptop. "Got it now. I'm getting a good Wi-Fi signal here so I logged in to the station." He looked up at the screen.

"Looks OK," he said. "There's a Dan Caughlan at the address they gave. Driver's license looks like him."

"Reckon we could have a hit man from Troy, Alabama?" said Blackbeard.

"Hit man? Now who's getting ahead of the facts? You going to be the one to tell the chamber of commerce we've got a mob hit in Emerald Coast Beach?" said Terry.

Blackbeard didn't say anything for a long time. He motioned for the technician to roll on. In the silence, finally, he said, "Maybe."

• • •

They finished up an hour later. Blackbeard put the video discs in a plastic evidence bag and looked at his watch.

"Ten o'clock," he said. "Late for me. BeaAndra's gonna be mad I didn't call."

"We done here?" said Terry.

"I am. Done with everything but a few hours sleep."

Terry grinned at Blackbeard. Ten o'clock was too early for anything to be happening at the club he wanted to hit tonight. "You want to get something to eat?"

Blackbeard looked at him like he was crazy. Then he nodded, yeah, sure, always.

FROM THE SHADOW of the Margaritaville restaurant at Pier Mall, Rolvaag sat in his BMW 7 with Fabbi watching the Hilton as the hot Florida summer afternoon burned away into night and night crept on toward midnight. Blue uniforms and technicians crawled into and out of the Hilton like a trail of ants.

"I still can't believe you left the damned money," said Rolvaag, sipping his fourth cup of coffee. Latte, this time. Mad at Fabbi for losing the money, Rolvaag punished him all afternoon by making him take the long walk through the stores and restaurants in the blazing sun to get him coffee that he didn't really need. The kid kept trying to make up for it by getting him premium coffee drinks. Last one had chocolate in it. Chocolate. Who puts chocolate in good coffee, for Christ's sake? Now this one had about a gallon of cream. If he'd wanted cream he'd have asked for cream. Kid's not much help, but what are you going to do? In this line of work, you take who you can get. Like he had a choice.

"In fairness," said Fabbi, "you never said bring the money. I accept responsibility, but you could have been clearer."

"You accept responsibility? What kind of talk is that? You leave two million of my money, your father's money, on the table, then say to me, 'I accept responsibility?'"

The kid looked scared and Rolvaag felt bad about getting on his case. It wasn't the kid's fault. Well, yeah, it was his fault about the money and Rolvaag had no idea how to fix that. He knew that he, not the kid, would be the one to pay if it came down to that.

Rolvaag had come to ECB five years ago, retiring out of a life of real estate banking in Atlanta to a life of sun and golf. But the market took his money, so Rolvaag had to take a job with a small out-of-state bank. He found out that commercial real estate was a rougher business here in Florida than in Atlanta. After five years of compromising the few principles he had, he found the bank had become a front for the Vegas mob. By then Rolvaag was in too deep.

The real owner of the bank—not the board members in their nice suits smiling in the picture in the annual report, but the big sloppy guy in Vegas with the dead eyes—had a son who had graduated from college with a degree in French literature. The kid had no prospects of a real job but a lot of exposure to the gritty side of his father's businesses. His father sent him to Florida to learn the banking business, do whatever needed doing, keep an eye on the bank and, really, to get him out of the old man's hair.

So here was Rolvaag, banker, trying to play mob boss assisted by a twenty-two-year-old hit man with a degree in French literature. Christ.

The boy shrugged. Rolvaag tried to hold back, had said it already a hundred times, but was about to say it again.

"I said, 'There's a guy coming to the Hilton bringing two million in cash to give to the Oasis real estate boys from the Sunshine Development boys. If Oasis gets the cash from them, then Sunshine gets to develop the last stretch of clear beach between here and Mobile. If you pop the guy, then we get the money and we give the money to Oasis in our name, and we get the deal. Your poppa gets rich and I get a big bonus and get to really retire again. What's not clear?"

"You never said, 'Bring me the money.' Back home in Vegas, you see two mil in cash all the time."

Rolvaag swore and the kid picked up a book by Moliere and went back to reading. Eventually, Blackbeard and Terry came out of the Hilton, and walked to their car.

"That's them," said Rolvaag, cranking the BMW.

"You sure?"

"Yeah. You haven't been down here long enough to have seen what I've seen. Florida cops are all dirty. The story, on the radio and inside the department, is that this is an ordinary death. No mention of money. So someone in ECBPD's got the money for themselves."

The kid didn't want to argue, still wanted to get back in the good graces of the only boss he'd ever had, basically a good man to work for when he wasn't mad like this.

"Yes, sir," he said. "If anything happens, sir, I'll take the linebacker. I'll leave you the little old man in the gray suit."

"I'd have thought that way when I first got here, too."
Rolvaag shifted in the seat and poured the coffee out the window on top of the other coffee. "No, that little guy in the cheap suit is named Blackbeard. He's an old time Florida native; tough as that lousy gator meat they sell down here that'll nearly break your teeth. He's scrawny, walks around with his head bent down like a snapping turtle. They dragged him out of the swamp, poured him into a cheap suit, and gave him a badge. He's probably got a hidey-hole somewhere in the swamp where he's got our money hid, or he's about to take it there. He's the one to watch out for."

Terry and Blackbeard pulled out onto Front Beach Drive. Rolvaag put the car in gear and pulled in behind them.

AFTER DINNER, Blackbeard dropped Terry at his condo at Portside SD6. Terry stood under a palm tree watching Blackbeard pull out onto Front Beach Road with the Gulf and the Portside pools behind him. A silver BMW pulled out of a parking lot and fell in behind Blackbeard. Terry leaned against the tree like he was resting, but followed the BMW with his eyes, keeping tabs on anything close to his partner. Beemers were unusual here. Portside was a working-class resort sandwiched between Mack's Diner and a donut shop, a place with more Fords and Toyotas than European luxury cars. But when the Beemer fell back from Blackbeard on Front Beach Road, Terry dismissed the driver as just an out-of-place tourist.

He stood in front of his door and took a deep breath of the salt air rolling in from the Gulf and then punched 7718 into the lock on the door. The "77" was from the old TV detective show, *77 Sunset Strip*. The show aired on TV long before Terry's time, but he had the 1958 season on DVD, with Roger Smith and Efrem Zimbalist Junior as cool L.A. private eyes. The "18," of course, was from F-18, the boat slip of Travis McGee, the greatest of all the fictional Florida detectives. Terry had read John McDonald's Travis McGee books over and over, until they fell apart in his hands.

He went past the small kitchen and the tiny front bathroom and climbed the stairs to the second floor. He stood in the shower longer than he meant to and realized that he was daydreaming, mentally calling to Keeper's missing second bag, dreaming that in some magic, psychic world the bag would call back to him, show him where it was and how it got there.

Of course that didn't happen. Terry dressed for the evening, left his condo and walked past Mack's Diner to a small pink cinderblock house with a detached garage over on Sundial. He punched the same combination into the side door of the garage, went in and pulled up the garage door, and sat down on the white leather seat of his blood-red 1969 Chevelle 396 convertible.

The engine started with a rumble and Terry smiled. Yeah, when they made the movie of his life, this was going to be one thing he would insist on: the first sound of the movie would be this sound, the growl of his big 396. Powerful, ready, eager. He eased the car into the driveway, got out, locked up the garage and looked back at the house of the man he rented the garage from so his baby wouldn't have to sit outside in the blistering Florida sun of the Portside parking lot.

Most of the windows of the house were small and set up high in the style of the old Florida houses, safe from hurricanes. But a broad bay window had been added at the front, and Terry saw a substantial man with one missing arm standing in the darkness watching him. Terry saluted Ron. As far as he could tell, Ron was always standing at the window, guarding the world against something real or imagined, armed only with a tall glass and determination.

Terry turned back to the car and ran his hand along the hood. He remembered buying the 396 when he was in high school. It was old even then, and in bad shape, and it was destined to be in worse shape a few years later, after being mistreated by him through his college years. But as he matured the car became a part of who he was, and over the years, little by little, he cleaned and fixed it up. It was perfect now, the red paint shining and the white top glowing in the moonlight. He cranked it up and put the top down, and eased down Sundial to Front Beach. Then he pointed the 396 toward the clubs on the East End. He drove past the Margaritaville restaurant at Pier Mall and looked up at the Hilton as he went by, as if it would speak to him and give him the answers he needed.

Terry turned into the parking lot of Danny's Oyster Bar, put the top back up, locked the 396, and activated the alarm. He nodded to a tourist coming out and found an empty spot at the bar. Then he ordered a Land Shark and a dozen baked Apalachicola oysters with Parmesan cheese and horseradish.

Just as his food came, he looked at the back table and saw that the regulars were already there, waiting for him. A girl named Sheri waved and he waved back, picked up his plate and his beer and started to walk over. He caught himself scanning the room and realized his mind wasn't on old friends or new girls tonight. He shoved eleven uneaten oysters and money at the bartender and stood up, waved goodbye to Sheri and walked out. Hero's work was waiting for him.

A few minutes later he was cruising down Front Beach with the top down. Traffic was slow. He threw an arm onto the windowsill and felt good. This was where he belonged: taking the beach slow, feeling like an old-time detective, cool and tough, searching his city for a killer on the loose. Yeah. The movie of his life that was always scrolling in the back of his mind was black-and-white noir tonight, with the tough-guy star tracking down a scary villain. On the road to glory

A boy who looked to be no more than eighteen burst out of the Spanky's parking lot and vomited on the road in front of the 396. Terry stopped a foot in front of the boy with a squeal of tires. The boy looked up at Terry and laughed a nervous laugh, puke still on the front of his dirty shirt. He threw up his hands and spun around in the street like he was doing a victory dance.

Terry pulled into the parking lot, got out and walked into the stinking exhaust fumes of the road and grabbed the boy's shoulder.

"ECB, hell yeah," yelled the boy.

"Hell, yeah," said Terry, guiding him to the curb. Terry looked at the front of the 396 to make sure the boy hadn't got anything on it.

"Sit down here, son," he said. The boy collapsed and leaned against a light pole.

Terry pulled out his cell phone and started to call a patrol car to come take the kid in. Before he called, he said, "You got a place to stay?"

"Sure. Staying with friends. Course they got mad and went back to Atlanta Tuesday, left me here."

"Where you staying now?"

"The beach. Here. Paradise." He waved his arms.

Terry looked at the kid. He smelled bad and there was fear in his eyes, even while he was laughing.

"So you got no place?" said Terry. "You figure you'll wind up sleeping somewhere on the street tonight? Good plan. When'd you last eat?"

"Had breakfast with Roscoe and Sadie before they left. They thought it was funny, driving away and leaving me in the parking lot. But I'll show them; I'm having funnnnn." He threw his arms up in a victory dance again and Terry took him by the shoulder, trying to avoid the puke, and held him still.

"Tuesday?"

"I guess. No, wait, sometime in there I found half a hamburger behind Mickey Dees."

"Great. Today's Wednesday."

"Huh."

"So you've made it almost two days on beer alone? You got any money left for food?"

The kid turned his pockets inside out. A few coins fell clattering on the sidewalk and he laughed.

"Can't waste money on food in ECB. Live on beer."

"Now you've got no money for beer, either." Terry looked at the kid a long time, still holding the phone in his hand.

"C'mon." He stood the kid up and walked him across the street to the Waffle House. The kid tried to order a Jack and Coke, but Terry ordered him a waffle and eggs and stayed to be sure he ate them.

"Let me see your license," said Terry.

"You a cop?"

Terry nodded. The kid gave Terry an oh-shit look and fished out his wallet and handed it to Terry.

"How old are you, son?"

The kid looked out the window and said, "Twenty-one."

There were two Georgia licenses in the wallet. One said twenty-one. The one that looked real said nineteen.

"Atlanta home for you, like it says here?" said Terry.

"Yeah." The kid was talking with his head down while he shoveled food in. He was starting to sober up, crashing on the down side of days of too much alcohol and too little food. His appetite was coming back, too, the bites coming faster and faster. "I mean, yes, sir. Go to school there. Georgia Tech." He looked up at Terry. "I'm smart, sir. Really."

Terry wanted to say one thing but instead he said, "Kid, we get a lot of smart kids that turn dumb down here. Let me guess, you're on some kind of scholarship."

"Yeah, really sir, I'm not like this."

"And if I bust you, your parents will have to come down and bail you out. You'll miss some school, maybe lose that scholarship."

The kid looked back at him, starting to realize that the trouble he was in was real.

"Maybe."

Terry looked at him a long time. Finally said, "We get you back to your family, can they look after you?"

The kid thought a minute. "Yeah," he finally said. "Yeah."

"Get you cleaned up, back in school?"

"Yeah."

"Wait here."

Terry stepped out the door and made a call on his cell. He paid the bill, collected the kid and walked him back to the 396.

"Those eggs aren't going to wind up on my carpet, are they?"

"No, sir."

Terry drove across the Halfway Bridge to a small frame house with a chain link fence and the lights still on. As he stopped the car in front of the gate, dogs started barking inside and the kid threw up on the white carpet of the 396.

"I'm sorry, sir. I'll clean it up." He started wiping at the puddle of eggs and waffle in the floor with the tail of his shirt, making more of a mess. Terry pulled his hand away and pushed him out the door.

"Jesus Christ," was all he said.

He went around and pulled the kid up the walk to the front door. A huge old woman with a face like John Goodman and an improbably bright red wig stood there in an old floral housedress.

"Watch him, Fran," said Terry. "He's already unloaded in my car. Might christen your carpet next."

Fran gave the kid a horrified look and handed him a bucket she already had in her hand. "Here. Last kid that missed the bucket wound up licking his puke up from my carpet while I sat on him. Sit there for now." She pointed at an old couch covered with an army blanket and the kid sat down.

She turned to Terry and laughed. "So this one dirtied up the pussy magnet?"

Terry smiled. "Yeah, guess so. Speaking of pussy magnets, where's Red?"

Fran jerked her thumb at an old Lazy Boy chair with the upholstery worn off one arm. A shriveled, gnome-like bald man lay on it snoring with his mouth open.

"Passed out watching Showtime porn. Jesus, Terry, they got gladiator porn on that channel now. What will they think of next? World War II movies where the Nazis are all topless women?"

"Red wouldn't miss an episode."

"Not a one."

A yapping Chihuahua ran up to Fran's ankles and she picked it up and held it like a baby.

Terry took some money out of his pocket and handed it to Fran. "So you'll get him up tomorrow and put him on a bus to Atlanta?"

"Yeah. I'll get these clothes cleaned up while he sleeps. Get Red to take him to the station when the kid comes to in the morning." She looked at Red. "When either one of them comes to."

Terry left and went back across the bridge. He found the do-it-yourself car wash and stood there in the early morning air scrubbing puke out of the carpet.

Two years, he thought. Two years and I'm quitting and striking out on my own. Just me and the car, travelling across the country looking for adventures, like in *Route 66*. Emerald Coast Beach is no place to be a real detective.

Two more years, he thought. *Maybe four.*

LIZZIE TOOK THE SHOTGUN, fishing rod, grocery bag, and a guitar down to the dock and loaded them into the work-boat next to the blankets and grocery bag she had already loaded. She untied the lines and climbed aboard, and kicked the boat away from the dock. She thought about starting the engine but decided to sit and watch the water, let the boat drift a while on its own.

Looping her legs over the side, she let her bare feet trail in the creek until she felt like a water creature coming home. The water was clear here and she saw a couple of small carp weaving in and out of the stand of eelgrass that fanned out from the dock. She wondered if Momma Crab from earlier was watching her. Water creatures all seemed wise and peace-ful to Lizzie, and she wished she could spend her days floating effortlessly in their cool dominion. She imagined her-self playing a concert under the sea with crabs swaying their claws in time to the music and shrimp dancing in the grass. Lizzie saw herself singing from the deck of an old shipwreck and wondered, what does a mermaid sound like when she sings?

The boat was drifting close to a stump and her simple wa-ter world would get messy if she crashed into that. She yanked her feet out and broke her bond with the water world, and cranked up the noisy, smelly diesel engine that let her come back to visit the water. Spinning the wheel, she took the boat out through the narrow mouth of the creek and into the West Bay.

She took the boat past the cabin owned by the Canadians who only came down for the winter, looked back, and hoped she was far enough away not to hear the money calling from her boathouse. When she found a good place to fish, she dropped the anchor overboard and let the boat drift in a small channel. In the slanting rays of the fading sun, she could almost see the fish below using the channel as their road to and from the creek.

The fishing rod never got baited, though. She sat cross-legged on the deck up on the bow, watched the sun set on the water, and felt the wind fill her up like a sail. Soon, she would call the bastards at the record company to find out where to send the check to get her life back. Soon, she would go back to where the water was dirty and cold, where her fans waited to hear her sing. The last ray of the sun pumped energy into her, and the energy commanded shape. She could already feel the beat of the opening song she would play in her first show back. It was coming.

But she could feel another beat, too. Even out here the telltale heart of the money tucked away in the boathouse warned her that she could not keep what was not hers. She knew the rhythms and tells of the world, and she knew when a storm was coming.

Lizzie sat there until the sun was gone and the wind off the water turned cold. Then she climbed back into the working well of the boat, wrapped herself in a blanket, and braced her back against the bulkhead so she could watch her house to see if anyone came looking for the money. She tore a piece of bread off a loaf in the bag and ate it with a square of cheese while she drank a beer. After, she picked up her guitar and strummed it quietly, humming a song with the blanket wrapping her feet into a mermaid's tail.

She sat through the night, watching and singing softly between naps until the dark night sky blossomed into red and purple and she headed home to get ready for work.

BLACKBEARD WAS SITTING at his usual booth in the back corner when Terry walked into Mack's Diner just as the sun was coming up. The Formica table in front of Blackbeard was littered with glossy eight by tens and a pile of interview summaries. Terry could hear Blackbeard grumbling at the photos as soon as he walked in the door.

A waitress with short blonde hair and a body that looked both strong and busty was scrubbing down a table up front, her arms bulging and her mouth set in a tight line. She was determined to get out a nasty stain left by a sweet but messy little girl from Knoxville the night before. The waitress stood up and was rubbing the back of her arm when she saw a customer standing by the please wait to be seated sign that nobody ever paid attention to. She smiled when she saw it was Terry, and then replaced the smile with the look of a harried mother that waitresses in diners always seem to save for locals.

"You know where he is," she said.

"Is he a permanent fixture here now?" said Terry, keeping his smile because he knew it was charming and he tried to be charming around women. "Kind of like that animated Santa Claus you guys had around here last Christmas who danced and sang Christmas songs for the kids?"

Julie smiled back. "I've started putting a cup of coffee at his table before we unlock the doors in the morning." She went back to scrubbing. Without looking up she said, "And Terry, I'm not going to tell you again about that 'you guys' crap. It's 'y'all,' or you can eat your breakfast at one of the big chain restaurants up on 98."

"Yes, ma'am." Terry kept his charming boyish grin. Julie grinned back but kept her head down.

Blackbeard hadn't raised his head to acknowledge Terry.

"What I got to do to get here ahead of you?" said Terry. "You got an old alarm clock with a special setting that says, 'ten minutes before Terry?'"

Julie slid Terry's coffee in front of him.

"What, no menu?" Terry looked hurt.

"You don't need no menu," she said. "You'll have what I bring you."

Terry turned to the photos. "Found anything?"

"Lots of pictures. No real evidence so far. Prints supposed to come back sometime today. Eric will call if anything jumps out at him."

Terry pulled a handful of photos toward him and started to arrange them.

"The killer came in here." He put a picture of the hall outside the room on his left.

"Killer or killers," Blackbeard corrected.

"Working loose here, trying to get a feel."

Blackbeard sipped his coffee and watched Terry.

"Our victim, Mr. Keeper, opened the door."

"If Keeper's his real name."

Terry gave Blackbeard a look and Blackbeard went back to his coffee.

"Keeper opened the door. Must have known the killer and let him in without a fuss. Or the killer already had a gun pulled out and Keeper went quietly. Let's say he went quiet.

"Not much happened inside. There's no glasses out and the bed didn't look like anyone had sat on it. Not rumpled." He looked at Blackbeard. "Killer walked in, maybe talked a minute, and pow. No complaints about noise, so he had some kind of silencer. Close range, one shot, no signs of a struggle."

"You should write for the TV."

"I told you, we're always writing our own story. Take charge of your story, or it takes charge of you. In this case, though, we want to find a story for Keeper that fits the facts."

"I think old Joe Friday had it right. Just the facts. Leave the story for you and the TV boys."

An older man came through the front door and Terry thought he was an early snowbird, someone retired from Canada or the Midwest, coming to ECB to escape the winter. The man recognized Blackbeard and came over.

"Make some room, Terry. This here's John Connelly. John's the head of security up at the Hilton."

"Sorry I missed the excitement yesterday," said Connelly. His face looked like it had more lines than it had years, and hung loose in the jowls like an old hound dog. He slid into the booth and stuck his hand across the table to Blackbeard, then turned in the booth to shake Terry's hand.

Connelly said, "Only excitement since I come down here, and I'm off at a damned required Hilton corporate seminar in Tampa learning what color my management style is. Like I'm going to change at my age."

Blackbeard said to Terry, "Connelly retired out of Birmingham PD and came down here to head up security at the Hilton. He sometimes acts like he knows what he's doing."

"Sometimes," said Connelly.

Julie sat down two plates of bacon, eggs, and grits and looked at Connelly.

"If you'd a told me you had a third coming, I'd have had coffee here waiting for him."

"What if I wanted tea?" said Connelly.

"You're a cop. You get coffee."

"Can I get some food, too?"

"Sure. Two eggs, bacon, grits, biscuits. I know you cops."

"Retired cop, so I eat better. What's in the seafood omelet today?"

"Fresh grouper and shrimp. Good today."

"Then let's go for good. And some sliced tomatoes, if you don't mind."

Julie left and Blackbeard shoved the pictures over at Connelly. Connelly shoved them back.

"I looked at the video before I came over here."

"So what you think?"

"If I'd been watching a lot of TV I'd say it was a mob hit. Of course, here in tourist-friendly ECB, the mayor and the chamber of commerce will insist that he died of natural causes."

Terry shook his head. "I'm tired of hearing that. This is a pro job all the way."

Blackbeard laughed. "Hey, I know you have a mob hit a day up in Chicago where you come from, but down here we don't have that sort of thing. The chamber of commerce says so. Sometimes they say it through the mayor. You see him on TV explaining that ECB is nothing but white sand, the warm, clear waters of the Gulf, and good fun. Can't be any sharks or hurricanes. Certainly no real crime. But even while he's talking, you see a guy from the chamber whispering in his ear, saying, 'Don't scare the tourists.'"

Connelly leaned in. "In Birmingham, we have gangs and street crimes instead of white sand beaches. But the criminals all have to have names like 'Tavaris' or 'Mohammed' to let the good white citizens know they're in no danger out in the suburbs where the money is. Even there, if you have anything look like its run by a family named something like 'Gambini' or 'Gallo,' the pillars of the community will be all over you to keep it out of the papers."

Terry leaned back. "So we're supposed to say what? A kid on spring break had too much to drink, decided to shoot off his gun in celebration, happened to hit a guy in a hotel right in the forehead?"

"Story'll be on page forty-seven of the paper, next to another story about how the new airport is a big success."

"Paper ain't got forty-seven pages down here."

"That's the point." Blackbeard folded his arms and looked at the door.

The door opened and two good-looking young women came in with their arms linked around an older guy. They appeared to be finishing up the night rather than starting the morning. The girl with silver blonde hair spotted Terry and waved. Terry gave his head a little shake as if to say, 'not now.'

It didn't seem to matter. She peeled off from the other two and came over to their table. Connelly and Blackbeard turned and watched as she came over. She walked with the easy roll of a woman soaked through and through with a night's worth of Mojitos.

She leaned on the table between Blackbeard and Connelly and brought her face down to Terry's level. She wasn't wearing a bra and she was swaying slow and smiling big and daring him to look her in the eye.

"The party's at Sheila's Friday night. Told her you'd be there." She picked up Connelly's spoon and licked it slowly.

"You need more sugar," she said, facing Connelly but watching Terry. "In your coffee, I mean." She turned with one last graceful shake and went back to the others.

Julie came over and poured more coffee for Blackbeard and Connelly, but ignored Terry.

Connelly pointed at Terry's empty cup. "What about our young friend?"

Julie glared at Terry. "I believe he's had enough."

Connelly looked at Blackbeard and smiled. "Think we got this all wrong, Blackie. Keeper didn't get shot at my hotel. He died at one of Terry's parties. Let me see those pictures again. Did he die with a smile on his face?"

BLACKBEARD SMILED, and then looked at Connelly. "Assuming you're wrong about Keeper being partied to death, we still got the question of how the killer got in and out of the Hilton. He could be one of the 783 guests we're working through, or the fourteen staff on duty that night, or one of the folks we see in one of these videos of the entrance." Blackbeard shoved a stack of photos across the table at Connelly.

"Yeah. I looked at the videos. I counted thirteen people coming and seven leaving in the period between an hour before Keeper checked in and an hour after. Oh, the hotel manager said to tell you not to disturb his guests any more."

"Yeah, right," said Blackbeard. "We've already got a little office set up in one of the conference rooms with a team processing guests as we speak. Nobody checks out without a gunshot residue check and an interview. Your manager's out of luck."

"Pretty much what I told him."

Terry stuck his head in. "I want to do something more. After each of these guys goes back home, I want their local PD to contact them and make sure they were down here. We might have a hit man coming in using the identity of a farmer from Eufala."

Blackbeard nodded.

"OK, so for suspects we got 783 guests plus fourteen staff plus maybe another thirteen or so random folks coming and going. When we get to the hotel, I want to get the team together and see how far along we are, see if anybody has turned up anything. Got to be one of these guys."

Connelly leaned back. "Or not."

"What do you mean, or not? Whether the shooter was one of Terry's Chicago hit men or even the drunk college student the C of C wants it to be, he had to be in the Hilton."

"Yeah. But he didn't have to show up on video."

Blackbeard and Terry looked at each other.

"You telling us we got a ghost?" said Terry. He turned to Blackbeard. "Maybe the C of C will like that one. The killer was a ghost. They can open a new tourist attraction, maybe a haunted house next to the pier. Charge tourists $14.95 to come see the killer ghost. Hire a kid to wear a sheet and rattle the chains in his cell so people will know it's not fake."

Blackbeard frowned. "Y'all get back to serious work. We're ruling out ghosts. Also vampires, terrorists, and whoever really killed Kennedy."

Connelly shook his head. "Can't do it. See, the video system has big holes in it."

"Yeah, your video guy yesterday told us some of the floors don't have cameras in them yet," said Terry.

Connelly snorted. "That's a big understatement right there. Truth is, the Hilton's only a year old and there's a lot of stuff not really finished. There's only about a quarter of the recommended cameras installed right now. Manager's been going to the C of C meetings, listening to that crap about no crime here. Maybe this will light a fire under his butt.

"But for now, some cameras were never installed because a bean counter decided not to be in a hurry to get them in. Some service doors are unmonitored, whole floors blind. It's basically a useless system."

"How many know about this?"

"Security folks, engineers. Jenkins Architects out of New York. Progress Bank here that financed everything. Basically, anybody who's ever had access to the blueprints can figure out where the blind spots are. Probably more suspects than tourists on the Fourth of July."

"Great. So we can't even eliminate ghosts."

Julie put down Connelly's breakfast. He poured Tabasco on the omelet, and looked up at Blackbeard and smiled.

"Can't eliminate ghosts. If it makes you feel any better, you can eliminate Kennedy's killer. Everybody knows that was Lyndon Johnson, and he's dead."

"Thanks." Blackbeard scooped up the photos and looked at Terry. "Come on. I got to go tell the chief we need a couple more guys to start interviewing ghosts."

They paid and went out to the parking lot. Then Blackbeard stopped and said, "Dadgummit."

The trunk lid on Blackbeard's ECBPD Impala stood open, still flapping from being jimmied. Terry ran to the street and looked both ways. A man was walking away along

Front Beach. He crossed Sundial and looked back at Terry. Then he broke and Terry took off after him.

"Hey," he yelled. "Police."

The guy reached a silver sedan sitting in the Emerald Isle parking lot with its engine running. He pulled the passenger door open and looked back at Terry again. He jumped in and the car pulled away as Terry got to the edge of the lot.

Terry watched the sedan scream away before he stomped back to the Impala.

"Would have thought it was a kid, if I hadn't seen the car they drove away in," said Terry.

"A kid breaking into a car at Mack's?" said Blackbeard. "When's the last time anything like this happened at Mack's? Half the customers here are local watermen and construction workers, the other half retirees. Nothing to steal, and liable to wind up with some waterman using you for bait if he catches you breaking into his car."

Terry looked back at where the car had been parked. "Got a quick look when he turned back. White. Young. Maybe five-eight, one-fifty. Baseball cap. Dark windbreaker. Car was a big silver luxury sedan, Beemer or Lexus. Florida plates, but couldn't get a number. Why break into a cop's car?"

Blackbeard shrugged and pulled out his cell phone. "Don't know. I still want the techs to come check it out. One more use of department resources to make the chief even madder."

He sighed as he dialed the number.

"Eric? Yeah, need you to come do a workup on my car in the Mack's parking lot. Bring a black-and-white with you to give Terry and me a ride down to the Hilton so we can start interviewing the staff."

• • •

Sitting in the BMW as it screamed down Cobb Street, Fabbi pulled off the baseball cap and said to Rolvaag. "Didn't think it would be there."

Rolvaag floored the throttle as they turned east on 98. He was sweating, even in the air conditioning.

"Money's got to be somewhere," said Rolvaag. "We didn't see him take it out of the car when we followed him home last night. Got to be somewhere. And we've got to get it."

LIZZIE DRAGGED HERSELF into the Hilton Thursday morning hung over but five minutes early, praying for a quiet day. But Yolanda was waiting at the door to tell Lizzie to get her ass down to the conference room and talk to the policemen first. First. Not "instead of cleaning her rooms" but "first." That meant—if the police weren't already waiting for her with handcuffs—Lizzie would spend hours going round and round, repeating the words she had carefully rehearsed a thousand times, saying everything real innocent and polite. Then, when she walked out of the interrogation room to take her first real breath of the day, the rooms would still be lined up waiting for her. *Shit.*

She tapped on the conference room door and went in, meek and cooperative, smiling with the wig neatly in place.

"Thank you for coming in, Miss Gaffney. I'm Detective Terry."

He was thirty-five maybe, wearing bright colors like a tourist. He might have been cute if he wasn't trying so hard to be cute. The older one with the dark gray, worn-out, J.C. Penney's suit, sat hunched over his notebook.

"Yes, sir," she said. "I only heard about this horrible murder on the news yesterday, but I'm happy to do anything I can to cooperate." The words didn't sound like herself to Lizzie but it sounded like something from an old *Dragnet* rerun, so that's what she went with.

The older detective looked up, startling pale blue eyes in a dark, tired face.

"Lizzie?" he said. "Ain't you Lizzie Gaffney? Doc's little girl?"

"Lieutenant Blackbeard?" She sat down and smiled. Her real smile, not the good-citizen smile she'd practiced in the mirror.

Blackbeard smiled back and turned to Terry. "I didn't recognize the name. The hotel roster may say this girl's name is Elizabeth Gaffney, but nobody ever called her anything but Lizzie or maybe Doc's girl. But once you hear that voice, you never forget it. How you been, girl?"

"Up and down. How about you, Lieutenant?"

"'Bout the same. Hasn't been Lieutenant in a long time, but that's another story for another day. I haven't seen you since your daddy's funeral." Blackbeard turned to Terry. "I used to go out with Doc on his crab boat sometimes. People called him Doctor Crab because he knew more about blue crabs than anyone else around. Actually wrote a book about crabs and crabbing, got a lot of attention back in the nineties. He never followed up on it, though; he liked being on the water more than sitting at a typewriter. That man could tell some stories. I still miss him. How long's he been gone, Lizzie, two years?"

"Three. Feels like yesterday sometimes. Time just slips away."

Blackbeard held up the personnel form. "Says here you're twenty-seven. You can't be more than twenty-one, twenty-two."

"As I said, time slips away. I'll be twenty-eight in February. I look young because I'm so little. Do you mind?" She pulled off the wig and fluffed out her mohawk. The new look got Terry's attention.

Blackbeard turned to Terry. "Lizzie's a singer, used to be one of the best around here. Sang under the name 'Lizzie Borden,' like the crazy ax killer. Really didn't sing much of the country crossover/ top forty stuff the bars around here favor."

Terry looked at Lizzie with his mouth open.

"I remember you," he said. "I've got your first album, *Forty Whacks*. You're on the cover walking a gator on a leash down Rodeo Drive. *Rolling Stone* even did a review."

Lizzie looked at him a little closer. "Yeah, well, you're one of about two hundred that own a copy of that CD. Right after it came out the record company was sold to a fruity guy who likes soothing new age music, same note over and over drawn out to relax you and let you see all the peace and love in the world. Not rock and roll. He doesn't want anything edgy. He pulled my CD, killed my stuff, and killed a lot of other good acts, too. His suits decided to keep the rights to all songs from the old label, including mine. They made me an offer: buy back the rights to my songs for a hundred grand. Until then, no songs, no music. Step on a stage as Lizzie Borden or even anything that sounds distinctive and they'd sue my ass. I told them I'd think about it, and hauled ass back here to raise the money."

"You miss singing?"

"Hell, yeah. Mostly, I miss those times when I'd stop in mid-song with a new idea and make up a new song on the spot, the band struggling to keep up and the crowd screaming while I scribbled the song down in the big leather notebook I kept next to me on stage. It was like I was the mother of the song, but the crowd was the daddy, and nobody loves a baby like their own."

She paused. "It felt like really great sex—great sex where you made a great baby." She looked coolly at Terry and said, "Yeah. I miss it."

Terry realized he was staring and he was supposed to say something. "Looks good on you, the mohawk, I mean. Attitude. Not many girls could pull it off, attitude and still look like a girl. Works for you."

Blackbeard laughed and broke their stares. "Didn't work for some of the local crowds. They wanted something more mainstream. I remember drunk guys, yelling, 'Play *Margaritaville.*'"

"Yeah." She sneaked a glance at Terry. "Thanks." *Maybe he was more like thirty.* "Yeah, I like my music a little grittier. Got Lieuten—Detective Blackbeard to blame for that. You gave me that old Johnny Cash vinyl record, remember? *Live at Folsom Prison.* I still listen to it, on the iPod of course these days."

Blackbeard turned to Terry, "I know you don't remember that one, made before either of you were born. See, Cash wanted to make this album, live, at a prison. Record company wouldn't let him—"

"Of course I know that one," Terry said, offended. "Every musician knows that one. Part I like best is when he says to the inmates, 'you know we're taping this live so you have to be on good behavior, not say 'shit' or anything like that.' Right away told them he was one of them, that this was going to belong to them and he didn't care if the suits liked it."

Lizzie leaned into him, eyes bright. "I liked when he threw the water glass down because the prison water they gave him wasn't fit to drink. He smashed it on the floor right in front of the men and the warden to let them know he knew they were getting crap. But, he wasn't going to take crap, and he wasn't going to give it to them. Every audience, everywhere, country, rock, even operas or guys in prison, knows one thing: if it ain't honest, don't bring it."

"Yeah," said Terry. "Hell yeah."

She saw the way Terry was looking at her and she couldn't decide if he liked her words or if he liked her looks, but either way it was a rush and she recognized it. It was the same rush she used to get onstage, but now she was getting it from just one guy. *Cool.*

Blackbeard flipped open his notebook. "Well, I'd love to sit here and tell stories about your daddy, but we got work to do and I'm sure you do, too. How about you walk us through Tuesday morning?"

"Yes, sir. I approached my seventh room of the morning, room 417, at approximately 8:47. I saw the do not disturb sign and passed the room, as required by company policy, and proceeded to room 425, the next room on my list."

"How did you know we were interested in room 417?" Blackbeard said, not looking up from his notebook.

"The TV news opened with a shot of the door with police tape on it last night. And everyone downstairs is talking about it."

Blackbeard nodded. "OK. But I need you to go back. Start with getting up Wednesday and coming in to work. Give me everything until you went home."

Well that's a curve, she thought.

"OK. My alarm went off at seven, set so I can begin my shift as scheduled at eight." She went on with Blackbeard nodding like every detail was the most important thing on earth, sometimes stopping her to clarify a minor point. She noticed Terry watching her, too, but only half listening to the words, paying attention to the little tells that she might give to show she was lying or uncomfortable. But he was staring into her eyes in a way that made it hard for her to concentrate.

She got to the part about the room and said the same thing over again, almost exactly the same words. Blackbeard interrupted her.

"So you didn't notice anything about the outside of the room. No mud on the carpet, nothing around the door, nothing?"

She looked at him. He looked impassive and maybe a little bored. No clue what he expected her to say. *What did I miss?* Was there blood on the floor that she stepped in, leaving tracks down the hall? She could imagine a trail of her own bloody footprints leading all the way from the room back to her house, with her sitting here playing innocent. Maybe they'd let her sing in prison, kind of like Johnny Cash in reverse.

"No sir." She made her choice. Stay in character and stick with the story. "Did I miss something?"

"No," said Blackbeard, scribbling in the notebook again, no sign of interest, just a man doing his job. "Sometimes somebody notices something that seems small at the time but that winds up helping us out. Just covering the bases."

Blackbeard closed his notebook. "I think that'll do it for us, Lizzie. I know you've got stuff to do."

"Yeah," she said, getting up. "Just another beautiful day in Panhandle Paradise."

"Still a nice place to live when you get out on the water," said Blackbeard, "but always hot here. Sometimes I think I'll move to Minnesota, see what it's like to stay cold."

Terry would have none of it. "You know, I love you people who grew up down here, but you don't know how spoiled you are. Those of us who grew up someplace else, shoveling snow, grey skies all the time, water so dirty you can't touch it, we're the ones who really see this place for what it is. May not be paradise, but it's pretty damned close. White beaches, like fine sugar. Water so blue and clear you can count your toes. And that's not the best part. The best part is the people. Down here, the water flavors the people, gets into their rhythms, and teaches them to slow down and laugh, sit back and take their time and enjoy a good meal."

Now Lizzie stared at him until he grew uncomfortable.

"Except, of course, for the real estate people. They can go to hell," he finished, trying to slide back into his tough detective character.

Lizzie reached over and grabbed Blackbeard's notebook.

"Hey," Blackbeard said, grabbing back but grabbing too slow. "That's police property."

"Oh, calm down," said Lizzie, tearing a blank page out of the back. "I'm not going to steal your precious police secrets." She handed the notebook back and pointed the pen at Terry. "I am going to steal your line, the one about the water flavoring the people."

"Can't let you steal, I'm a cop," said Terry. "But I can give it to you. I'll give you a guitar riff or two to go with it, if you want it."

"You play?"

"Chicago blues, when I was in Chicago, when I had time. Club work, a little studio work here and there."

Lizzie handed the pen back to Blackbeard and stared evenly at Terry. "We ought to get together sometime. My daddy built a studio for me in our garage, years ago."

"Chicago blues and Johnny Cash. Might be an interesting mix."

"I ain't Johnny Cash. We'll see about the mix." She got up. "You've got my number. Call me." She walked out.

Terry smiled, liking the way she said "call me," not like a request or a whine, no girlish cuteness at all, nothing but a flat statement that she expected him to fulfill.

Blackbeard saw Terry's look. "Don't get your hopes up partner, that one's tougher than she seems."

"Nobody's tougher than that one seems."

"Just saying, be careful. You think your ex did a number on you. That one can chew you up and spit you out."

"Might be fun."

Blackbeard rolled his eyes.

"She's right about one thing, though," Blackbeard said. "The audience can tell when it's not honest. That little girl's holding something back."

"Oh, she was just enjoying the conversation. Being honest is important to that girl."

Blackbeard thought a minute. "Lot of ways to be honest," he said.

TERRY WENT OUTSIDE the hotel to make a call to the Chicago PD while Blackbeard went to the lobby to check on other officers who were interviewing guests. When Terry walked back into the Hilton lobby, a guy wearing a green Parrot Head shirt with the price tag still on it had his face an inch from Blackbeard's.

"You really think my six-year-old son killed the guy upstairs?" the man snapped. "Jesus."

Terry stood and watched.

"You small town cops need to bring in some pros and let us guests go home. Be midnight before we get back to Nashville at this rate."

Terry started to wedge in between the guy and Blackbeard but Blackbeard looked at him and gave his head a little shake. No.

"I'm sorry, sir," said Blackbeard without moving. "It's procedure. We need to fingerprint everyone who was in the hotel Tuesday night and ask you a few questions, with your permission. We'll get you out of here as soon as possible."

Blackbeard tried to smile politely, but on Blackbeard, a smile looked forced. The man swore and went back to the table to wait his turn.

A police aide sat at a table trying to handle intakes and complaints. She had more complaints than intakes. Blackbeard turned to her and said, "Becky, try to keep them off me for a few minutes."

Becky shrugged. "What you want me to do when they demand to talk to the man in charge?"

"Send them to Brandon. See what he can do. I'm going to the coffee shop with Terry for a few minutes and pretend I'm a cop instead of a concierge."

When the coffee came, Terry said, "Long day for you, Blackie. Car jimmied, then playing tourist greeter."

Blackbeard shrugged. "It all pays the same. It ain't the ones that complain that worry me. The complainers just want to go home, same as you or I would. The guy that did this will smile and thank the police for doing their job—if he's here. Besides, working the meet-and-greet line before I turn them over to somebody else for the questions gives me a chance to see each of them, look them over. Lot of the time, you learn more from that first look than from all the questions."

"How about the questions you're getting from the chief?"

"For that I could use combat pay. Called me this morning and wanted to know how much this will cost. Told him it depends on whether he wants the guy caught or not. Won't tell you what he said to that."

"I think I'm too young to hear it."

"Yeah. Anyway, you hear anything out of your friends in Chicago?"

"Heard they already got snow. Old friend offered to trade jobs with me."

"Reckon your old chief up there would take you back?"

"Probably not."

Blackbeard sat and waited.

Terry said, "My guy said they've got no record on anybody with a name of Keeper. Said the address on the driver's license looks fake, too. He'll know more once we get the prints up to him. Maybe we'll get a real name then."

Terry leaned over and blew on his coffee. "My guy back in Chicago says we need to find some way to lean on the local wise guys down here. Somebody knows who did this."

Blackbeard smiled. "Let me know when you find the local wise guys here, maybe sitting around the back of someplace like Pasta Grill, drinking Chianti and calling each other 'Guido.' Ain't like that here, Terr. The only mob down here is the real estate developers, guys in nice suits with nice smiles. You can find people down here that will sell you cocaine and stuff, but the white powder that people fight over here is white beach sand. You go looking for the mob here, you'll find them at the ECB Rotary Club meeting with the mayor and the governor. You want to threaten them, tell them you plan to vote for a Democrat."

Terry swirled his coffee and sighed. "To think I came down here to be a simple beach bum."

Blackbeard took a sip of his coffee. "You came down here to be a hero, figured us small town folks would be dazzled by your big city skills and fall for your story."

Terry smiled. "Told you, it's important to have a story. My story in Chicago was same shit, different day. Clean up a gruesome file on your desk and three more like it would be there the next day. I remembered ECB from vacations down here when I was a kid, how clean and bright and beautiful everything seemed. Wanted to come to some place where my story would end with me looking at something good at the end of the day and saying, 'I had a hand in that.'"

Blackbeard sipped his coffee.

"So I ain't going back to Chicago," said Terry.

"Didn't the chief up there kind of insist you stay gone?"

"There *was* that problem."

"And your ex-wife."

"That, too."

Terry thought about the part of the phone call he hadn't told Blackbeard about. He had thought his former partner was a friend, but there was an edge to their talk, one too many comments asking how Superman was doing in Hicksville. When Terry was in Chicago, he was the youngest homicide detective ever—hot until he crashed. Young and hot and arrogant, he knew now. People love hero stories. Even more, they love stories about the hero who goes too far and crashes, and becomes the butt of jokes. Good story, and apparently his story in Chicago. Not the story he wanted here.

The manager of the Hilton was coming toward them across the coffee shop, walking fast and hitting a rolled-up newspaper against his thigh like a swagger stick. He did not look as friendly today as he had been yesterday. Terry put on a polite smile and started to say hello.

"What the hell are you trying to do?" the manager said.

Blackbeard said, "I'm sorry, sir, but we need to talk to each of your guests."

"Don't mean that. We talked about that. I'm cooperating. You didn't tell me about this." He threw the paper down. Terry leaned over and saw the headline, "Mob Killing at the Hilton?" on the top of the fold on page one. Blackbeard picked up the paper and scanned the article.

"We didn't do this, sir. Nobody in our department knows enough to characterize this crime yet."

"Well, somebody sure as hell characterized it for this reporter. I got ten cancellations already." He paused. "Your chamber of commerce promised Hilton this was a business-friendly town, everybody at city hall would do whatever it took to get the tourists in and make them happy. I'm going to talk to the C of C, see what they can do about this."

He left the paper and marched away. Terry looked up to see Becky striding across the hotel lobby toward them, trailed by a crowd of men in beach shirts and ugly shorts. One tall woman in a straw hat leading the mob.

Terry watched them come. "Good thing they don't sell pitchforks and torches in the gift shop."

"I think they plan to beat me to death with sand shovels."

"Want me to take it for a while?"

"No. You go on and do some police work. Try to find out something about Keeper." Blackbeard looked at his watch.

"I'll stay here another hour or so, then I got someone I want us to talk to." Blackbeard stood up and gulped the rest of his coffee. "Besides, if I let a hero like you handle this crowd, you'll probably kill somebody."

BIG MAMMA'S BREAKFAST was run by Mamma Louise, who wasn't big, which was the joke, such as it was. It was nicer than Mack's, and that's why it wasn't on Blackbeard's usual morning list. But Mamma Louise did know everything there was to know in Emerald Coast Beach, so Blackbeard drove them over there for a second breakfast. She came over to their table while Terry and Blackbeard were arguing whether omelets counted as eggs or not. She pulled up a chair and broke off a piece of Terry's muffin.

"Hey," he said.

"Hey yourself. So how come you think y'all have solved that Hilton thing so fast?"

Terry looked at Blackbeard.

Blackbeard said, "We ain't solved nothing yet."

"Must have. The early edition of the paper was all fired up about Al Capone personally coming to take over the beach. Two hours later, the late edition has one little story on page seventeen, police working an unspecified death at an unspecified hotel. If you read the story, you'd think it's a junkie overdosed in a flophouse, probably somewhere up near Tallahassee."

"The power of the press," said Terry.

"Power of the C of C," she said.

Terry pointed at the sticker in the window. "Says you're a proud member."

"Says I get blackmailed a couple hundred bucks a year to buy a sticker." She broke off another bite. "So what you think you know and what you think you need to find out?"

Terry leaned back and pointed a finger at her. "How come you think you know more about this than we do?"

Mamma Louise opened her mouth in outrage and Blackbeard put his hand on her arm to slow her down. Blackbeard grew up around here; his mom had been friends with Mamma Louise for many years. Growing up, Blackbeard lived with the certainty that his mom would know everything he did five minutes after he did it. He also grew up knowing that Southern men do what they think are important things and run the world. And, that Southern women talk among themselves, know everything there is to know, and sit back and shake their heads in amazement as their men run around in circles until they wind up right back where the women knew they were going all along.

"I know there's only one thing around here that people want bad enough to kill someone for," she said. "Now that beach real estate is hot again, everybody and his brother is sniffing after Hole in the Beach, that one stretch of undeveloped beach across from Portside."

"I know that beach," said Terry, eating what Mamma Louise had left of his muffin. "I live in Portside. We enjoy the last unspoiled view of the Gulf, and pray to God nobody comes along and puts another twenty-three-story slab there and takes away our sunshine."

"Then you better find a better church to do your praying in. Oasis owns that sand, and word is they are going to develop that stretch of beach, and get Sunshine Development to do the building. Sunshine was supposed to have a big announcement about it today, but I reckon they cancelled it out of respect for the dead."

Terry said, "Yeah, a lot of respect for the dead in those companies."

She gave Terry a look that said she was about to go to the back and get the big flyswatter and take it to his behind if he didn't shut up. Never said it. Never had to.

"Well, I assumed you brilliant detectives would figure it out if there was some other reason. Being a Christian woman, I gave you the benefit of the doubt and assumed you were working, instead of wasting money good taxpayers like me give you for doing next to nothing but sitting on your butts eating. However, Jesus has not blessed my heart with enough charity to allow me to assume you know when something's going on that smells like two-day-old bait."

"You think something's going on at Sunshine? You got anything to prove it?"

Mamma Louise stood up. "That's your job. And I think you should go do it."

GOING TO SEE CAPTAIN DAVE seemed like a better idea last night than it did now to Lizzie. It was Thursday afternoon, her shift at the Hilton had finished, and she was driving the pickup up the gravel road to the old marina where the captain lived. The few fishing boats still docked at the marina hadn't been on the open water since dope smuggling went out of style and the only weed here now were the ones growing up through the gravel road. The old place looked like what it was: a floating retirement home for old fishermen past the point of living at sea but damned sure not going to live on land. She pulled up next to an old Mustang with a bumper sticker that read "save a fish, eat a tourist" and another that read "f big petroleum." That car had been hot once, but now it sat on two flat tires and mostly served as a place to lean an old red bike. Lizzie stood in the sun looking at the broke-down boat in front of her.

"Hey in there. Permission to come aboard?"

She repeated it a couple of times and heard a clatter like falling pots and pans from inside the boat's cabin.

"Go away. I don't want nothing."

"I ain't selling nothing. Captain, I need to talk to you."

"Then call me on the goddamn phone."

"You won't answer it."

"Why should I? Nothing but lawyers and telemarketers on the phone lines. Which are you?"

A shaggy gray head stuck out of the passageway and blinked in the sun at Lizzie's mohawk. "You supposed to be some kind of a Indian?"

"No. It's just a haircut. Captain, put on your glasses and open your eyes. It's Lizzie. Doc's girl Lizzie."

He looked at her a long time.

"Well, damn," he finally said. "Lizzie with a mohawk and a Hilton shirt. What have you got yourself into, girl?"

"Well, damn, yourself," she said. She stepped aboard without waiting to be asked. They would have hugged, if either one of them hugged folks.

"You want a beer?" he said.

She looked at the blazing Florida afternoon sun. "Looks like the sun's started heading down, at least somewhere. Good enough for me."

He disappeared inside and came back with two Dos Equis and two Coors. He handed her a Dos Equis and a Coors and she set her Coors down. He turned up his Coors and drained it.

Lizzie smiled. "I forgot the Captain Dave rules of beer drinking."

He threw the empty Coors bottle into a recycling bin on the dock and looked at her. "See, some folks say you should start with the good beer and switch to the cheap stuff once you've lulled your taste buds to sleep. I say use the cheap stuff to get you kick-started, then cruise easy with stuff you can taste."

"Right." Lizzie picked up her Coors, chugged it and threw her bottle into the bin and looked back at the captain.

"Now can I enjoy my Dos like a civilized person?"

He shrugged and took a sip, slow now that he was on good Mexican beer, and looked at Lizzie.

"Little Lizzie. The first time I saw you, you were what? Fifteen?"

"Fourteen. And scared shitless." She thought about it and took a long sip of the Dos, then held the bottle in her hand like a theatrical prop the way smokers use cigarettes. They sat in the shade of the cabin, both sipping their beers and quiet for a long time.

The captain pointed his beer at the gravel road and laughed. "Your Daddy and I had a bet on whether you would make it or not. I thought he was touched, asking a little sprout of a girl to drive his truck, knew I was going to pick up easy money from him when his truck showed up with fresh dents. Doc said, 'Don't ever sell Lizzie short.' We sat right here and watched that truck turn onto the gravel road and he said, 'See.' I looked out at you fighting the truck, kicking gravel from one side to the other like a waterspout kicking up sea water and said to Doc, 'She ain't made it yet.'"

Lizzie smiled and set her bottle down on the deck. "Cut me some slack, Jack. It was the first time I'd ever driven a car or a truck. I was scared to death."

"So was I. Your Daddy said he was too drunk to drive home but too broke not to take his boat out and make a living that day. I thought he was calling a grown-up to come get him. I offered to take him myself when I found out he'd called a kid that had never drove."

"Daddy probably made the right choice in turning that offer down. You were probably farther gone than he was," said Lizzie. A pale green lizard had climbed up on her bottle and she was watching to see if it would take a sip.

"He thought you could do anything," said the captain, watching the same lizard and wondering if he should bet Lizzie on what it would do next.

"Probably why I thought it, too. Although, with the benefit of hindsight, his confidence was probably a little over-stretched in that instance. I told him I couldn't drive and he told me to turn the key and let the truck drive itself. I found out pretty quick he had too much confidence in the truck, too."

"Probably."

"In fairness to Daddy, that was the summer Momma died. Everyone was always offering to help in one way or another. He didn't want us to take help from anybody. So, he fished and visited Momma in the hospital while she was hanging on, and didn't do much of anything else."

"Except come here and drink with me and the boys."

"Except that, and that was mostly after Momma died." The lizard decided it was too early for beer, and skittered across the rusty white railing and vanished in a green flash. Lizzie picked up the bottle.

"I figured the truck out and got Daddy home and into the boat without hitting anything. Well, without hitting much. By the end of that summer, I was a pretty good driver."

"Practice makes perfect. Speaking of practicing, how's that singing coming? Saw your name in the paper a while back. Even went and stood in the back of the crowd when you sang in Frank Brown Park."

"That was the last show I did here before I took Horace Greeley's advice and went west. That show was a lot of fun."

"So how'd L.A. work out? Land of fruits and nuts like most folks say?"

"And then some." She laughed. "Kind of like here, except not. Just as many fruits and nuts here, present company included. Only difference is that here they know they're nuts, and proud of it. Out there, the fruits and nuts have money, and think they're gods."

The captain waved at the line of pink condos down along the beach. "It's coming here. People used to come here to go to the beach, go fishing, get drunk and smuggle grass. Now they smuggle condos. I'm afraid to go to sleep at night for fear I'll wake up and find three new ones in my back yard. They gave me a big four-bedroom unit up near the top of that one over yonder to make up for some land they took to build it. I won't sleep in it or have nothing to do with it. Who wants to sleep in something called a 'unit?' The crooks in the old days knew they were crooks. The crooks that build these new places think they're saints and civic leaders."

"Yeah, well, I may need your help with some of those crooks."

He smiled. "Why come to me for help with crooks?"

"Daddy always said you were the most honest crook he knew."

"What a compliment. Better than being the most dishonest citizen, I guess."

"Yeah, maybe. But what if one of those honest citizens were to come across some cash money—all legal, mind you?" She paused and thought. "Well, it ain't illegal."

He smiled over at her. "Is it yours?"

"Nobody else's."

"Not the same. Your daddy was always big on not wanting what wasn't his."

"Yeah. Daddy was always hardheaded about that. Me, too. Was, I guess. Anyway, if that honest citizen is sitting there with a pile of money and needed a way to turn it into something they could use, how would they do it?"

"If it's legal, take it to the bank and deposit it. Like an honest citizen."

"I never said it was that legal."

The captain smiled. "In the old days, I'd take it to a dope smuggler. They had guys on their payroll to make things look legal when they weren't."

"And now?"

"Now those same guys are called real estate development bankers."

"So I take it to them, they take a cut, and I've got a legitimate investment?"

"You don't take it anywhere. I do. A bad crook will only trust another crook. And these boys are so bad they belong to the chamber of commerce and the rotary and the city council. Places that only take crooks so bad they think they're good, and have their pictures smiling in the paper to prove it."

"I thought you'd say something like that." Lizzie reached into her back pocket and pulled a stack of bills out and threw them to the captain. He caught it and counted it.

"Ten grand?" he said.

She nodded.

"Looks like bank money," he said.

He waited but she didn't say anything.

"So how much of this do we need to clean up?"

"Enough to write a legal check for one hundred thousand dollars."

He sipped on his beer and looked at her.

"You could give me the whole hundred grand now."

Lizzie thought, *I'd like to give you the whole two million, get it out of my house.*

But what she said was, "Daddy never said you were that honest."

ROLVAAG SAT CHEWING ROLAIDS inside his BMW, parked in front of Blackbeard's house on a blazing Florida afternoon with the air conditioning on high. Fabbi tapped on the window and Rolvaag growled and punched the button. The window slid down with an expensive muted whir. Hot air and bugs poured in from the scrub brush.

He waved furiously at the air and glared at Fabbi for making him open the window. "Damned mosquitoes."

"Technically, sir, I think they're gnats."

"Yeah. Whatever." He waited for Fabbi to say something worth listening to.

Fabbi said, "Nobody home. Knocked three times, like you said. No one's home."

Rolvaag looked at the house, a typical old Florida cinderblock backing up to a stand of sawgrass in the bay, hidden in the pines a mile from the nearest neighbor. It had probably started small, was maybe even a hunting shack, with rooms and outbuildings added on over the years by cousins and brothers, probably without permits or inspections, until it sprawled loose now from one end of the clearing to the other. Not the type of thing Rolvaag's bank would finance.

"What kind of flag you reckon that is?" Fabbi said, pointing. "That there ain't no American flag." Rolvaag gave him a look. Fabbi was trying to broaden himself by reading colorful books about Florida swamp heroes, working hard to try to talk like he thought the crackers down here talked. Worked about as well as a mullet haircut on a French poodle.

"That's some of the local color you need to pick up down here," said Rolvaag. "That's a Florida State Seminole flag. College football team. Down here, you better be a Seminole fan or root for their hated Florida Gators rival. People get killed for rooting for the wrong team in the South. Look at the way that flag pole is cared for with a nice circle of white rocks bordering a bed of oyster shells painted garnet and gold, Seminole colors. They probably bow toward Tallahassee when they raise the flag every morning. If you're gonna live down here, you're gonna have to choose."

Rolvaag got out of the car, handed the kid his toolkit, and turned and locked the door.

Fabbi cocked his head the way the hero in his Florida book did and said, "Why lock the only car in the only driveway of the only house for a mile either way, out here in a swamp where nobody but one of these crazy Florida natives would live anyway? We thinking a gator's going to come sauntering by? A gator thinking, I'm tired of walking around all day, dragging this long scaly tail behind me. Think I'll take this nice unlocked BMW into town for a brew."

Rolvaag glared back and said, "You read too much."

"Yes, sir."

"Remember, go around the back and find a way to get in. Come through and let me in the front door. We'll find where this redneck cop hid the money and get back to the office with smiles on our faces in time for a late lunch."

"Yes, sir."

"Remember. Anything goes wrong, we're from the Florida power company, conducting an energy audit."

"Yes, sir," Fabbi said.

Rolvaag thought, "Please just play the idiot, son. Play the polite, smiling idiot and don't mess this up."

Rolvaag stood on the porch for a couple of overheated minutes before he knew Fabbi had screwed up somehow. He heard a high-pitched scream and wondered who the kid had hurt this time before he realized the scream was Fabbi's. Fabbi burst through the front door and ran past him with a twisted, screaming face and a garden hoe stuck in his rear end, trailing him like some kind of tail. Rolvaag turned to follow Fabbi and was knocked down by a big woman in a wide straw hat waving a shotgun as she ran after Fabbi. The woman reached down and yanked Rolvaag up with her free arm.

"Excuse me, sir. My momma raised me to be more polite than this, but I'm chasing me a Florida Gator cretin right now."

Rolvaag looked up, dazed and bewildered, and remembered their cover story about working for the Florida power company.

"Florida Power, ma'am?" he said.

The woman's face distorted and she waved the shotgun at Rolvaag.

"Another Florida fan," she yelled. "Stop yelling those Florida Gator cheers and get off my land." She pointed the shotgun at him and Rolvaag took off running after Fabbi.

The first blast went into the ground behind Rolvaag's feet. By then Fabbi had made it to the car, pulling on the locked door handle.

"Let me help you with that," yelled the woman, shattering the back passenger door window with the next load. Fabbi dove through the broken window and landed with his legs and the hoe sticking out the window and waggling up and down as he cringed on the seat. Rolvaag made it to the car, jumped in the front and cranked the car as another blast put a hole in the front fender. The car spun away in a cloud of gravel, bouncing down the road with the hoe waving goodbye to the woman standing in the road. She yelled "Go Seminoles!" and waved the shotgun like Chief Osceola about to plant the flaming spear in a football field at the start of a Florida State football game.

• • •

Blackbeard yelled into the phone, "I'll do my dagnabbed job."

He slammed the phone down so hard the receiver snapped in two. Terry looked across their desks. Blackbeard was glaring at the phone like it was the phone's fault and said nothing. He saw the other cops in the squad room pretending not to be interested while they peeked at Blackbeard and listened in. After a long minute, Blackbeard said, "Dagnabbed chamber of commerce," and stared at Terry.

Terry thought Blackbeard wanted support.

"Damned bastards," he said.

It didn't help. Now Blackbeard glared at Terry.

"They called me up with a list of who they consider to be likely suspects. Probably a bunch of homeless guys they've been trying to run out of town for not buying souvenirs at Alvin's. Arrest one of them, close the case, and move the story out of the paper so the tourists won't see it. Wanted to know what they could expect from me."

"Good answer."

Blackbeard's phone rang. He tried to pick up the receiver, but the two pieces dangled in his hand while the phone kept ringing. He finally punched the speaker button and spat out, "Blackbeard."

BeaAndra's voice boomed across the squad room. "Well of course I know you're Blackbeard. I know my own husband's name when I call him."

"Bea, this is not a good time. Let me talk to you when I get home tonight."

"No sir, you need to know about this right now, in case somebody calls up complaining."

"Bea, what have you done now?"

Blackbeard cradled his head in his hands. A couple of other detectives drifted over to the desk next to Blackbeard's and shuffled papers, but their heads were cocked toward Blackbeard's phone.

"Nothing. Not a blessed thing. Except defend myself against a couple of Florida Gator fans trying to break in and tear up our house because they don't like my Seminole flag."

"Bea, I told you, nobody takes football as serious as you think they do. How do you know they were Gator fans?"

"They told me so. Kept yelling 'Florida Power' right in my face, but not right away. I was out back in the truck patch when I saw the young one sneaking around the back of the house. I thought he was another one of those inspectors, come to give us a citation."

"Bea, you promised to leave those guys alone and let me handle them."

"And I was prepared to do just that. But then he started climbing in the back kitchen window and I thought, 'Well that's just rude.' So I picked up a hoe and hit him in his hind parts. On the third whack, the hoe got stuck in his belt so I ran inside and got my shotgun."

"Tell me you didn't kill the boy."

Several patrolmen had joined the detectives around Blackbeard's desk. Blackbeard looked up, scowled at them but nobody was leaving this show.

"Of course not, I promised you I'd leave those inspectors alone. But when I got the shotgun, he started yelling 'Florida Power' and I started chasing him through the house yelling, 'Seminole Chop' and chased him out into the front yard where there was another one yelling 'Florida Power.' He probably was planning on burning my Seminole flag."

"Let me get this straight. Two men broke into the house, and you attacked them with a hoe and a shotgun."

"I didn't attack them. I was defending myself. Stand your ground, and that applies to defending your football team. Or ought to. I didn't shoot them, neither. I put a hole in the fender of their car, but I didn't shoot neither one of them."

"You should have called me."

"And what would you and that knight-in-shining-polyester partner of yours have done? Showed up in time to find my lifeless body, probably painted blue and orange by them Gator terrorists?"

"BeaAndra, don't make me come arrest you."

"Remember the last time you arrested me? Wound up marrying me. What we going to do this time, make another baby?"

Blackbeard looked around. The room was packed now and he wished he'd never answered the phone.

BeaAndra went on. "Got me thinking, maybe the kids can go to church with Momma this evening, give us some alone time. Make sure you bring those handcuffs home with you tonight."

Blackbeard punched the disconnect button and banged his head softly against the desk.

BLACKBEARD SAT GLARING at the phone as the crowd thinned out. A couple of people laughed, but nobody was ready to ride Blackbeard about this. Not yet.

"Here." Terry unplugged the handset from Blackbeard's phone and took it over to an empty desk. Picked up the handset from that phone and plugged it into Blackbeard's. Blackbeard nodded tersely without looking up.

"Blackie, we need to do the afternoon stand up on the Keeper case," said Terry.

Blackbeard stood up and stomped off toward the conference room. Brandon and a couple of others were standing by the coffee pot waiting for him.

"C'mon," said Blackbeard, with his head down. "Status time."

Brandon pulled his cuffs off his belt. "Gonna use these to take me into the meeting?"

"Might." Blackbeard brushed past him and into the conference room.

The room was half full of patrolmen, detectives, and techs waiting to go over the daily status.

"OK, Terr," said Blackbeard as he got to the front of the room. "You want to catch everybody up?"

Terry stepped forward like a kid giving a report in school.

"Our guy's not named Keeper, or at least Chicago PD can't find anybody by that name. They're checking his prints against their locals, see what they come up with. We know Keeper—whoever—came in with two bags, but we only found one. Know Oasis and Sunshine had some kind of big development deal fall through, and now the Oasis guy's nervous about something."

"Wait a minute, Terry," said Detective Benson, one of the detectives pulled in to help. "You ain't saying that has anything to do with this, are you? That's two big businesses that employ a lot of people. And Sunshine's based out of a church, that big pink one up on 98 that runs the Christian resort for kids so they can have godly beach vacations. They only started their construction company as a way to provide jobs for folks. We ain't accusing these guys of nothing are we?"

"We're not accusing anybody of anything—yet." Terry nodded. "But Sunshine is also one of the biggest companies around the panhandle. Even church groups get into the wrong stuff sometimes."

Benson turned to Blackbeard, "Blackie, Terry's from up North and don't know no better. You're from around here and know we take our churches mighty serious. We go messing around Sunshine with no reason, folks ain't going to like it."

"You're right," said Blackbeard. "It may be nothing. But Keeper was into something important enough to get him killed." He paused. "Or it looks that way right now. At the same time, something big fell through or got delayed or whatever at Oasis or Sunshine. Now we've got a report that Chop Raines is nervous enough to hire a bodyguard."

Brandon laughed, "That's a lot of body to guard."

Blackbeard said, "That's the point. He don't scare easy, and he's scared now."

"I still think Sunshine ought to be off limits," said Benson.

"Maybe that's the point," said Terry. "If somebody tough is trying to muscle their way into the beach they might pick a partner that nobody will question. But we're not saying they're connected, not right now. Hell, who knows, maybe Keeper was just here to go to the beach."

Blackbeard said, "Didn't bring a swim suit. At least, no swim suit in the one bag we inventoried."

Somebody hidden in the back said, "Maybe he was a nudist."

People laughed, loosening them up and making them bolder. A young guy next to Brandon said, "Maybe Mrs. Blackbeard shot him, thought he was a Gator fan."

More laughing. A couple of guys made comments under their breath. Blackbeard glared and waited for it to die down.

"Johnny." He said the name loud to get everybody's attention, and turned to a man in the back. "You've been pulling together all the interviews from the hotel itself. Anything jump out?"

"Maybe, sir." Johnny was a rookie, which was why he got stuck collating interviews. Clerical work, but somebody had to do it.

"There was a man named Claude Lee from Statesboro, Georgia, interviewed by Sergeant Matthews. Lee said he came in the hotel with his date about the time Keeper checked in. Said his date saw somebody in a Hilton shirt following behind Keeper, carrying two bags for him. Said his date wanted him to get a bellhop to carry her purse."

Terry looked at him. "She wanted a bellhop to carry her purse?"

"Lee said she may have been intoxicated, sir."

A few people laughed, but at least nobody made a BeaAndra joke out of it.

Matthews shook his head. "I'm the one who interviewed him. He said they were both three sheets to the wind. You can't rely on anything he remembered."

"Still," Blackbeard looked at him. "Could be something there. There was only one bag in Keeper's room. Did you interview the girl?"

"She was gone."

"Follow up?"

Matthews shrugged, "Nothing to follow up. He couldn't remember her name."

Blackbeard glared at Matthews. "I need to know stuff like that as soon as you hear it."

Johnny said, "I called Mr. Lee and got a description, sort of. He said he met her at Alley's. Thought I'd check around there, sir, if you agree."

"Yeah," said Blackbeard. "Long shot, but, yeah, try everything. That's our job, keep turning over rocks. Good job,

Johnny." He saw the kid smile. "I mean, good job, Officer Coram."

He turned to Eric, the tech who was working the case. "Anything new from y'all?"

Eric started to say something but Brandon interrupted him.

"Yeah, we found prints from that hot young quarterback the Florida Gators got playing this year. Detective Blackbeard—I mean the real Detective Blackbeard, Detective BeaAndra Blackbeard—has already lit off to arrest him, lock him up before they play Florida State."

A couple of people laughed but more looked away, getting tired of the joke and wanting to focus on actually solving a murder.

Blackbeard looked at Brandon and said in a flat tone, "You know Brandon, your ma still don't know the full story of how her truck got tore up the year before you got your driver's license."

He stared at Brandon till Brandon looked away. Then he looked at Eric.

Eric cleared his throat. "No, sir, nothing new. It's all in the report I gave you yesterday. No prints in the room except hotel staff. It's still a new room, and the Hilton does a pretty good job of cleaning up. Sometimes, a hotel room has so many prints we can't sort anything out. But this one was still pretty clean."

Blackbeard thought a minute. "You got the prints laid out by location?"

"Yes, sir." Eric riffled through the report until he came to a floor plan of the room with numbers showing where prints had been found.

"Where'd you find Keeper's prints?"

"Didn't. Got his prints off of him, not from anything in the room."

Blackbeard turned to Terry and went, "Huh."

Terry nodded. "So they walked into the room and, pow."

Blackbeard said, "Maybe." He turned back to Eric. "How about the outside of the door? Either Keeper opened the door, or our mystery bellhop did. One of them hung that do not disturb sign on the door. Either way, prints on that sign ought to be interesting."

Eric hesitated. He didn't have to look at the report for this one.

"We don't have those."

The shuffling in the room stopped and there was a long pause.

"I thought I told you to get outside the door. Fact, I know I told you to get outside the door."

"You did, sir. And I did." He hesitated again. "Lieutenant Randle said not to process anything outside the room, sir. Said he wasn't going to pay overtime for unnecessary work when you've already got enough evidence."

Everyone watched Blackbeard.

"Enough evidence?" Blackbeard started to pace with his head down, talking to the floor. "He felt there was some kind of magic card in the room, something that would say, go here and collect the killer? You listen to me and you tell Randle this ain't no drunk college prank. Tell him to do his job." He pointed his finger at Eric. "No. You tell him I'm coming down there to tell him to do his job."

He looked around the room.

"Every blessed one of you," he said, pointing at Brandon. "Stop making jokes about my wife and go do your jobs. Do your jobs or get off of my case and go back to cleaning up drunk puke off the beach."

He yelled, "Dismissed" and turned his back on the crowd.

Terry looked at the side of Blackbeard's face and saw his teeth grinding. "They'll forget about it, Blackbeard."

Blackbeard turned his head to face Terry. "What I'm afraid of, partner. This is just another Dogpatch-on-the-Beach caper for them. But it feels like bad things are coming. May take more than a shotgun and gumption to protect Bea. Or the rest of us, for that matter."

Terry looked up and saw the chief standing in the door and wondered how long he had been there. The chief looked around and saw a room full of men resenting being chewed out. Blackbeard saw it, too. He put his head down and brushed by the chief, almost knocking the chief out of the door in a hurry to find Lieutenant Randle. Terry hurried to catch up, but he did at least say, "Excuse me, sir," as he rushed past.

seventeen

LIZZIE PULLED the Hilton shirt off as she walked through the side door of her house. She almost bumped into the door-jamb in her hurry to get rid of the damned thing, her skin was cracking and her head was bursting with songs that had to be written down right now. She dropped her wig and shirt in a pile on the kitchen floor, pulled the pen out from the spine of her notebook and started writing as she sang. She kicked out with her right foot, her hand still writing, and sent the wig flying across the room.

"Rock and roll, hell yeah," she yelled, finding a new song in the middle of the one she was trying to write down. "Future, hell. Here and now belongs to me today, and ain't nothing better."

Her voice screamed and her pen flew and she stood there dancing in her bra and polyester Hilton pants. She looked down, outraged that she still had anything of the uniform still on. She ripped them off, panties coming with them, and she danced in just her bra, imagining she was singing in concert, the songs coming so fast that she couldn't finish even one, the imaginary audience going crazy and loving it. She looked down at her nearly naked body and thought, yeah, no wonder.

Lizzie went back through the house, holding the note-book in her right hand and trying to write with her left while she looked for something. She found it, her old Bama concert shirt, buried deep in the cardboard box that was her laundry hamper. When she pulled it on the shirt was barely long enough to cover her ass, but she danced back to the kitchen anyway.

She wrote until the words finally stopped coming out of the pen, and then she opened a cold Tecate and held it against her forehead. Yeah. This felt more like home. The morning with Blackbeard and the young detective reminded her of the music world where she came from and where she still belonged—where she was going back again, and damned soon, too. The day was coming when she could march into Yolanda's office, throw the uniform at her, and tell her to clean her own damned rooms. Maybe she would walk out of the Hilton bare-assed, too. Though, come to think of it, with what some of the rich young girls in the hotel wore to the beach, maybe no one would notice. And that would deflate her ego.

She giggled. Today she was funny and smart and full of herself. She thought about taking the boat out, finding a quiet place and taking off her clothes and lying there alone in the hot sun for the end of the afternoon, just her and a six pack. Maybe think about that detective, Terry, while she was out there.

But no, she had work to do, so she decided to take advantage of sunset-on-the-bay mojo. The instant the sun touched the horizon, she was calling L.A. She wished she could be there to see the look on the faces when she told them she had the money. She was coming back to free her babies.

Lizzie dug out her cell phone and checked to make sure the number was still there. She had never called it, but it had been carefully transferred from phone to phone, waiting for the day when she would have something to say to the people at that number. Today was that day. Looking out the window, she could see it was almost time.

She took two Tecates out of the fridge and skipped down to the dock. Then she sat there with her bare feet dangling in the water, grounded like a lightening rod waiting for the strike she was about to call.

As the big red globe touched the horizon, she pushed the button on the phone and put it on speaker so she could yell.

Someone picked up and she yelled, "You took my joy and I want it back." There, give them good old Lucinda Williams. Nobody, including Lizzie, did angry and bitter like Lucinda. For now.

After a long pause, a soothing female voice on the speaker cooed, "Peace and Light Music."

Lizzie calmed down a little. "This is Lizzie Borden. I want my joy back."

"Well, you certainly should have your joy. How can I help you with that?"

"You can put the weasel on the line in charge of letting artists have their songs back."

"That weasel would be Mr. Montevallo." Lizzie thought she had lost the connection or the phone had broken, but no, she was listening to the kind of soothing music the company sold now. She waited while one note slowly flowed into another.

"One Mississippi, two Mississippi, three Mississippi . . ." she started counting and got up to fifteen before the next note. She was singing scat over the top of the next note when she realized there was a voice on top of her note, so soothing and mellow it could have been part of the song. If this deserved to be called a song.

"Hello?" she said.

The voice chuckled and started over.

"Greetings, fellow voyager on the warm sea of life. Peace and Light Music welcomes you to our fragile vessel and bids you a safe and fruitful voyage with us."

"What?"

There was a pause and the voice said with a little more grit, "How can I help you?"

"You said something about a voyage?"

Another pause and more grit. "Look, lady, you called me. Whatchawant?"

"'Safe and fruitful voyage?' Jesus, y'all need some new writers out there."

"Are you applying for a job? Let me put you in touch with our personal growth department."

"No! I want my music back, and I'm ready to pay your ransom to get it. This is Lizzie Borden."

"Oh." Then there was a pause and the voice said, "Oh" again like it meant it. "Funny you should call right now. I was just on the phone about you with Lady MaraJane, you know, the artist who takes other people's songs, sets them to a dance beat, and makes them hits under her name?"

"You wouldn't."

"She's interested in 'Get Off My Land.' Though the test marketing group is having trouble with the castration verse. Seems the men dance funny when they get to that part."

"You can't do that to my song."

"Our song. Did you read the stack of contracts you signed when we took over?"

"Not well enough. And I sure didn't know the lawyer I let you recommend would wind up working for you."

"My brother-in-law. And, as he would tell you, we can do whatever we want. Really, we would all benefit from creating a little more beauty in the world, don't you think?"

"How much were you going to pay me for this?"

"Technically, it's not your song anymore."

"That means I don't get Jack Shit, right?"

"There's no need to get ugly. Think of it as your contribution to a better world."

"Better world my ass."

"Have it your way. Yes, Jack Shit is exactly what you'll get. But you'll be part of something creative."

Lizzie suggested something physically impossible and very creative to Mr. Montevallo.

He said, "There's no need for that either."

Lizzie kicked the water and said, "There's no need for any of this. I'm ready to buy my music back. I just need to know where to send the check."

The voice squealed. Lizzie thought the voice was male earlier, but now she was less sure.

"Oh how perfectly lovely. We are always so happy to help our artists spread their wings and fly on their own. I happen to be in the process of helping Len Avil reacquire an interest in his music."

"I remember him. He was going to be the new Bob Dylan, only not as commercial, until you shut him down. Glad he's coming back."

"We've mellowed him a little. OK, I see your file here. Yes, we just need two hundred thousand dollars. I am so excited to be able to help you."

"It's one hundred thousand."

She watched the orange and red streaks on the water as she heard typing on a computer. "Oh, I see. Yes, one hundred thousand dollars. Plus another hundred thousand personally to Mr. Tush, the owner, for his working with you to develop your talent. That's a very good rate."

"Sounds high."

"Avil paid it."

"Still sounds high."

"Not for forty-nine percent."

Now Lizzie paused. She pulled her feet out of the water and stood up on the dock.

"Forty-nine percent?"

"You get forty-nine percent interest in your music and we retain fifty-one percent. An excellent offer. I think we'll work together swimmingly. We'll pick the songs and tell you what to sing, and you get to sing them for us and get rich."

"How much more for one hundred percent?"

"We don't normally do that," he said and laughed. "At the best, we would have to negotiate." He drew "negotiate" out long and smooth, like one of the notes in their music.

"Perhaps we could negotiate my going out under a new name, like Prince did, and leave you without a penny."

"Prince had some lovely lawyers. So do we. You don't."

"Listen to me, you high-voiced son of a bitch."

"This is becoming confrontational."

"You bet it is. You took my joy and I want it back. I want what's mine."

"This no longer belongs to you, and won't until you get a better tone of voice."

Lizzie screamed something decidedly confrontational in a very fine tone of voice and threw the phone as far out into the blood-red creek as she could.

OASIS DEVELOPMENT'S OFFICES were in a pink condo above a water park on the first floor, with cartoons of water droplets splashed across the walls and walkways. Blackbeard parked in the lot across Front Beach Road and he and Terry walked across the skyway, following a German family pushing a loaded-down luggage cart. At the bottom of the waterslide a kid slapped Terry on the butt with a wet Styrofoam noodle and grinned.

Blackbeard knew where he was going and Terry followed. They took an elevator to the second floor, walked past a reception area and down a hall with rose-colored walls and piped-in music until they came to a compact reception room hidden away from the tourists. Terry looked at the walls and saw the pictures of palm trees and sailboats had changed to autographed pictures of football coaches such as Pat Dye and Bobby Bowden, and paintings of football players straining to push the ball across the goal line or reaching up one more inch to block a kick.

A young woman, with a figure and tan that God and the sun had never given her, looked up at Blackbeard.

"May I help you, sir?" Then she saw Terry. "Oh." She smiled big, the same smile Terry himself often used. "Bradford. I haven't seen you since the party last week."

Terry smiled back but Blackbeard was smiling, too, a rare smile. Blackbeard spoke before Terry could say anything.

"Bradford? Didn't know you had a first name."

Terry started to say something to Blackbeard, but this time the girl interrupted him.

"Only his very close friends get to call him Bradford." She leaned over the desk. Her thin sweater was tight and it was the same bright, unnatural blue as her eyes.

Blackbeard pointed at the door. "Chop in?"

"I don't think he's seeing anyone."

Blackbeard walked in anyway and Terry followed him, nodding at the girl as he went.

The room featured a walnut desk the size and shape of a fishing boat on the far side of an acre of sand-white pile carpet. *Nice*, thought Terry. The sun pouring in the wall of windows made it feel like they were hanging out at a shipwrecked boat on the beach. He realized, too, that walking across all that carpet made one feel intimidated and small.

A man big enough to make the desk look small jumped up with fear in his eyes as Blackbeard burst in. Terry saw another man, smaller, but still big, stand up in a corner hidden behind the door and reach for something on his hip.

"I wouldn't do that," said Terry, stepping quick toward the guy behind the door. His boss nodded and the guy took his hand away. Terry turned so he could see the desk without taking his eyes off the man with the gun.

Blackbeard and the boss faced each other across the desk.

"Detective Blackbeard," said the boss. "Didn't it used to be Lieutenant?"

There was a long pause.

"Terry," Blackbeard finally said without taking his eyes off Raines, "meet Chop Raines."

"Charles," said Raines. "My name's Charles."

Blackbeard said, "They called him 'Chop' when he played at Auburn. Famous for chopping other guys' knees, take them out for the game or maybe their career."

"I play to win."

"Sometimes it ain't playing."

Raines shrugged. Then he smiled at Blackbeard, the fake salesman smile you give somebody when you need something from them.

Terry decided Blackbeard needed a good cop so he smiled back at Raines. "Look, Mr. Raines, we're trying to get a feel for what's going on around town. Detective Blackbeard said if there was anything to know about beach development, you'd be the man. All we want is a little background on the beach development business."

Raines turned to Terry and kept his smile.

"People have been hanging on here since the market crashed, barely getting by," he said. "Now we got a few deals opening up. The Hole in the Beach deal is the biggest thing in years. We're brokering it for the owner; Sunshine's going to develop it." He hesitated. "Sunshine or Progress Bank. We were supposed to pick a winner yesterday. Looks like maybe

tomorrow, if either one of those two can get their acts together. Look, for all of us, if we can get a piece of that, and if
the tourists keep coming back, we might make some money."

He turned back to Blackbeard. "You don't mind if we
make a little money, do you?" Then he looked back at Terry.
"Detective Blackbeard has a grudge against people making
money—unless they do it with a fishing pole or a shrimp net.
Sometimes he has to be told to get his cracker nose out of
the business of the good people here who are trying to make
money for us all." He smiled back at Blackbeard. "Maybe we
really can come out ahead, if we don't spook the tourists with
all this talk of mob killings."

"I didn't tell nobody we had a mob killing."

"You didn't say we didn't. You kept everybody lined up
at the Hilton like we had a terrorist attack. You ain't helping."

"I do my job. Don't like it, you and the C of C can talk to
the chief."

"Dammit, Blackie, we grew up together. We fished together—"

"Now we're different." Blackbeard jerked his chin toward
the guy with the gun. "What you got yourself into, Chop?
Guy big as you never needed a bodyguard before."

Raines looked around like there was someone in the room
they couldn't see. Then he came around the desk. "C'mon."
He walked out and said to the girl, "Sharon, tell the restaurant
we're coming." The gun scurried to get in front of Raines. He
looked like a blocker leading a runner in a college football
game, except that their sizes were reversed.

Blackbeard and Terry followed Raines and his bodyguard out of the office and through an open area to a restaurant with glass walls looking out on the beach on one side and the water park on the other. That way Mom and Dad could have a nice meal while keeping an eye on the kiddies. Or, Mom could keep an eye on the kiddies and Dad could keep an eye on the girls on the beach. Whatever.

The manager was waiting for them at the door, but Raines walked past without acknowledging him, and headed to an empty table in the far left corner. Waiters scurried around, moving families that were sitting close to the corner over to the other side of the restaurant, offering them free meals to keep them happy. In a few seconds the whole quarter of the restaurant was clear and Raines sat down. The gun took a table between them and the door, and Terry sat with him.

"You got to try this new thing the chef's got, Blackie," said Raines. "Grouper dusted with a mix of coffee and habaneras. Make your hair stand on end."

Blackbeard shook his head but Terry said, "I'd like to try that." He smiled at Raines, friendly.

Blackbeard grimaced but looked at the manager. "You got any fresh snapper back there?"

"Got some good looking pink snapper came in half an hour ago."

"Grill it with a little Old Bay. Let me have some mashed potatoes and fresh tomatoes, if you don't mind."

"And give me a double Bloody Mary with my usual," said Raines.

Raines made small talk until the food arrived and the servers withdrew out of earshot.

"Blackie." He leaned over and talked quieter, almost in a whisper. "You need to wrap this thing up, arrest somebody and recover what that guy was bringing down."

"Who said he was bringing anything?" said Terry.

Blackbeard gave him a look to be quiet and let Raines talk. Terry turned back to his plate, took a bite of his fish and thought, *damn, this is good and hot*. He had a quick image of a cartoon cowboy jumping up and draining a horse trough of water to quell the fire. Then he looked toward the entrance to the restaurant. A small gang of young men with baggy pants and ball caps turned backwards, looking like a gang ready to cause trouble, were trying to get in, arguing as the manager shooed them away. Terry tensed, but the gun showed no interest.

Raines paused. "Just assumed," he said, looking at Blackbeard. "There's bad things going on, Blackie, and you get paid to protect us."

"So you want Terry and me to get a hammer," said Blackbeard, "join in with you and the C of C in building a grand high rise to cover up that ugly Hole in the Beach so tourists won't have to see how the beach used to be with sand dunes and sea oats instead of white tablecloths and waiters in tuxedos?"

"C'mon, Blackie. Look, maybe the Hole in the Beach deal falls through. The property owner's already mad because he feels like Sunshine and Progress aren't keeping the commitments he expected. He's making noises about just taking the whole property, from the beach all the way back to 98, and giving it to a charity a buddy of his from California runs, make it some kind of a retreat for kids, bring together kids with potential from different places around the world. Maybe try to grow a generation of leaders who can work together rather than fight. Who knows?" Raines leaned over. "But if the owner gets pissed and turns do-gooder, all of us lose a ton of money."

Blackbeard said, "So you got to do something fast."

"No, you do. Wrap this thing up so we can move on."

Terry saw a couple of guys in suits walk into the restaurant, walk right by the manager and come toward them like they owned the place. The gun straightened up and paid attention, pulling his gun out and holding it in his lap under the table while he watched the suits. The suits ignored him and sat down at a table, just businessmen looking for a quick lunch.

Terry turned to Raines, "This guy's going to get somebody killed waving his gun around like that."

"Where'd you get him?" said Blackbeard. "Yellow pages?"

"He's one of my sister's nephews."

One of the suits stood up and the gun pointed the gun at him under the table.

"Oh, for crying out loud," said Terry. He reached out and swept his hand under the table, and came up with the gun in his hand. He checked the safety and put it in his pocket as he stood up.

"Hey," said the guy who no longer had a gun.

"Do what you do best," said Terry. "Eat."

Raines stood up without touching his lunch. "Fine. Be the tough guys. But Blackie, the folks coming in now are pros. Going to take more than a couple of small town Barney Fife's to stop them. You need to get this done or call in help."

Blackbeard looked at Raines with no expression until Raines got tired of waiting for him to say something.

Raines leaned over Blackbeard. "Fine. Have it your way. But a storm's coming. A bad storm's coming, Blackie, and it's your job to protect us from it."

LIZZIE SAT IN THE KITCHEN picking out crabmeat and putting it in a Cool Whip container to go into the freezer for another time. After the talk with Peace and Light, she was too upset to eat. So, she dropped a big chunk of back fin meat into the tub and picked up her Tecate. Too upset to eat, but not too upset for a beer. Or several.

"See now, you're mine." She waved the beer at the pile of white meat streaked with orange spices. "And you're mine." She waved the bottle at a line of empties beside the steamer of crabs. "Ain't no fruity lawyer gonna tell me you're not."

She sat there for a long time, then screamed at the window.

"I get it. You danged Gods of Honesty are telling me that money ain't mine either and you won't let me buy my music back with something that ain't mine. I. Get. It."

She giggled at herself. "Good thing we Gaffneys can hold our liquor." After she had thrown her phone off the dock, she'd gone up to the house and had a beer. And another. Then she went into the studio and tried to play, but everything she played sounded New Age to her today and reminded her of Peace and Light. That made her feel like a traitor.

After, she went down to the dock and thought about diving in and retrieving her phone.

"To hell with it," she said. She thought about it a minute and threw her arms out wide and screamed, "To. Hell. With. It," screaming each word separate like she was announcing the name of a band or a song at a concert. Might be a good song.

But not a song for her today. The writer in her was gone now, replaced by a pitiful creature who reminded her how powerless and unimportant she was, even with stolen money.

She had pulled up the crab trap. If you don't check the trap every day, Daddy taught her, then the crabs die in a cage, wasted, and that was just wrong. The trap was full today, a ball of beautiful swimmers waving their claws at her. Attitude, she thought. That's what takes a little bitty handful of nothing but shell and grit and turns it into a fearsome thing of beauty.

And good eating. She threw back the sookies and the ones too little to keep, dumped the rest into a basket and took them up to the house to steam.

"Good eating," she said now, sitting at the table with the beer in her hand and a nearly full container of sweet, white crab meat. "Maybe not tonight. But another night I'll be hungry and you'll be there for me.

"You'll be there because I worked for you. Not just caught you and cooked you. Fed you every time I threw scraps out in the water for you. Waved to you every time I took the boat out. I contributed to you, and the gods rewarded me with the best eating anywhere. Hell, I've eaten so many crabs, my body's probably mostly crab itself now. So in a way, I belong to you."

She looked at the crab on her plate. "And you belong to me." She giggled and clinked her beer against an empty bottle. "And you and you and you . . . and especially you," she said, clinking her beer against each of the dead soldiers in turn.

She thought of something in the boathouse that didn't belong to her. That stack of money had seemed like a ticket to freedom and honest music. Now it was a magnet for trouble that wouldn't even buy back full rights to her own music.

"Ain't that the way of the world," she said, "Earn it or leave it alone." *Another good song in that line,* she thought. But there weren't going to be any songs written now. She drained the beer and went to the refrigerator for another.

The refrigerator was empty. Facing a night with no beer and no music, she thought about driving to the store but shook her head. "Getting too old to drive around drunk," she said. "Ain't fourteen no more."

The phone rang just then, but at first, she didn't recognize the sound. No one called on the house phone; anyone who knew her knew to call her cell. She wondered where her cell was, then remembered, and she giggled again.

"Sleep with the fishes, Peace and Light," she yelled. *Another good line for a song. Damn.* Lines were all over the place when you didn't need them.

The phone kept ringing so she picked it up.

"Elizabeth's Pity Party," she said. There was silence on the other end. After a few seconds, she said, "Hello?"

"Is this Lizzie Gaffney?"

"Maybe. Today I'm not too sure."

The voice laughed and said, "With a voice like that, the rest of us are always going to be sure who you are."

Lizzie laughed, "And that's a good thing?"

"A very good thing. Ms. Gaffney, this is Brad Terry. We met the other day at the Hilton. My partner, Detective Blackbeard, and I talked to you."

"Yes," Lizzie stood up a little straighter. *See now, that evil pile of paper in the boathouse was coming for her.*

"I don't have nothing here the police want," she said. "Not nothing a 'tall."

She grimaced. *Lies on top of lies.* See now, that's what happens. You take one step away from being honest, then you take another and another, and soon you're as phony as everybody else. Might as well fish the cell phone out of the water, call Peace and Light back, and see if they'd give her a job answering the phones or something.

Terry laughed. "Well, I don't want to mislead you. This call's not really about official police business."

"It's not?"

"No. When we talked, you and Detective Blackbeard indicated that you used to be a pretty good musician."

"That's right," she said. "Used to be."

"So I did some looking around. Found a YouTube video of a concert you did in San Diego."

"Oh yeah." Lizzie smiled. "That was a good one. Got three new songs that night. Two of them are going to be on the next album." Lizzie listened to herself, realized she had said there was going to be a next album.

"I'll buy a copy. You're good, real good. I've never seen an audience go crazy like they did when you came up with 'Sand in my Shorts.'"

"That one was fun. I tied together the water back here in ECB and the beach in San Diego where I was giving the concert. And it talked about how I felt then, how I could not sit still for anything. There was too much to get done. Sleeping more than a couple of hours seemed like a waste to me then."

"Good thing," said Terry. "If that's what it takes to get you to come up with songs like those, someone should keep your shorts full of sand all the time."

Lizzie paused. Maybe this wasn't the police. Maybe this was just the cute guy she'd met. Maybe that was a line he was giving her. Course, if it was, it was one of the strangest lines she'd ever heard. Of course, strange didn't scare Lizzie.

"You mentioned getting together to jam sometime," said Terry. "Wondered if I could come by after work tomorrow, make a little music with you."

"Sure," said Lizzie in her best I-don't-care-if-you-do-or-don't voice of a girl talking to a guy early on. But then she realized that she needed to add something more. "Be here at nine. Don't be late." She hung up the phone before he could give her any backtalk.

Might be good to make a little music.

"Make a little music, make a little music," she hummed as she walked through the house to the studio. Only two lines, but it was a song that belonged to her.

IT WAS RAINING when Terry walked into Mack's on Friday morning. Not a real Florida downpour, it was light enough that Terry looked out the patio door of SD6 and said to himself, "Nah, don't need a jacket for this."

Of course the walk was longer than he remembered. And of course he was wet and chilled by the time he walked in the door. Julie threw him a dish towel and muttered something about sense and rain.

Blackbeard sipped coffee and watched as he sat down. After a couple of minutes, Blackbeard threw the paper across at him.

"See today's news yet?"

Terry set down his fork down and picked up the paper.

"Perfect weather this weekend. Good time to walk down to the beach, see what's shaking at the Tiki Bar."

"Like I said about what's your full-time job and what's your part time job. No, scan the front page. What do you see?"

"Nothing."

"Exactly. Yesterday morning, the lead story was about a possible mob killing at the Hilton, full of a breathless mangling of the facts. By midmorning it was just a small story;

police still don't know what happened. Today, look at page three."

Terry opened the paper. "Nothing here."

"Look again."

Terry found something.

"Hey, how come we didn't hear about this? Headline is, domestic dispute at hotel. We're supposed to be informed on domestics in case next time it gets worse . . . oh."

Blackbeard smiled at Terry. "Yeah. You figured it out."

Terry read. "'Police now say the death of Albert Keeper at a hotel Tuesday night was a probable domestic dispute.'"

Terry looked up at Blackbeard. "Domestic dispute? The guy came down here alone. We didn't say any of this. Hell, we don't even know his real name. Jesus."

"Read on."

"Out of deference to a sensitive family situation, a police spokesman said the remaining investigation will be handled privately."

Terry slammed the paper down, and got eggs and hot sauce all over the front page.

"Police spokesman? You mean Keller, the moron who takes the reports we write up, changes a few fragments, throws in a couple of 'whoms' where they don't belong, and sends it to his buddy at the *ECB News*?"

"You do have a lot of fragments in your reports." Blackbeard was enjoying Terry's outrage.

"Adds punch. Want my story to have punch and meaning, something worth reading. Read Elmore Leonard sometime, man can't write without fragments."

"Yeah, I get it. Glamour and excitement is what we're about."

Terry pulled the paper out of the mess and fumed at it.

"Know what that means?" Blackbeard said.

"Someone can't write?"

"That too." He leaned toward Terry. Blackbeard's eyes had the same cold blue fire Terry had seen when Blackbeard was about to nail someone in an interrogation.

"Means they're coming for us, partner. They can't print this stuff and leave us on the case."

Terry wadded up the paper. "They don't know who they're messing with. We're going to go Serpico on them, call up the Tallahassee and Atlanta papers, give them the real story. Get some real reporters down here. We stand for the people. We're going to bust this case wide open."

"Yeah, yeah." Blackbeard fixed him with a stare. "What we're going to do is, we're going to do our job. Just keep doing the job, day after day, and don't quit."

Terry was still fuming when Blackbeard said, "You going to finish them eggs?"

Terry looked at him like he was crazy. "Too juiced to eat now. We got a battle to fight."

Blackbeard pulled the plate over. "Then I'll eat them."

When they walked into the station, Terry saw Brandon lounging by the side door, out for a smoke. Terry caught his eye and waited for Brandon to make a smart comment, but Brandon just looked away like he didn't know them. Everyone seemed to look away as they walked in, and no one spoke as they went to their desks. Then the lieutenant walked over.

"Chief wants to see you."

Terry stared at him. "Tell the chief to come out here. Anything he's got to say, he can say to us in front of everybody."

Blackbeard put his hand on Terry's arm and said to the lieutenant, "We'll be along in a minute." Blackbeard hung up his coat on the second slot of the rack, just as he did every morning, then jerked his head at Terry and walked toward the door.

"Jesus, partner," he said over his shoulder, "was getting run out of Chicago so much fun that you want to get run out of here, too?"

"Maybe."

"You think fighting with the people in charge is part of your job description?"

"Sometimes."

"Well, try it my way this time. Just do our jobs. Don't quit."

"Looks like we're being fired."

"Can't control that. Can control whether we quit."

They walked in on the chief talking to a city councilman. The chief saw them and said to the councilman, "We'll finish this later."

The councilman said, "We just need to get clear on—"

"Later." The chief stared at the councilman until the man shrugged and left. The chief sat down behind his desk and motioned to two chairs. Blackbeard just stood there, so Terry did, too.

"You're off the Keeper case." The chief looked at Blackbeard for a fight, but Blackbeard said nothing.

"Not my call," said the chief after a minute of waiting. "Not entirely. The city's going to hire a couple of outside experts to handle this. I'm supposed to call them later today."

"Yes, sir," Blackbeard said.

There was another awkward pause.

"You know I don't like this anymore than you do."

"Yes, sir."

"Blackbeard, I worked with your father, way back when. He was a good cop."

"Yes, sir."

"And I'm a good cop."

"Yes, sir."

The chief picked up a letter opener, an award he'd won when he was a young cop, and started balancing it. He looked up at Blackbeard. Blackbeard stood there like a statue that could stay rooted in one spot forever, if need be. The chief then looked at Terry. Terry was fidgeting, and wanted to tell the chief what a good cop could do with that letter opener. The chief smiled, ready for Terry to give him the fight he wanted. But, Terry looked at Blackbeard and straightened up, stood tall and started staring at nothing in particular.

"I am a good cop," said the chief.

"Yes sir," Blackbeard said.

The chief drummed the letter opener on the blotter on his desk. Finally, the chief put it down. "Look, take the weekend off. I'll have Burress keep working the loose ends over the weekend. We'll talk again Monday."

"Yes sir." Blackbeard turned and walked out of the room. Terry looked at the chief one last time, and and then followed.

Terry's phone was ringing when they walked back into the squad room. It was the only sound in the room.

He snatched the phone up. "Terry."

"You mean Superman?"

Terry recognized the voice from Chicago. "Yeah. Funny. How are things up in the Windy City? Still laughing at me about the no-name guy from Chicago I got down here?"

"No. Nobody's laughing at you up here now. I'm supposed to stay in touch, give the brass here daily briefings on what's going on down there. You caught a big fish.

"Your guy ain't no nobody. Name's Mex Carmex. Or Jonathan Jefferson Carmex, you want the full handle. Local fixer for the wise guys here. They send him places to make things happen. People up here want to know what he was making happen down there."

"You mean he's an enforcer?"

"Enforcer when he needs to be, businessman when he needs to be, negotiator, you name it. Kind of like a free safety, but a big one. He goes someplace, things get done. Usually followed by an army of guys coming behind him to finish things up. You got trouble coming your way, Terry. You may have left Chicago, but Chicago may be coming to you."

Terry said, "The bag the guy had—what'd you say his name was again, Carmex? Anyway, he had two bags when he came to the hotel, but only one when we found him. We're assuming it was money. If he was down here as an enforcer, it could have been weapons."

"Could be. You think a guy with connections can't get a carry-on bag with guns on a plane in Chicago? I'm faxing you his jacket now. Look, Superman—"

"You know I hate that name."

"Yeah, right." Jordan laughed, a little nervous. "Yeah, right. Terry. Whatever." He paused. "Look, the brass here are watching this, want to see what you turn up that they can use. Some of them are thinking, hey, what the guy did before wasn't so bad, just a little aggressive. Maybe they could use some aggressive now. You make a play on this thing, give them something they can use and there might be an opportunity for you here. There's talk of opening an organized crime section, real Elliot Ness kind of thing. Even some talk about bringing you back for it. Could be a break, if you come out of this thing a hero."

"Yeah. Thanks."

Terry hung up.

He looked at Blackbeard sitting at his desk with his eyes down. *Maybe two years to spend here in the minor leagues,* thought Terry. *Maybe less.* He looked past Blackbeard, out the window to a patch of white sandy soil where the grass wouldn't grow. *Maybe snow wasn't so bad.*

An aide came in and dumped a stack of file folders on Terry's desk.

"Chief says you're supposed to go through these closed cases, clean up any paperwork that needs fixing."

Terry looked at Blackbeard. "What do we do now?" he said.

Blackbeard reached over and took the top half of the pile. "Do our jobs, partner." He shoved the lower half across to Terry's desk. "Do our jobs."

twenty-one

SATURDAY MORNING, Rolvaag took Fabbi to the walk-in clinic on the other side of Pier Mall from the bank. Really, he didn't want to take him anywhere, but Fabbi had showed up at work Friday morning complaining about being in so much pain that he couldn't sit down. He drew so much attention standing up and whining that Rolvaag knew he had to do something. He thought about taking him somewhere out of town, Tallahassee maybe, in case the cops were looking for a guy with a hoe wound in his ass. But really, what were the chances that the cops were canvassing hospitals and clinics looking for a victim of a garden hoe attack? Besides, he was tired of playing master criminal and wanted to go back to being a development banker and fill out paperwork and smile at the boys at the chamber of commerce meetings.

So here they were at the clinic.

The doctor was a cute young blonde woman who looked about fourteen—except for the flare around her hips and bust.

"So tell me," she said in a breezy Russian accent. "How you get this?"

Fabbi tried to say something, but he was lying face down on the hospital bed and his face was in a pillow.

Rolvaag said, "He fell on the fan blade of my 309 while we were working on it." No point in letting Fabbi make up some hero story and make things worse. "We were pulling the engine out of my Chevy Charger." Rolvaag hitched up his pants because he felt like it went with the story. "Dang thing got away from us and he fell back, caught his keister on a fan blade."

She looked at Rolvaag, her eyes a brilliant pale blue. Right now, they were working hard to not show her disbelief.

"He not wearing his pants while you work on car?"

"Well, of course he was. What you think? Danged blade cut right through his jeans."

She paused, but showed nothing. "That some fan blade. What kind of engine you say this was?"

"309. Flathead. Hemi. Full Bore." He didn't know what any of it meant, but it sounded good.

She nodded, seemed to file the details of the story in her head for later, at happy hour. Then she turned back to the problem at hand.

"You lucky. Fan blade just cut skin. Baby cut. Sharper fan blade cut big gluteus muscle, you bleed like pig and maybe die. Will clean you up, put in few stitches, you be OK. Hurt when you sit down for few days." She looked back at Rolvaag. "Wear tougher pants, next time you do whatever it is you two do."

She went out of the room.

Fabbi hissed at Rolvaag, and Rolvaag bent down to hear him.

"Why the hell did you tell her that story? I wanted to tell her I was attacked, cut by a guy with a knife, get her sympathy. She's the cutest thing I've seen since I've been down here."

"You think telling her some guy stuck you in the ass is going to turn her on? And if it does, you sure you want to go back home with her?"

Fabbi was quiet. The doctor came back in with an assistant who was holding a metal tray. She took a big needle off the tray.

"This may hurt little bit." She jammed the needle in hard next to the cut. Fabbi stiffened and clutched the sheet, but he didn't say anything. "Not like fan blade," she said. "But little tingle."

"I go out now," she said. "Let anesthetic work, then we do stitches."

She stepped out and Fabbi hissed at Rolvaag again.

"I told you to take me to a real hospital. She almost killed me."

"Stop your bellyaching and be glad I took you anywhere. Told you yesterday, go home, lie down, let it heal."

"I did. Still bleeding today."

"Then be glad I took the time to bring you here."

"Back home, we'd have people to take care of me."

"You aren't in Kansas anymore, sport. Neither of us are."

"Yeah, well, I talked to Dad last night. You don't find that money and get this deal done, he's sending people out here. Might not be a bad idea to get some pros in here. We may need some Vegas pros here if the Chicago guys are coming in."

"We don't need that. You Vegas pros are just going to wind up with a little old lady's hoe stuck in your ass." He glanced at Fabbi and saw him grimace.

"Yeah, that's about it." Rolvaag leaned into Fabbi. "Locals down here are tougher than you think—sure a hell of a lot tougher than you, and you got the mark to prove it."

Fabbi was glaring now, as much as you can glare while you're lying on a hospital bed with your bare ass up in the air. Rolvaag was enjoying it.

"You and your dad have to understand that the guys that have his money are cops. You can't just walk up and break their legs and demand payment like your dad used to."

"Hey," said Fabbi, raising his head so he could look Rolvaag in the eye. "If you think guys from Vegas aren't tough enough to get the job done, you've got another think coming. Cops can die, too."

Rolvaag looked up and saw the Russian doctor standing in the doorway with her assistant standing behind her. No emotion showed in the doctor's pale blue eyes.

"C'MON," SAID BLACKBEARD, closing a folder, moving it from the hulking stack of reports he had left to the smaller stack of reports he had done that day.

Terry looked up. His stack of finished reports was smaller than Blackbeard's. Every time he'd looked up today Blackbeard was grinding away, one report after another, no complaints, no sign of resentment. Terry kept expecting Blackbeard to jump up with his jaw locked and march back into the chief's office, tell the chief what he could do with his paperwork. Terry was primed to go with him, but it never happened.

"Barely three o'clock," said Terry. "You never knock off before six."

"Today I'm leaving early. You coming?" Blackbeard ignored him and pulled his jacket off the rack.

"Sure." Terry unfolded his jacket and followed. "Where we going?"

"To Steamers to get some blue crabs. Don't usually have time to go that far out. Figure we'll take advantage of working regular office hours rather than chasing a case."

"You buying?"

"I'm driving."

Blackbeard pulled the Impala out onto 79 and headed north toward the bridge that spanned the Inland Waterway. They followed signs through a trailer park, and past a little primitive church, to a small compound of old buildings set in the live oaks on the banks of the waterway. Off to the side, down by the water, sat a tin-roof shack with an airbrushed sign, ride the airboats while you wait for your table. Terry waved at a guy with a dyed blonde mullet who was loading a family of six onto an airboat. The guy brightened when he saw Terry.

"Hey Terry," he yelled. The man settled the mother into her seat and came running up the crushed oyster shell path.

"Look, Terry," he said when he got to them. "Can you take this one for me? I need to call my ma to let her know I'm going to be late getting home. I been busier than a one-legged man in an ass-kicking contest and ain't had no chance. You got your certification on the airboat out here a while back. If you can take this one for me, I'll owe you."

Terry grinned and looked at Blackbeard.

"Sure, kid," Blackbeard said. "Go play. I'll get us a table inside the shack and get them started on a pile of blues."

Terry turned back. "OK, Jason. Want me to take them out and drown them?"

"Just out to the edge of the bay. Run them over to that creek the Canadians live on and bring them back. This one's a quick trip, one of those thirty minute rides we give folks while they're waiting for a table up at the big restaurant."

Terry and Jason walked down to the dock. Jason reached under a small wooden counter and pulled out a pair of goggles and a windbreaker with a life jacket sewn inside. Terry waved the goggles away and fished a pair of wrap-around Oakley sunglasses out of his jacket pocket and put them on. Then he peeled his jacket off, tucked it under the counter, and pulled on the windbreaker.

Terry looked around and realized that he was looking for a mirror to check out how he looked with the black jacket and the black sunglasses. Smiled at himself for his own vanity and climbed up on the high pilot seat behind the paying customers.

"Ladies and gentlemen," said Jason. "You have the rare privilege of being escorted today by Officer Terry of the Emerald Coast Beach Police Department."

"Detective," corrected Terry.

"I thought officer was higher than detective."

"No, it's—never mind." He stopped himself, realizing that he was still looking around for the mirror, but in a different way. He turned the key. The Chevy 502 engine roared to life, and the propeller at his back turned into a blur. Jason threw the coiled rope into the bow and kicked the boat away from the dock.

Terry ran the throttle up to about a third and pulled the stick back to turn the nose of the boat left and out into the waterway. The humid air quickly turned into a fresh wind as the boat picked up speed.

He stood up with one hand on the stick and one bracing on the seat. He leaned into the wind and felt like he was flying, skimming along just a few feet over the water like some giant bird of prey.

A young boy in the front seat of the boat looked up with a grin at the big man in the black jacket and dark glasses, standing tall and protecting the boy's family as they flew over the water. Terry gave him a salute and the boy saluted back proudly.

The Inland Waterway itself seemed wide, but when they came out into the West Bay it felt as if they had entered a huge water world. The only land they could see was an insignificant ring of rock and salt marsh far away on the horizon. Terry spotted the creek by the Canadians and turned into it, turning the wide-open water world into a narrow tunnel that was covered in scrub pines. He throttled the airboat down as slow as possible and let them drift into the creek. With the engine quiet, Terry pointed out the features of the creek and the salt marsh around it.

Then he let the boat drift into a stand of spiky brown grass.

"They call this stuff sawgrass," he said. "It's one of the oldest plants known to man, and one of the toughest. There's just one problem with it."

He dug a tissue out of the locker under his seat and dragged it across the grass. The paper came up in shreds.

"It's sharp as razors."

The boy said, "Cool."

Terry smiled at him and said, "Be careful of this stuff. Sawgrass rings nearly every mile of Florida Panhandle salt marshes. The salt marsh protects its own."

The boy's mother smiled at Terry and said, "You must be a native."

Terry smiled and guided the boat away from the sawgrass. After they passed the Canadians' house, he spun the airboat around twice, showing off, and brought them back to the dock. He tied up the boat and thanked the passengers, gave Jason his jacket back, and headed off across the crushed oyster shell parking lot.

The airboat stand shared a dock with a sprawling restaurant with tin roofs and unpainted wood and colorful signs sprawling up from the water. It was good, but it wasn't where he knew Blackbeard would be. Terry climbed up the parking lot, hiked across the narrow road that led to the section of the old bridge that had been left as a fishing pier, and went into the pines until he found a shack with the words steamers on top.

Blackbeard was waiting at a picnic table out front. Terry walked up to him still grinning.

"Thought you were doing Jason a favor?" said Blackbeard. "Looks like he did you one."

"Felt good out there."

A little girl no more than three years old, wearing pigtails and a sunburn, dropped her fork and Terry ran over to pick it up. He wiped it off and set it back on the table with a flourish. Then he walked back to Blackbeard and grinned.

"To serve and protect," said Terry.

"One day one of your fictional detectives is going to leap off the page, kill you, and bury you out in the Nevada desert. And I won't lift a finger to stop him."

Terry leaned in and wiped the corner of his mouth with the back of his hand, like Bogart used to do in the movies. "Sure you would," he said. "'Cause you're my partner. You're supposed to feel something for your partner."

"I feel like my partner reads too many detective books and watches too many superhero movies."

Terry sat down. "You wouldn't be able to call me on all the quotes if you didn't do the same."

Blackbeard didn't say anything. Terry pointed at the pile of steamed blue crabs between the two of them. The table had a hole in the middle and under the hole was a trashcan. That way diners could throw the shells away without getting up. Terry looked at the large pile of half-eaten crab in front of Blackbeard. "Thought you were going to wait for me?"

"Was. Except you got to have crab meat to go with beer." He waved a bottle of Killian's.

"Thought you didn't drink?"

"Got to have beer with crab meat," he said. "But don't tell Bea."

"After what she did to those Gator fans, I'd be afraid to tell Bea anything other than, 'yes, ma'am.'"

"Good idea."

Terry reached over and picked up a crab, all hard shell and claws and legs covered in brown-orange spice, and broke it in two. Waved one half at Blackbeard.

"So," said Terry. "How's it feel to be without a case?"

Blackbeard looked out at the water and smiled. Terry was surprised. Maybe Blackbeard was enjoying being an office worker.

Blackbeard ignored the question. "So what you think," he said, "happens to the case now?"

"Now that we know real wise guys are definitely involved?" said Terry. He was starting to pick out the meat, making a mess and having fun. "I think the C of C is going to have to get out of the way, let whatever hot shots they bring in chase this thing from Chicago to wherever it leads down here, no matter who it embarrasses or how many big real estate deals crash and burn."

"They ain't going to like it."

"They'll just have to accept it," said Terry, "if they're honest."

Blackbeard leaned back and picked up his Killian.

"See, Terry, there's all kinds of honest in this world," he said.

"There's one kind of honest, or there's none at all," said Terry.

"No, that sounds like a line from your detective books, but it ain't true. In the real world, everybody's got their truth, and they'll defend it, and that's what they mean by honest.

Tell a preacher there's no God, and he'll get his back up. That's his truth.

"Look at this place here. You tell the two young guys trying to make this little shack a success that they don't know how to run a business, and they'll shrug. But tell them their crabs have too much Slap Yo Mama seasoning on them, and you'll have a fight on your hands. Don't mean they don't want to make money. Someday they'll have a bank, an accountant, an IRA, and everything just like every member of the chamber of commerce. But their food is their honesty.

"The chamber's honesty is just money. You tell the owner of one of the big condos down on the lagoon that your room stinks, and he'll smile and offer you another room. A voice in the back of his head is saying to you, 'Yeah, pal, but I made more money last month than you did this year.' Pride in his product ain't personal to him, just another business cost.

"I don't fault them for it. I like money, too. It just ain't my honesty."

They finished eating. After they paid the bill, Terry looked at Blackbeard.

"So, what is your honesty?"

"My name."

"What? Like the pirate? That makes you honest? You going to get an eyepatch?"

"Yeah, that sounds like me. No, it's one of those honest/dishonest things where you have to decide where you want to make your stand. When I was twelve, we went to meet some cousins I hadn't met. Except their name was

Blackburn, not Blackbeard. I asked Daddy about it later. He drew a big breath and said, 'Son, I reckon it's time you knew. There's a lot of Blackbeards scattered around coastal regions where Blackbeard the pirate never set foot. And we ain't related to each other and we ain't related to the old pirate himself. Somewhere along the line, somebody decided they wanted the swagger of a pirate name, so they changed theirs. In our case, it was my grandfather who started calling himself Blackbeard instead of Blackburn. And that's why we're Blackbeards.'"

He glared at Terry, daring him to make a joke. Didn't get one.

Blackbeard sighed. "I was outraged to learn I had been lied to, that I had spent my life lying to people about who I was. I vowed to change my name back as soon as I could."

He paused.

"But by that time, Daddy was gone. I decided that my name and my belief in honesty were the best things he had left me, so, while Blackbeard may say 'pirate' to most people, it says 'Daddy' to me."

Terry said, "Your own kind of honesty."

"Only kind that matters." Blackbeard stood up from the table. "C'mon, let's take a ride out to the new airport while we're out this way. It's only about three miles away and I've never seen it."

"Sure."

• • •

The new airport was supposed to open up the whole Emerald Coast, if you believed the publicity. Blackbeard parked in front, in a no parking zone.

The two partners walked into a lobby that was still shiny-new. They paused and Terry looked around and said, "Looks nice." He had never seen Blackbeard play tourist and he wasn't sure what else to say.

Blackbeard said, "Real pretty," and turned and walked away. Terry hurried to catch up. Blackbeard walked back to a bar tucked in front of the security area. A young man, wiry and dark, looked up.

"Hey, cousin John Christopher," he said to Blackbeard.

"Never heard anybody call you anything but Blackie," said Terry.

"That's cause this here's a Blackbeard, too. Terr, meet my cousin Earl."

Earl stuck out his hand. "This is the famous Terry? One you were bragging about?"

Blackbeard's mouth got tight. "Never bragged about him."

"Yeah you did. Just a few months back at church, at the baptism, you said this new partner might be half-decent. For you, that's bragging."

"Aw," said Terry. "You care."

"I never said that," said Blackbeard, turning red and looking at Earl. "Don't make me forget why I come here."

He pulled a paper out of his coat pocket.

"Earl, were you here late Tuesday night, flight from Chicago and Nashville come in?"

"You know I was. I'm always here."

"Seen this guy?" Blackbeard spread a picture of Carmex out on the counter. Terry looked at Blackbeard and saw the Blackbeard he knew, tight-mouthed and serious.

"Huh," said Earl. "He didn't have a bullet hole in his head when I saw him."

"So he was here."

"Yeah, last guy of the night. I was getting ready to close up after the last flight. He walked in and ordered a double double and I figured it was worth it to stay open."

"Must have been thirsty after the long flight."

"Yeah. Said he had to sow his wild oats tonight because he was going to church tomorrow. Kept laughing at that, like it was a funny joke. I said something about most churches here having Wednesday night services and he said he had to go to a special prayer meeting early the next morning—that would have been a Wednesday."

"Remember his bags?"

"Yeah, 'specially one of them. He had a suitcase he kept down on the floor. But he had a black leather gym bag he kept on the counter. I tried to move it to clean and he got a real nasty look for a second. Then he smiled and said, 'Don't touch that. Manna from heaven.' Real funny guy. At least he seemed to think he was."

"Thanks." Blackbeard turned and walked out. Terry caught up to him in the lobby and stopped him. Outside, the sun was setting, which caused the windows to swirl magnifi-cently with bright oranges, reds and purples.

Terry said, "So the chief telling you not to work this case is like telling that preacher you mentioned that there's no God? And you call me a phony."

"I do my job," said Blackbeard. He looked at Terry and Terry could see that he wasn't smiling any more. "We both do our jobs."

ONE OF THE PROBLEMS of being a real estate banker in Florida was that some pretty questionable characters turned up at the office. Usually unannounced, usually late on a Friday, usually smiling a goofy smile and hoping you'd invest in their get-rich-now scheme. Like this one coming into Rolvaag's office now.

Rolvaag looked at his watch and thought: *I don't have time for this. Got to find some way to get two million dollars before help arrives from Vegas, the kind of help that would leave me not just out of a job, but out of oxygen, too. Need to grab Fabbi, get out of here and go to work.*

He smiled a banker smile at the man leaning on the door-frame.

"How can I help you, sir?" Rolvaag said. What he meant was, "How can I help you out the door fast?"

"I understand you have some unique investment opportunities here," said the man. The man wasn't smiling and didn't seem crazy. Old, unshaven, and disinterested in social niceties, but not crazy.

Rolvaag smiled. "Let me introduce you to Mr. Edwards. He can tell you all about our CDs and mutual funds. I'm sure you'll be very happy you dropped by to see Progress Bank."

Rolvaag stood up and went to the door but the man walked past him and sat down in Rolvaag's guest chair.

"A Mr. Rove out in Rosemary Beach told me about an opportunity you had here."

Rolvaag remembered the name, and the deal. He walked back around the desk, sat down in his chair, and looked at the old man, slow and careful this time. The man was looking at him in the same way.

"I don't believe I know a Mr. Rove," said Rolvaag.

The man was still looking at Rolvaag with the same stare that a cowboy used before a gunfight in an old western.

"He said he invested ten thousand with you and only got back eight thousand," said the man.

"Doesn't sound like a very good deal for Mr. Rove."

"Like I said, it was a unique investment. Rove said he was happy. I'd like to be happy, too."

Rolvaag considered. "You know, I don't know Mr. Rove personally, but I believe he has done business with the bank. Let me call him to see if he can refresh my memory." He ignored the Rolodex on his desk and reached into his desk drawer for a small notebook. While he was dialing, he looked at the man.

"I don't believe I caught your name, sir."

"Dave. Most folks call me Captain Dave."

Rolvaag nodded. "And your line of work?"

"Retired."

"Not in law enforcement? You look like a man with a background with the law."

Captain Dave smiled. "Not employed by law enforcement in any shape, form or fashion."

The phone was ringing but no one was answering. Rolvaag looked at the clock and realized that five o'clock was too late in the day for Rove to still be sober. He looked at Captain Dave and wondered if he knew that, too. He decided to play the hand out.

"Mr. Rove?" he said as the phone kept ringing in his ear. "This is Mr.—ah—Smith at the bank. I have a Captain Dave here with me who says he knows you." He looked at Captain Dave for a reaction. The captain smiled and Rolvaag knew the man could tell he was bluffing, which he probably wouldn't know unless he really did know Rove. So maybe there was something worth listening to here.

"Well, ah, yes, thank you very much, sir. You have a nice day."

Rolvaag hung up and looked at the captain. "So you have ten thousand dollars to invest?"

"Yes sir." The captain took a brick of bills out of his fishing pants and drummed it on his knee. "Cash. And Monday morning I'll have an account here in my name with eight thousand in it, *and* documentation showing the eight thousand was deposited a few years ago as a result of a legitimate, documented real estate transaction."

"Yes, sir." Rolvaag reached across the desk for the money, but the captain held on to it.

"And in the future, if I had more money to invest?"

Rolvaag sat up. "How much more?"

"Let's say a lot more."

"I'd need some notice and a rough idea of the amount so I'd know how to set up the transaction. More money, more notice. Might need to decide if you sold a quarter-acre of cheap sawgrass, or a shopping center."

"Let's say a medium-sized beach house. Out in Rosemary Beach or maybe Sea Oats."

Rolvaag looked out the window and watched the traffic go by as he tried to stay calm. Even after the downturn, houses out in Rosemary Beach and Sea Oats were worth millions.

"And when would you want to do this?" he said.

"Next week. Perhaps."

"I think we could do that." Rolvaag reached into his desk and pulled out a business card, a different one than the ones in the little tray on his desk. He passed it to the captain.

"Now, if we could conclude today's transaction."

Captain Dave tossed the brick onto Rolvaag's desk. Rolvaag looked down and saw the paper band around the bills. The band read, First Chicago Community Bank. Rolvaag stood, smiled his banker smile, and put out his hand out to Captain Dave.

"I think I'm going to be very happy you dropped in," he said.

twenty-four

"YOU DON'T KNOW a thing about music," Lizzie said to Terry, which of course meant he knew one hell of a lot about music, enough to open Lizzie's eyes to a style she didn't know well.

"Maybe you can teach me," said Terry, which of course meant he knew that she knew he knew music. If Lizzie was impressed enough with his music to challenge him directly, rather than give him the polite pat on the head he would have gotten if he really were a talentless amateur making a brave effort, then maybe he had impressed her enough that maybe there was something here. When men and women talk, there are always subtitles below the conversation, as if the five hundred thousand words in the English language weren't enough, or maybe were too much. In any case, for the moment anyhow, Lizzie and Terry were reading each other's subtitles.

"Let's try something. I like your Chicago Blues some." Lizzie paused, realized that she wasn't getting the subtitle right, and was sounding way too positive. She then said, "I like the Memphis Blues a whole lot more, but Chicago is all right. I think it needs attitude, though. Everything needs attitude." She reached up to the rack of guitars behind her. The rack was rough, made from leftover lumber when Daddy replaced the dock years ago. The guitars themselves, though, were all shiny fiberglass and metal. She pulled down a bright blue bass and said, "All right. Gimme 'Sweet Home Alabama,' but Chicago Blues style. You do know it?"

Terry grinned, remembering back to junior high when he first played the song. He had learned it on the spot when he had to fill in with his brother's band for a show in a converted gas station. Yeah, he knew the song, about twenty different versions.

"That's it," she said as he played. She liked his version, but she was frowning, needing to touch it herself, change something. She played along, following to get the feel of what he was doing. "Yeah, that's it. But it's all wrong, too. Kick some ass with this. Thing I don't like about the blues, it's too hangdog. It's a guy taking the crap the world gives and muttering under his breath. I want to hear him yell back. Rip you up. Gimme that."

Terry cranked the volume up, sped it up, stomped on the beat and threw it back at her.

"Yeah," she smiled, accepting his challenge. Terry was glad to see it and wondered what was coming next.

She cranked up the volume on the bass, caught up, shook the garage with him, and they played. Not just guitar, but played: chasing each other like puppies in a field, Terry leading off in one direction, showing Lizzie something new, then Lizzie would catch it quick and take off in her own direction. Terry grinned when he heard her add something he'd never thought about. Finally, they got together, found something new to both of them. Lizzie started singing the words in a new style that was a little bit of them both. They were sweating together now, bodies working as hard as they could, but their minds were relaxed, the way something is when it's really good.

They finished and Lizzie left the last, "Lord, I'm coming home to you" hanging in the air. Terry turned to the monitor and added a Jimi Hendrix-style squeal at the end for good measure, jumped up, and came down to the concrete floor in a split as he fist-pumped an imaginary audience.

Lizzie screamed, "Hell, yeah." They were both panting hard, bright eyed, worn out and excited.

Terry pointed at the tape machine that filled the back wall, and said, "We should have rolled tape on that one. I think you've got a hit."

Lizzie's face changed. "I don't do redneck rock. People say I do, but I don't."

"Florida girl, panhandle girl, doesn't do redneck rock? Thought that was genetic down here."

"See, that's the point, the 'down here.' Everyplace has got its assholes. In L.A. they dress cool, smile, and take your money. Then they ask you to thank them for taking it. In Chicago, where you come from—I don't know—maybe they're guys named Guido who carry guns in violin cases.

"Down here, they ride around in the back of pickup trucks, singing songs about the southland and chucking half-full beer cans at the funny-looking daughter of the backwater crabber. Least ways they do until the crabber catches them. There's a hell of a lot of good down here, and it's the only place I'll ever call home. But there's a real streak of cowardice trying to act brave, pushing around anything too small to fight back, whether it's black folks or people who think different, or little girls who want to sing something different than, 'Stand by Your Man.' That's redneck. And I don't do redneck. I do Florida. I do South. I don't do redneck."

Terry looked at her and she looked away. "You've got your share of cowards down here, and I think you've got a good handle on them. But I got here just in time to see this area stand up to Hurricane Michael. Lot of people working together, lot of courage."

"Yeah. Emerald Coast Strong. Damned proud of that. That's what I sing about. Florida songs, panhandle songs, swamp songs. Hell yeah. But no redneck songs. You want a Tecate?" She opened the fridge in the corner of the garage and held up two bottles and a half a lime.

"As you said, hell, yeah," said Terry. He wished he had worn shorts for the heat, but he knew the soaking wet pale blue T-shirt made him look good, too. The wet shirt on Lizzie made her look even better.

"But, you know, you've got it wrong," he said. "I mean you've got it right, too. I see the people you mean every day. They keep me in business. If somebody came along and fixed them all up with a good shrink who cured them of their problems, I could read the paper all day and not have a job. And you nailed it when you said what they are: bravado wrapped around cowardice. Not too many stories about the Klan attacking a fortified position of black men, both sides with guns, both sides with the law backing them up in an even fight. No, it's always bullies, bullies who strut around trying to pretend they're tough. Good psychologist would have a field day with them all.

"You got that part right. What you got wrong, is the word itself. Redneck ought to be a proud word. Originally, proud men who worked in the hot sun all day, carving homes and cities out of swamps filled with creatures that wanted to eat them for breakfast got red necks. Those boys didn't have time to strut. Those boys, the ones who fought back against the land and made this place something great, well, they fought back against the very bozos you're calling rednecks. And many of those boys—the real rednecks—had black skins. And a lot of them were girls. And are, today.

"What I don't understand is why you guys down here just give up and let the bozos have the last word. You're the real rednecks here, Lizzie, you and the others who stand up and fight whether you're outnumbered or not, hell, particularly when you're outnumbered. Folks like you can't even sing a song without fighting about it. Make them give your name back. Call them 'yellownecks' or 'yahoos' but you guys ought to be proud to be rednecks. You're that kind of redneck, Lizzie, and the proof's right here. You're standing here, sweaty as any worker in any field, fighting for your song, screaming your heart out the same way. Only difference, these days, you've got SPF 200 sunscreen to keep your neck from turning red."

"Maybe." Which was as close as Lizzie ever came to saying someone was right. "Daddy always said, show 'em what you are, show 'em something better than anything they ever imagined."

Terry thought about it. "Yeah, that's it, you got to be something. Find your story and show it to 'em. Know about that. Only thing is, there's a cost to that, too. One thing I like about life here, panhandle style, is you got a lot of people just enjoying what they've got, like the food people cook in a couple of places here. Nothing fancy, and they never want to be fancy, but it's good and they're proud that it's good. Actually, it's enough for them to know they made your day with a plate of barbequed shrimp made a way nobody else can make it."

Terry decided he was preaching and decided to drop it.

"Anyway, what's that you said, back there at the start. You had a phrase I liked, what was it? Oh yeah, 'rip you up.' Liked that."

Lizzie smiled, "Got that from a momma crab the other day. I'll steal from anybody. Gonna be an album title, someday."

"Rip you up," said Terry, picking up his guitar, using the Tecate bottle for a slide, picking out something in their new style with the coolness and sass of blues, but in-your-face aggressive, too. "C'mon," he said. "Let's make something special, like nobody's done. See how far we can take it, nothing but the idea, "Rip You Up." Lizzie put a rhythm on from the drum machine, picked up her bass, and they jammed.

It took half an hour to get just the feel right, Lizzie stopping things every few minutes, yelling, "No, no, no, goddamn it. It's all wrong." Terry just smiled and said, "Try a little of this," and showed her something without getting in her way. But they got it, got the sound first and then Lizzie started to stick in a few words. She needed no help from Terry for that part. She'd sing a line or two, then stop and write it down. Terry stopped playing the first time she did that but she said, "No, keep the groove. Don't let us lose the groove here," so he played while she wrote, caught up while she sang, banging hard when she got to the chorus, a good, strong chorus that was both angry and protective. Playing the music, Terry felt like the ghosts of a million proud and defiant Southerners, felt like a Northern boy who wanted to be something big. Rip you up. It was good. He convinced her to roll tape at the end to catch the last good run, and they had it down.

Lizzie put down her guitar and picked up a towel. "That's all there is; there just ain't no more. Lesson one's over."

Terry grinned and read the subtitle, which said there might be a lesson two.

ON HIS EARLY SATURDAY MORNING RUN Terry pushed it hard all the way down to the Winn-Dixie at the corner of Front Beach and 98, a sweating, grunting four-point-seven miles from Portside. He ran out on Front Beach Road itself, sharing the skinny bike lane with locals on electric bikes and a couple of fall tourists huffing and puffing in the still-humid Florida October early morning heat. He cut through the gate marked Beach Entrance 96 and ran back along the beach, harder here with the sand sucking his feet down into the earth with every step.

He loved it. He loved the effort, the feeling of achievement with every step, and he loved watching the sun rising out of the water along the shore to the East, just he and a few early morning shell seekers and surf casters. When he got back to the Sand Dollar Market, he crossed back over to the road and jogged the last hundred yards to Tommy's Donuts.

A line had already formed at Tommy's. Even in the slack season of October, if you wanted the prize donuts at Tommy's, the apple fritters or the key lime cremes, you had to be in line by six-thirty. Terry got in line behind a teen-aged boy with bushy blond hair and a boogie board under one arm. Terry tried his smile on the boy.

"You with the church camp up the road?"

"Shit, no," said the boy.

Well, that smile was wasted. Terry shuffled along with the line until he made it to the front.

"Out of key lime, pina colada, and Boston cream," the girl behind the window said before he could open his mouth.

"You still got fritters?"

"Not fritters. Fritter. One."

"Let me have that, and a cup of black coffee."

He took the overstuffed fritter and the paper cup over to one of the picnic tables, set his back to the rising sun, and watched the road.

It took a while, long enough to go back for more coffee and a baloney biscuit, but Terry got what he wanted. Four young teen-aged boys walked up Front Beach from the west, bouncing like ping-pong balls. With a lot of jostling and tough talk, they got their doughnuts and sat down. Terry went over.

"Hey, you guys from the church camp up the road, the one run by Sunshine Church?"

"Yeah. We're down here on fall break." One boy, tall and gangly, appointed himself spokesman and the other three watched him.

"Mind if I ask how you like it? My nephew wants to come down next spring."

"It's all right."

"They got a lot of things to do there?"

"Pretty much. Beach, of course. Trips into town for the water park and that amusement park thing built like a house turned upside down in an earthquake."

"Ain't an earthquake," said the smallest of the group, a red head with a bowl haircut. "See, the whole idea is that gravity's gone crazy in there, and—"

"Might as well be an earthquake. But, yeah, camp's OK. Plenty to do."

"How churchy is it? Just Sunday/Wednesday services, or preaching every day?"

"Sunday and Wednesday night service. Get together every morning to say the Prayer of Jabez over and over."

"Jabez?"

The kid rolled his eyes at Terry. "Yeah, man, you know, the one that if you say it enough and really mean it, God will make you rich. They get Brother Roberts to come in and lead it. He's a big shot. He took the prayer and built the church real estate company into some kind of million-dollar deal. Keeps telling us if we say the prayer, we can be just like him."

"Tell him about Wednesday," said Red.

"That was cool." The kid leaned back and stretched to tell the story. "Wednesday morning they put us on a bus and took us up to the big pink Sunshine church itself for the prayer. Brother Roberts said we were going to see a miracle. We were going to say the prayer until manna flowed down from heaven. Really said that. So we started saying the prayer, over and over. At first, Brother Roberts was full of fire and brimstone, yelling and singing the prayer. Soon he started staring at the back door, chanting the prayer like some crazed zombie, and not even noticing that we gave up a long time ago.

"Finally Brother Joe, the guy who drove us up there, tapped Brother Roberts on the shoulder and said, 'Sometimes, God doesn't give you what you want.'"

"Kind of like the Rolling Stones?" said Terry.

"Who?"

"You know," said the redhead. "Old guys. That rock band your grandpa always brags about seeing, trying to make us think he's cool."

"What about them?"

Terry looked irritated. "You can't get what you want, but if you try sometimes, you get what you need."

The kid nodded. "Justin Bieber wrote that."

"Yeah," Terry looked out at the water, "when he was very, very young."

"Anyway, Brother Roberts shook off Brother Joe and picked up more steam, screaming the prayer and looking at the door. Finally, he gave up and walked out. We stood around until Brother Joe gathered us up and took us to the beach."

"Yeah," said Red. "Tell him what Brother Roberts said as he stepped out of the pulpit before he turned off the microphone."

"He said that f-word that we're not supposed to say."

"Yeah," said Terry. "I know the word."

Red said it anyway, just to be sure.

twenty-six

LIZZIE LOOKED AT TERRY across the Formica tabletop. "So this is the famous Mack's," she said. It was
Saturday morning, late. Late for the locals; early for the few
tourists down at this end of the beach. Lizzie had come to
Portside to go to the beach with Terry on their day off, the
day after their music night. They had walked to Mack's for a
late breakfast before hitting the beach.

"This is the famous Mack's," said Terry.

Julie put down two plates in front of them.

"Actually got what I ordered this time," said Terry.

"You upgraded your table from Blackbeard."

Terry turned to Lizzie. "Lizzie, this is the famous Julie.
Famous for bringing you food you didn't ask for. Permanent
fixture at Mack's, kind of like the fryer with the original grease
from 1942."

"I ain't no permanent fixture. I got a life." Julie marched
away.

Lizzie giggled. "I believe you perturbed that girl."

"That girl stays perturbed."

Lizzie took a bite. "Pretty good seafood omelet."

"Best in town."

"The one I make at home's better."

"I'll have to try yours."

Lizzie laughed at him. "You come up with better lines when you have a guitar in your hands."

"Funny," he took a bite and then looked at Lizzie. "Funny how that works. Not just better lines, but a better life. I'm a different person making music with a guitar in my hands. Know what I mean?"

"I feel the same way, only more so. I'm only really alive two places: making music or on the water. The rest is just like a break from living."

He was silent for a few minutes. Lizzie thought, *Well, there's another one you've run off with your weirdness and your honesty. Might as well learn now.*

Terry said, "The beach."

"The beach?"

"Yeah. I'm alive on the beach. You locals here take it for granted. Everybody here has to have a beach chair, pay some hotel thirty bucks for a piece of wood to hold their ass up in the air off the sand for a day. Not me. When I lie down on the beach, I like to burrow down in that beautiful snow-white powder we have here, let the heat flow from the sand into me until I can't stand it.

"Then I jump in the water, particularly when the water's cool. Keep my eyes closed until I'm completely under. Open up and find myself in another world. Better than time travel or science fiction. Funny little fish swimming by, looking like they're dressed up in their Sunday best, smoking some kind of long cigarettes in holders. Sea cucumbers. Urchins. Things that don't even have names, least no names I know."

"Yeah," said Lizzie. She put down her fork and stared at him. "There are beaches all over the world, but nothing like ours here."

This was more serious than Terry wanted. "Course, even if you stay under water as long as you can, eventually you have to come up and hear a twelve-year old from Birmingham standing ankle deep whining, 'Ma, can we go to Walmart now?'"

Lizzie laughed, tough and cynical again, "Thank God for rednecks. Or yellownecks. Whatever."

Julie came back with more coffee, even though they didn't need any.

She looked at Terry. "Sheila's friend came in early, looked like her crowd was finishing up the night instead of starting the morning. Said to tell you she was mad at you for missing the party last night."

"Got caught up in something more important."

Julie looked at Lizzie. "Looks like you made a good choice." She turned and said over her shoulder. "For once."

Lizzie said, "I'm done. Let's go."

Terry wanted to protest that he wasn't done, but Lizzie was halfway to the door so he paid and caught up.

"That tip I left," he said to Julie as he opened the door, "was out of habit. Not earned."

"Can't handle it when folks are honest?" she said to his back.

He caught up with Lizzie in front of the Island Market art shop and walked with her through the Portside gate past the pool with the waterfall to SD6.

"Boy, this is bright," said Lizzie, standing in the long living room/dining room/kitchen combination that made up the first floor. The walls were bright yellow and the couches a tropical blue-green pattern.

"I'm not afraid of color."

"Guess not. I like it, though. Feels fun and open."

"Figure if you're going to live at the beach, might as well look like the beach." He walked to the stairs. "Here, I'll give you the guest room to get changed."

"You have guests?"

"Sometimes."

They were at the top of the stairs by then and he motioned to the room to the left.

"I guess your guests don't need to sleep," said Lizzie, looking around the guest room. There was an old black bedroom set, minus the bed. The wall opposite the window held a rack of guitars.

"I had to make room."

Lizzie crossed to the guitars.

"Man, you've got a collection."

"Little of everything. Gibson. Fender, of course. That cheap acoustic there was the first guitar I ever owned."

Lizzie turned to the battered black dresser that was tucked under the window. There was a gun case on top. Lizzie picked out a gun.

"Uzi," said Terry. "That's my weapon collection."

She looked at the guns. "Next time the Emerald Coast Chamber of Commerce talks about going to war with Mobile, I'm coming here."

Terry took the gun out of her hand and clipped it back in its place. "Think you better stick to guitars."

"Yeah. Shotguns and crab traps are about as lethal as I get."

Terry went to change in his room and Lizzie closed the door and stripped off her shorts and T-shirt and pulled a blue bikini from L.A. out of her bag. She stood there, naked, looking at Terry's guns and thought about which one she would want to have to protect herself. Just until she got rid of the money in the boathouse. She pulled a mean-looking little machine pistol off a rack. Just for a little while.

She walked to the mirrored closet door and pointed the gun at herself, a little, naked girl trying to look tough. She giggled, something she seemed to be doing more lately than she usually did. She choked off the giggle, didn't want Terry in the room next door to wonder why she was laughing in a room full of guns.

But it was hard not to laugh, looking at herself standing in the mirror wearing nothing but a big gun. Maybe an album cover, if they arranged everything to block out the dirty parts.

No, that wasn't her. She looked at the gun in her hand. This wasn't hers, either. She put the gun back and pulled down Terry's original guitar, imagined him a pimple-faced kid struggling to force the guitar to make something that sounded like music, until he learned that you have to let the music come out of the guitar, ride it like a wave. The girl in the mirror looked like her, a little girl with a big guitar, but with a look that told you they belonged together. Maybe this was the album cover. Plenty of girls out there could pull off a sexy look like this, girls who really were actresses, and who had producers who knew how to auto tune their voices for the fan boys who bought the album just so they could look at the cover of the almost-naked actress on the CD.

Not her. She put the guitar back on the rack and looked in the mirror, nothing but her there now. It had been a long time since she had really looked at herself naked, a long time since her looks had mattered to anyone, including her. Her body was fuller than she remembered, curvier than the girl she still imagined herself to be. She thought, *I wonder where this is going, here with Terry at the beach?* Nowhere good was the answer that came back. These things always end badly. If this was a thing. Maybe this day would end up to be nothing but a sunburn. Maybe, if she was really lucky, she'd get a song out of it.

She put on the suit from L.A. and went downstairs. Terry stood up from the couch when she entered the room, and she liked that.

"Didn't have you figured for one of those girls who could take forever to put on a swim suit."

"I'm not. Let's go."

She caught him looking as she turned to the door, and she liked that, too.

twenty-seven

THE BEACH ACROSS FROM PORTSIDE was an empty space between two condos, the so-called Hole in the Beach. Lizzie and Terry found a place a hundred feet away from anybody else. Terry spread out a thick beach towel for Lizzie and rolled his up into a pillow beside hers.

"You're not going to spread out?" she said.

"No, told you, I like to feel the sand."

She thought for a minute. "You can do it; I can do it." She picked up her towel, rolled it up, and laid it beside his.

He smiled. "You ready for a drink? I can walk up to the bar at the yellow condo there and get us a couple."

"Maybe something later. Anything that doesn't have an umbrella in it." She lay down on her back on the bare sand, and heat flowed into her. "This is going to take some getting used to."

Terry was looking at her. She closed her eyes and imagined him looking. She hoped she wasn't smiling—and hoped he was.

"OK, let's make this right," she said.

She started wiggling and scooting down into the sand until she was half buried, completely held by warm Mother Beach. It felt good. Terry stopped looking and scooted down beside her, making his own little cubbyhole.

"So how'd you get all the way down here to ECB?" she said, her eyes still closed.

"Kind of didn't," said Terry. "Really just got down to Portside and then adopted ECB as home. My wife—I was married at the time, not now—won a week at Portside, off-season. Lucky for me it was off-season. If we'd come down in the middle of summer I think all the screaming kids would have driven me crazy. As it was, most of the people in the Portside townhouses that week were owners who had come down to relax. All folks in no hurry, with more easy smiles than errands on their to-do list.

"You couldn't sit out on your patio with your coffee without somebody stopping by. Sometimes they'd just say hi. Sometimes at the end of the day they'd still be sitting there, telling you their life story and listening to yours when you turned out the lights. By the end of the week I told my wife I knew the life story of a hundred people down here and only knew stories of about two people anywhere else."

He rolled onto his side, facing Lizzie, and squirmed until he got the sand right. Lizzie knew he was watching her.

"I'd always been a real intense, let's-go-save-the-world kind of person. This wasn't just a different place; this was a different me. A few years later, when everything blew up in Chicago, I came down here for a week to get my head together. The week became a month, the month became a year. I found myself down at ECBPD one day applying for a job. Woke up a couple of years later lying on the beach with a pretty girl."

"Aw," said Lizzie without opening her eyes. "Like I said about your lines."

"Yeah, well."

Now she turned onto her side and faced him. "What happened to the wife?"

"Didn't work out."

Lizzie propped herself up on one elbow and stared down, letting him know she expected more. He laughed, not the funny laugh, but the bitter one.

"There was this girl," he said.

Lizzie threw herself back on the sand and stared straight into the blazing sun.

"I knew it," she said.

"Not like that." He laughed the bitter laugh again, going back in his mind.

"I had just made detective, youngest detective in Chicago history. Thought I was a real hotshot. Before that, when I was a beat cop, there was this one woman, a Russian bride brought over by a small-time politician who had connections with some tough guys. Every Friday night he'd get drunk and beat her up. Every Friday night, the neighbors would call. We'd go over and break it up. Every Saturday morning, she'd lose her memory and recant her story.

"The first Friday night I went over there after I made detective, the woman opened up and told me her husband and his friends had made her do things, bad things. That if she ever went to the police, they'd tell the police what she'd done. She'd go to jail, or back to Russia. I tried to get her to tell me what she had done, but she just shook her head. So, I went to hubby, told him if he ever touched her again, I was coming back personally.

"Next Friday, same thing again. I got in his face, and he got in mine. It got out of hand and he wound up in the hospital. I wound up with a lawsuit against the department and encouragement to seek other employment."

Lizzie sat back up. "They got upset over that? Just putting a few bruises on a wife-beater?"

Terry smiled. "They tend to take vigilante violence seriously up there. Silly Yankees."

"Huh," Lizzie lay down and then popped back up.

"Your wife left you over that?"

"I went back while the hubby was in the hospital. Told Svetlana to pack a bag. Took her to the bus station, bought her a ticket west and gave her some money. Told her to find some place far away and start over clean.

"My wife's boss saw me giving money to a blonde in a bus station. My wife blew up and walked out. Made more sense to me later when I found out my wife had been sleeping with her boss for more than a year."

"Oh," said Lizzie. She felt like she needed to change the subject. "Miss it? Chicago, I mean."

"Sometimes. Miss the hustle and bustle, everybody trying hard to be something, do something."

"I know what you mean. I miss L.A. But this will always be home for me. Coming back made me realize that I never want to be away from here for long." She paused. "Maybe you could be something here."

"Yeah. Sounds pretentious and corny, but I still want to do some good."

"Wasn't that a line from *The Untouchables*?"

He raised one arm up in surrender. "Got me. Can't even come up with my own lines. What about you, though? Gonna be hard to be a rock star without going back to L.A."

She looked at him. "You think too much." Then Lizzie jumped up, shook sand on Terry, and ran for the water.

He caught up to her when she was waist-deep, just crossing the line where the little waves broke. They dove into the water together. She glided for a while, opened her eyes and saw him there beside her. It was cool here in the water, an infinite cool that stretched all the way to South America. Cool, like good and relaxed. Cool, like gently wiping away the heat and sweat from the land world.

He angled close to her and their faces almost touched. Lizzie knew that all she had to do was turn her head and they would kiss, and that it might be just a kiss or it might be their first kiss.

No. Or at least, not yet. She turned away and stayed cool.

twenty-eight

"I'LL SHOW YOU my water later," Lizzie told Terry.

They were having lunch in a tourist restaurant, an expensive place made out of weathered wood to make it look casual.

She held up a forkful of crabmeat and waved it at him. "My crab's fresh. This is from a tin can," she said it like she'd just found out the chef was a child molester. Lizzie pushed the plate away and picked at the fries.

Terry looked at her sitting there with the Gulf behind her and passion up in her eyes. Beautiful to see, even if the passion was just for a small, spirited, hard-shell creature not treated with proper respect. She looked up to see why he was so quiet. For a moment he was startled. The clear green-blue of her eyes matched the Gulf so well that she looked like a special effect from a movie, with the water showing through her.

"Mother, mother ocean," Terry found himself singing the line without realizing it.

"Don't start singing Buffett," she giggled now, a feisty little girl again.

Terry grinned, a little embarrassed. She seemed to do this to him, throw him out of the rhythm of his coolness, make him feel like a little boy.

"Nothing wrong with Buffett."

"Nothing at all wrong with Buffett," she said, pointing a French fry at him. "Made up a whole new kind of music, right out of thin air. Best music that ever came out of this part of the world." She paused. "Well, until me." No false modesty, no cute little smile to show it was just a joke. Just the facts, sir.

Terry wondered if she had any false modesty. Wondered if she had any false anything.

She fixed him with her eyes and said, "Buffett's great. Problem is the ten thousand Buffett imitators who have flooded into Florida like some kind of zombie invasion, stumbling around the bars with their eyes glazed and their souls dead, muttering 'Margaritaville, Margaritaville' like some kind of religious chant."

Terry stretched out his arms with his hands down like a zombie and said, "I have heard you call," in a flat voice with no emotion and no music.

"No," Lizzie's face clouded up like a storm. "You don't make fun of good music."

He put his arms in his lap and they sat there, quiet for a time.

Then Lizzie said, "You sing? I did all the singing the other night."

Terry shook his head. "No. I can hit individual notes, but I never developed my own voice. Know what I mean?"

"I do."

"You've got a voice. A hell of a voice. I mean not just distinctive range and tone. They could take you singing a soup commercial, grind it up and autotune it, and everybody'd still say, 'That's Lizzie Gaffney.'"

"Lizzie Borden. I sing under Lizzie Borden."

"You do if you ever get your name back. Really, when did you stop singing like everyone else and find your own voice?"

She didn't have to think about it. "The summer my mom died. My dad was real independent. And fun. And wise. You'd have liked him."

Terry nodded.

"Anyway, the summer Mom died, Dad didn't want to accept help from anybody. Except me. I was just fourteen, but he leaned on me, hard. I liked that. I didn't like Mom dying; that part was hell. The day Mom died, I looked into the mirror and saw that I had the same tight little lines around my mouth that Mom and Dad both had, a look that said, 'Don't screw with me. I take care of what's mine.' I liked it then, like it now. Makes me look fifty, if you look around the mouth. But I wouldn't give that look up for all the Botox in the world."

Terry nodded. He knew he should say something complimentary about Lizzie's mouth, point out that it made her look like some movie star or another. But his heart told him that was the wrong thing for Lizzie, and the wrong thing for whatever was on the horizon between them.

"Anyway," Lizzie waved a French fry again. "I had been playing with a band down the road, sneaking out of school to do covers of Joan Jett and Patti Smith and Lucinda Williams, driving my Mom crazy. That summer, I didn't have time to learn the covers, with everything I had to do to hold Dad together. So I walked into the garage one day with the band waiting and told them, 'We don't have time for this shit anymore. I'm gonna sing my own stuff from now on.' Then I just opened my mouth and a song I'd never heard or imagined came out on its own. The band caught up. At the end, they all screamed. I hear that same scream, even now, when it's right with the audience. That's what I sing for: the scream, all over again, forever all over again, everything in one moment."

Terry stared at her.

"So that's today's charming story about how the little girl found her voice," she said. She finally popped the French fry, which was a little worse for wear, into her mouth.

"Bitch," they heard a guy at the bar say. It was an ugly word and he was an ugly guy in a Toby Keith shirt and a rolled-up cowboy hat. Both the word and the guy stood out. Everybody in the restaurant turned and stared at the pretty, skinny girl in front of him. She hung her head like she, rather than he, should be ashamed of the word. He laughed at her. She didn't know what to do so she slapped him, a weak, half-hearted little girl slap. He laughed an even nastier laugh.

Terry started to get up but Lizzie was halfway across the floor before Terry cleared his chair. The big ugly guy turned to her and smiled down at the tiny young woman who barely reached his chest.

"This," Lizzie said to the crying girl in front of her, "is how it's done."

The slap started from the point where her heel was rooted in the plank floor, gathered steam coming up her leg and turned into a storm through her twisting hips and burst out her open palm and smashed the smile off his face in the blink of an eye. His head jerked and he crashed backward over the bar in a shower of broken glass.

Lizzie turned back to Terry. "We should leave now."

• • •

They drove out through the scrub pine and sawgrass to Lizzie's place, with Terry following Lizzie's truck in his own car. She walked down to the dock and he followed.

"This here's real crab." She pulled up the crab trap and a half dozen pair of claws went to clattering.

"Hear that?" she said. "Hear the rhythm? Sounds like applause."

Terry laughed. "You boil up your audience and serve them for dinner?"

"They'd love it if I did."

Terry pointed back up at the house. "Never saw houses like that till I came down here. Looks like it grew right there, rather than was built."

"That's about the way of things here." She pointed at a cinderblock square in the middle of the structure. "That's the original house, built by Granddad way back when. Said he and Grandmom lived on their boat while they built it, going out early to crab, then stacking cement blocks all afternoon and evening. That section over there was added on when their kids came. That one there, my dad added that one when I was born. Said he wanted me to have a place that was mine, not something handed down from somebody else. I still sleep there, even now with all the other rooms empty."

"Everything down here have a story?" said Terry.

"Everything."

Terry pointed at the boathouse. "How about that?"

The lines came back around Lizzie's mouth. "Nothing there." She dropped the trap back into the water, grabbed a line, and stepped onto the boat. "Get aboard," she said.

Terry jumped on. The tightness stayed around Lizzie's mouth as they headed out and Terry figured she was concentrating on the boat.

"There," she finally said, pointing into the water on her side. Terry had to lean across her, their faces almost touching.

"Where?" he said. He focused on the water with the sun bouncing off it and saw nothing but a background of eelgrass. He focused again. This time, he saw a big blue crab scuttling across the bottom, keeping up with their shadow like a dog chasing a car.

"Oh," he said when his eyes focused and he saw clearly, saw the crab, the grass, and the little turquoise fish playing. There was a whole new world at his feet. He leaned across and braced himself with one hand and let the other dangle in the water, grounding himself in the ocean.

"Now you got it," she said. Her smile was back. "See, now that belongs to you. You played with Daddy Crab, he played with you. He'll go back to Momma Crab tonight, they'll be sitting around watching crab TV and he'll say, 'saw the little girl in the big boat today. Said to tell you hi.'"

Terry felt the water flow around his hand, a connection between him and the crab. "I always thought of a boat being something *on* the water," he said. "This is more like a boat *in* the water."

"Yeah," she said. Then, "Here, take the wheel." She stepped away without waiting for him. He straightened up and grabbed the wheel.

Lizzie was writing what Terry said in her notebook.

"You know," he said, "sometimes you can just remember a line, not write everything down."

"Then you might lose it. If something belongs to me, once," she looked at him, "I don't lose it."

They cruised around while the sun set as Lizzie pointed out sights from her childhood. As the sun fell in the sky, she pulled into a secluded cove and cut the engine. She pointed to a house on a nearby point of land.

"That's where Paul and Marie, the Canadians, stay when they come down for the winter. Nicest folks you ever met, even if they talk funny."

Terry looked into the little creek at the base of the cove and realized he had been here the night before in the airboat. Funny how different things looked tonight, down at water level rather than flying over it.

Lizzie pulled off her T-shirt and shorts, and jumped into the water in her swimsuit. Terry pulled off his shirt and followed her in.

The water was black and warm here in the bay with the sun fading. He tried to catch up to her, but she swam faster and climbed back into the boat. He climbed in behind her.

"You're hard to keep up with." He lay on his back on the white-painted floorboards and laughed, beaten and breathing hard.

"You have no idea," she said. Then she stood over him, straddling him.

He looked up at her and said, "I smell like I've been out in the sun all day."

She lowered herself slowly until she was sitting on his hips.

"If you can't handle a body's smell then you got no right to the body."

She reached back and untied the top of her swimsuit and let it fall away. After, she leaned forward and kissed him.

"I like your smell," she whispered.

Terry took a deep breath, and he had Lizzie's smell, all Tabasco and sweat and salt water, and it was better than all the perfume he had ever smelled. And then, in a minute, they had each other.

In the middle of it all Terry screamed and he looked at her and saw her smiling, and knew this was now one of her moments and he was now one of hers.

• • •

Paul the Canadian brought the binoculars in from the deck and slid them back on the shelf next to the sliding doors. Marie was still unpacking in the kitchen. She smiled at him.

"Well, you're back home on the water for the winter again. Glad we decided to come down in October this year. What'd you learn from sitting out there watching the water for two hours?"

"Lizzie's got a new boyfriend," he said.

"About time," said Marie, drawing the vowels of the first word out until it sounded like "a-boot."

twenty-nine

ROLVAAG PUT HIS HAND on the Las Vegas Prep Swim Team gym bag in Fabbi's lap to stop the kid from getting out of the car.

"You sure this is the place?"

"Yes," said Fabbi, pushing Rolvaag's hand away. "I followed the old guy, just like you told me. He left the bank, stopped at Publix, got two cases of beer and came here. Like I told you twice already."

Rolvaag put his hand back on the bag and looked out at the old marina behind the convenience store. "Just get him to tell you where the money is. We don't need to hurt anybody else."

Fabbi glared at the hand until Rolvaag took it away. It was close to midnight on a moonless night, but the look was still clear.

"I know my business," Fabbi said.

"I know. Your dad told me. Why you think he called today, anyway? He never calls."

Fabbi looked at him. "You lose his money, maybe he loses his development deal. In Vegas, we're not the kind of people to sit back."

"I didn't lose it, you did," said Rolvaag.

Fabbi had been acting differently since the phone call from his dad. Now, he and Fabbi sat in Rolvaag's Beemer in front of Captain Dave's old boat.

"Whatever," said Fabbi to Rolvaag. "Money's still gone. Dad wants it back. You can't get it, Dad told me to get it."

"I want the money as bad as your dad does. Just saying, we don't need a trail of bodies. Make it clear to this guy that it's in his best interest to give up the money. Maybe we can give him a home loan at a good rate, get him out of this crappy boat."

Fabbi smiled. "Home loan? Yeah, I'll try that."

He started to pull the bag away.

"What's in the bag?"

Fabbi brushed Rolvaag's hand from the bag. He yanked the zipper and pulled out a book.

"French existentialist. Something you never heard of." He smiled. "Figured I might get bored."

"What else?"

"Tools. Persuasion tools."

Fabbi opened the door, got out, and walked up to the boat. Rolvaag backed out, throwing gravel to get out of the parking lot before the kid got into the boat.

He drove down to 98 and headed west to 30A. He parked behind the Mexican restaurant at the Villages and walked down along the beach to the little outdoor bar behind High Point.

He smiled at the young girl tending bar and said, "Do you know how to make a Screaming Multiple Orgasm on the Beach?"

He watched her and saw the sour look he wanted. The girl paused, wondering if the tip was worth flirting with the old guy, then decided she was too busy and bored to play the game.

"Sure." She went away, but Rolvaag knew she would remember him if he needed an alibi later. She came back and banged the drink on the bar and stood there until he paid. He wanted to leave a big tip by way of apology, but he left nothing but a quarter just to piss her off to be sure she would remember.

He took a sip and made a face. Jesus, he thought, if this is an orgasm, I'm swearing off sex. He sat there listening to the gentle crash of the Gulf surf and thought of escaping his life. All the lies and deception. Now murder. He remembered the first time the voice on the phone from Vegas had overruled him and told him to approve a loan that made no business sense. After that came deals that were outright illegal. All with his name on them.

Now he went to Saint Bernadette's Catholic Church every Sunday and prayed for forgiveness. But every Monday, he went back and did as he was told. Like every tourist listening to every Jimmy Buffet song, he looked out at the sea and dreamed of sailing away. He switched to Heineken and sat there until his cell rang.

"C'mon back," was all Fabbi said on the other end.

Rolvaag slogged back across the sand, got the car, and headed back to the convenience store by the marina. Fabbi opened the door before the car had stopped.

"Go," he said as he closed the door.

They drove in silence until they got away from the lights of the convenience store and Rolvaag could stand it no more.

"Got it?" he said.

"Course not. Stupid idea." Fabbi stared out his window. He was trying to look cool, but the lines around his mouth were tense.

Rolvaag almost stopped in the middle of the road.

"What do you mean, 'course not?'"

"It's your fault. You didn't tell me about the guy. You never told me he was such an old guy. He died on me. He died, it's your fault, and Dad's going to know it. You never tell me what I need to know."

Rolvaag brought the car back up to speed, but it was hard to concentrate.

"Jesus."

They pulled out onto 98.

"Jesus. Can't you do anything but kill people?"

Fabbi turned slowly and stared at Rolvaag. "That's what I did in Vegas. I was supposed to learn something new out here, pick up some business skills from you. Fine teacher you are."

"What the hell did you do to him?"

Fabbi still stared, but started to smile. "You really want to know?"

Rolvaag started to say "no" but it was too late. Fabbi unzipped the bag and took out a long thin knife. It had been carefully cleaned and was still a little wet.

"See this? Down here they call this a fillet knife, use it to cut long strips of meat off a fish. Back in Vegas, we just used a steak knife, but hey, this is pretty good."

He turned it back and forth in his hand.

"So, when he came to the door, I hit the guy in the head and knocked him out. Didn't take much, he was mostly drunk anyhow. When he came to, tied up and gagged, I told him I wanted the money. That I'd make it easy on him if he told me fast. I pulled down the gag, just a little so he could talk but not scream. Know what the son of a bitch said?"

"No."

"'Banker's got it.'"

Fabbi paused for that to sink in.

"Pulled the gag back up and hit him across his eye, hard enough to rip his eyelid off. Asked him if he had a better story and he just shook his head, no. Took out the knife and showed it to him, let him think of all the things I could do with it. In Vegas, the guy who taught me this had a lot of stories. Said you take the knife and peel the guy's skin away. Won't kill him, but works every time. Sometimes takes longer than other times, but they always talk."

"Jesus," said Rolvaag. He thought of the prayers he had said in Mass the last time he went. It seemed like an eternity ago.

"So I started with a middle finger for laughs. He just stared at me with that one bloody eye.

"Split the skin at the knuckle. Kept peeling up so it would hurt more each second. He was crying, that one eye filling up with blood and tears. Still not making a sound. Peeled it all the way off until his forearm looked like something you'd see in an anatomy book. Pulled the gag down and you know what he did then?"

Rolvaag shook his head and didn't say anything.

"Puked on me. Son of a bitch puked on me. You got some screwed up people around here, man. Like he'd been waiting. Puked on me on purpose and laughed.

"I hit him again and washed myself off in his sink, let him think about it. Let him know I wasn't going to lose my temper and kill him, let him off easy.

"I just smiled at him. Took the knife and started again. Told him, 'I can do this all night, Pops.' Got up to the elbow with another long strips of skin hanging off like some costume. Looked up at his face. He was white like he had no blood in his whole body and his chest was rattling like dry leaves. Figured he was ready to give me a better story."

Fabbi paused and opened his bag. He put the knife in and took out his book.

"I pulled down the gag again. He looked at me, said, 'Thanks,' and died on me. Just died on me. Son of a bitch died on me." Fabbi glared at Rolvaag, a flat stare with pure hate and maybe a little fear mixed in. Rolvaag saw the look and started to panic.

"You never told me he would do that," said Fabbi. He reached into the bag for something. Rolvaag panicked. His eyes darted to the road, looking for anything, maybe a telephone pole that he could hit, thinking he had a better chance of surviving a wreck than living through whatever Fabbi was going to pull out of that bag.

Fabbi pulled out his book and opened it. Rolvaag had slowed down, the car barely moving, other vehicles honking at him as they went by.

"Searched the boat," said Fabbi. "Nothing there. Was so mad at the guy for cheating us like that, on the way out I picked up an iron skillet and smashed his face in."

Fabbi turned to his book.

"Think I'm going to read now. Dad's going to be mad at you."

LIZZIE AND TERRY WALKED up to the house from the boat, stumbling in the darkness and giggling every time they bumped into each other.

"I'll fix you a crabmeat and sweet potato omelet," she said. "Show you how to treat Mr. Crab proper."

Lizzie pulled the big, blue chipped ceramic steamer pot onto a burner. One by one she took half-empty leftovers from a line of beer bottles on the counter and emptied them into the pot.

"If you drink a beer around here, you've got to leave some for Mr. Crab," she said. "Crabs steam better in stale, flat beer. So when I drink a beer, I leave some here, waiting for cooking time."

The beer boiled after a few minutes and she dumped the crabs in. She pointed to a five-pound sack of shrimp boil seasoning sitting on the counter in front of Terry.

"Feed them some of that," she said.

Terry took a tentative pinch and delicately shook it into the pot the way he had seen it done on a cooking show on TV.

"Hell, no," Lizzie said. She dug both hands into the bag past her wrists, scooped out a double handful and threw it into the pot. Then she laughed and wiped the leftover orange-brown powder in a diagonal slash on Terry's shirt.

Terry laughed. "Gonna boil me up too?"

"You wish."

He pointed at the word Hilton that was stamped on the bag. "Where'd you get that?"

"I stole it."

She turned her face toward his, defiantly. When he just smiled, she said, "Actually, they were throwing it out. Too hot for the tourists. I'm going to take it to a friend later, a guy who never thinks anything's too hot. At least, if you have enough beer—and he always has enough beer."

When the crabs turned bright orange, she took the steamer outside and dumped the crabs onto the picnic table. Then she and Terry sat under the rising sun and she showed him her ritual: thanking each crab before starting to harvest the meat.

"Tell me you don't really think the crab hears us when we do that," Terry said, "believe that our thanks goes up to some great crab-god in the sky?"

"No." Lizzie was serious. "It's praying, and praying's not for God, it's for you. It's your way of recognizing that the crab belongs to you and you belong to the crab. Without it, it's just grocery store food."

Terry looked down at the orange shell in his hands.

"Thank you, brother crab." He twisted the back leg and a big chunk of snow-white meat flecked with orange spice came out. "Crab, meet body. Body, meet crab." He popped the bite in his mouth.

Lizzie reached over and pinched him with a crab claw. "Stop eating the meat. Save some for my omelet." She pointed to the plate he was supposed to be putting the meat on.

"But it's good," he said.

"Then let's make it better."

· · ·

Terry was gone and the dishes were cleaned up. Lizzie was humming something tuneless as she loaded up her daddy's truck.

She threw the bag of shrimp boil in the back and headed down the road, still humming the same little tune. She smiled as she drove to the marina, thinking of the first time she'd made this drive, filled with terror and excitement, but mostly filled with pride because Daddy believed she could make the drive on her own.

Lizzie pulled into the marina as quietly as she could, knowing that no one there would be awake at this hour of the morning. She giggled, thinking how Captain Dave would bitch when he saw her standing over his bed, probably waking up from a drunken stupor. Stepping over the rail, she set the bag of shrimp boil on the deck and went to the door.

The smell should have tipped her off when she cracked the door open slowly, but she was too wrapped up in her prank to notice the body odor and the smell of blood. She stepped inside and stopped to let her eyes adjust to the darkness, finally noticing the odor.

"Dang, Captain Dave. You need to do some cleaning around here."

She smiled when she saw him, sitting slumped back in a chair in the dark. The old coot hadn't even made it to his bed, just fell asleep dead drunk in his chair. She reached for the light switch behind her and flicked it on.

One staring, lifeless eye hung out of a smashed face of red pulp. Lizzie started to scream and then choked it off into something like a sob. It seemed like a bad joke. Maybe that was it: Captain Dave had heard her coming and put on a fright mask to scare her. It had worked.

"Captain?" she said softly, timidly. He said nothing.

She reached out to check his pulse and saw the long peel of flesh from his arm and the blood running down to the floor. Her hand jerked back just as if she had reached for a snake. Slowly, she forced her hand to Captain Dave's other wrist and held her fingers to the base of his thumb. Nothing. The skin was growing cool.

She pulled back and looked around. There were no signs of a fight, just the clutter she'd normally expect around the captain's place. On a counter she saw his wallet, money and keys. Next to it was a business card. She turned it over with a fingernail, careful not to touch anything with her fingers.

The card read, PROGRESS COMMERCIAL BANK. Underneath was a name: Ken Rolvaag.

Lizzie backed out slowly and wiped the light switch and door with her shirt sleeve as she went. She stepped down to the dock and got in the truck. Then she started the truck and headed down the gravel road with the lights still off.

Halfway down the road she breathed for the first time. With the breath came the sobs. Loud, gut-wrenching sobs. She pulled onto the blacktop and turned on the lights in the bright morning sun. Turned up the radio loud and screamed and screamed.

"Why?" she yelled. "Why, why, *why*?" Then she was quiet.

She knew why. She had lied. It was a lie when she took money that didn't belong to her. It was a lie when she took Terry and didn't tell him she took the money. And the lies had called out the demons and the demons had led to the sneering voice from L.A. that would not give her music back. Now the demons had taken Captain Dave.

She had called the demons up from hell with her lies. She would have to put them back.

thirty-one

YELLOW CRIME SCENE TAPE BLOCKED the gravel road into the marina. Terry parked at the convenience store, took his coat off, wadded it up in his left hand and jogged along the edge of the road. It was hot, the kind of hot that means a strong change of weather is coming. Terry was soaked with sweat by the time he got to the crowd around the boat. When Terry arrived, Blackbeard was arguing with the lieutenant, Blackbeard's boss.

"Blackbeard, I am opening up this lot. You can have the boat itself, but I need the lot to get vehicles in here."

"Not until Eric has lifted every set of tire tracks he can find."

"In a gravel lot? In dry weather? You know you ain't going to find nothing. And it will take all day."

"Probably. But we're going to do this one right, and clear it. If we'd cleared the Hilton case already, this man wouldn't be dead."

"I'm opening it up. And you don't know that, anyway, about the Hilton."

"You don't get the lot until you take this case away from me."

The lieutenant tried to stare down Blackbeard, but it didn't work.

"Jesus," he said. "Don't know why the chief said to call you in. Specifically said you're in charge 'til he gets here. All right." He started to walk away but turned and shook his finger in Blackbeard's face. "But we ain't wearing those booties you like in the parking lot."

The lieutenant walked away and Blackbeard looked up at Terry.

"When did you eat?"

"When did I eat?" said Terry. "Is this a lunch call, go get some barbeque or something? Thought we had an S-5, dead body and all that."

"We do. When did you eat?"

"I don't know. Breakfast. Early, I guess. Haven't had lunch yet."

"Good." Blackbeard turned and walked toward the fishing boat. He paused at the rail of the boat and put on a pair of paper booties from a box. Terry didn't need to be told to do the same. They pulled on gloves and stepped onto the boat.

"Here. Take one of these." Blackbeard reached into a cardboard box of plastic grocery store bags. He handed Terry one and kept one for himself.

"What do I need this for?"

Blackbeard looked up and saw a patrolman smoking on the edge of the lot, way off on the other side.

"You!" he yelled, pointing at the patrolman. "Get that dadgummed cigarette butt off of my crime scene." He glared when the patrolman was slow to move. "In fact, get your sorry butt out of here. Go on, go back to the donut shop. I don't need you in the way."

Terry started to make a joke but he looked at the red rim of Blackbeard's eyes and decided to keep quiet.

Blackbeard walked to the hatchway. Eric was standing with his back to them, taking pictures of the inside.

"Give us a minute, Eric," said Blackbeard. Eric backed out.

"I've got Swen taking tire tracks and footprints from the parking lot," said Eric. "See that little dirt road out the back? Told him to check that, too, just in case."

"Good job."

Blackbeard stepped in to the cabin and off to the left so Terry could come in. Terry took one step in and stopped.

"Jesus," he said.

The man in the chair had no face. Instead, he had a mass of smashed-in bloody meat with one eye hanging out, pointing right at Terry. Both arms were tied to the arms of the chair but one arm had a long strip of flesh hanging down like some kind of hideous decoration.

Terry tasted the bile in his mouth and opened up the plastic grocery bag in case he needed it. He forced himself to look at the body like he was far away, as if he was looking at a crime scene photo.

"Thanks for the barf bag."

Blackbeard nodded. "First guy in didn't have one. Lucky for him he made it out to the rail or I'd have him cleaning it up with tweezers to restore my crime scene."

Blackbeard let Terry take it in, then said, "We've got to put a stop to this, partner. People are dying on our beach."

Terry couldn't take his eyes off the body. He wanted to close his eyes and make it all go away, but he couldn't look away, either.

Blackbeard said, "I can't stand it in here for more than a couple of minutes at a time. Look around a little more and we'll step outside and talk."

Terry hardened his mind and started to scan the room slowly, trying to feel like a superhero searching for truth with his x-ray vision, rather than just an ordinary man who was just as vulnerable as the body sitting before him.

There was a bottle of Dos Equis next to the body. Terry reached over and put one finger in the neck and lifted it carefully.

"Half full," he said. "Doesn't seem like the kind of guy to leave a bottle half full."

"Wasn't. Captain Dave never left enough for a gnat."

"Captain Dave? So we got a name already." Terry held the bottle up and touched the bottom of the bottle with the wrist of his other hand.

"Warm. Hoping it was still cool."

"No," said Blackbeard. "Cold as this guy is, this happened sometime last night."

He lowered the bottle back to the counter and looked at Blackbeard.

"Much as I can stand, for the moment," said Terry. Blackbeard nodded and they went outside. Blackbeard motioned to Eric.

"Do me a favor. Take the temperature of the beer next to the captain. Take the temperature of other liquids in the room, too, see if there's any difference."

Eric nodded and went back to his van for equipment.

Terry breathed in and looked out at the line of condos along the beach in the distance. "Wish I smoked,' he said. "Anything to get that smell out."

"Smoking would ruin that Captain-America-save-the-world-five-days-a-week-in-the-gym thing you've got going," said Blackbeard. He was leaning on the rail looking off at the beach, too. Looking anywhere but back at the cabin of the boat.

"Gonna take superpowers to solve this one," said Terry.

"Gonna take hard work."

Terry smiled for the first time since he'd arrived. "The hard work's going to be keeping this one off the TV. Chief and the PR officer have the tough job here."

Blackbeard said, "Don't care about their job."

"OK," said Terry. "Catch me up here."

Usually Blackbeard pulled out his notebook for these kinds of questions, but he didn't need it here.

"This here is—or was—Captain Dave Ankerson. Legendary waterman and drunk. Friend of my father's when I was growing up. Inspiration for a couple of Buffett's songs. Also a drug smuggler, small time crook, and occasionally unsuccessful politician. Made a lot of fans over the years, pissed a lot of people off, too."

Terry said, "Don't think one of them did this. Whoever did this was way beyond pissed off."

"Don't start thinking anything yet. Just do our job, let the facts do the thinking. Get this thing wrapped up."

"Some hard facts in that cabin."

"True that," Blackbeard pointed over at a sailboat without a mast two boats down. "That's the guy that found him. Said he went over to see if Captain Dave was sober enough to go fishing. We'll talk to him later. I don't know him, but he's bound to know somebody I knew sometime, so we can get a read on him." Blackbeard looked at Terry. "Ready to try it again?"

Terry nodded.

They turned to go back to the cabin and Blackbeard noticed the five-pound bag of shrimp boil sitting on the deck.

"Huh," he said.

He bent down, careful not to touch the bag.

"Hilton." He stood up and looked at Terry. "Why would anybody leave a bag of spices outside like that? Rain comes along and ruins it all. Little bit of dew overnight would have done the same thing."

Terry looked down at the bag and thought of a shirt with an orange stain he had back home. Thought of where the bag of shrimp boil had been this morning. Thought of where Lizzie had been all night, even when Dave was being killed. He started to say something but kept quiet.

Blackbeard turned and waved at Eric, who was standing in the parking lot talking to a guy lifting a footprint. "Eric." Eric turned and looked at the bag of spices Blackbeard was pointing to. "Take special care with this. Make sure you get pictures and prints and make sure nobody disturbs nothing around it until you do."

Eric nodded.

They walked back to the cabin door and stepped inside. It was easier the second time, now that Terry knew what to expect. Easier, but not much. They stood there, shoulder to shoulder, in the narrow cabin.

"OK, Terr, tell me what you got."

Terry's mind was back outside with the bag of shrimp boil. He shook his head and focused, looked back at the cabin door for a minute and let the story come to him as he scanned around the room.

"Maybe." He paused. "Somebody had a grudge. Maybe a drug deal gone bad, something like that. Maybe they felt like they needed to make an example."

Terry held his hands up like he was framing a picture. "OK, so a couple of them came in here."

"Why a couple?"

"Drug scum always work in groups. They like to have a witness so they can go back and brag about how tough they are. Also, they don't have the balls to handle things man to man. Fair fight's the last thing they want."

Blackbeard nodded. "Can't be more than two. Crowded in here right now with just us."

"Yeah." Terry looked around. "Even with just two people, hard to see them doing this without knocking something over." He scanned the piles of dishes and beer cans in the cabin. "Though it's kind of hard to tell if they did."

"Another thing," he said, "if they did this to send a message, why not trash the place more? I mean, this just looks cluttered and lived in, not demolished."

"Agreed. So we got a vicious but neat drug thug. Shouldn't be too many of them around to check out," said Blackbeard.

They both stood there silent for a minute.

"Vicious but neat," Terry repeated.

"Yeah."

"Kind of the definition of a pro," said Terry. He turned to Blackbeard, but Blackbeard watched him without saying anything.

"Like the Hilton." Blackbeard finished the thought.

"OK," said Terry. "Let's try this. The guy's a pro. Comes in alone. Could just pop Dave, but he doesn't. Vicious pro, pro who gets his kicks torturing people? Maybe, but that's mostly on TV. Real pros get in, get out. Like the Hilton."

He stood there a minute. He would have paced, but he didn't want to mess up the small room so his eyes did the pacing.

"No. He wants something." Terry was working it through. "He tortures his victim," he continued. "gets whatever it is he wants. If he's a pro, then he puts a bullet in the guy's brain to make sure it's over. Why smash his face? Makes it hard for him talk, but no guarantee he's going to die. Don't know."

Blackbeard pointed at a cast-iron skillet in the sink. "I'm guessing that's what did his face."

"So we got a pro that uses a frying pan instead of a gun?" said Terry. "Don't know how much sense this is making right now."

They both scanned the room.

"Huh," said Terry. Blackbeard looked at him and waited for more.

Terry nodded at the counter. "Wallet, keys, a little money. And a business card. He leaned over and read it to Blackbeard.

"May be something," said Blackbeard. "May be nothing, too. Lot of these old timers own little bits of beach property here and there, brokers and development guys always chasing them for it."

"Maybe," said Terry. "Or maybe we got a pro who uses a frying pan instead of a gun and leaves business cards."

Blackbeard thought. "And delivers shrimp boil on the side."

Terry looked away. Seconds later they both heard someone behind them.

"Jesus," said a voice.

They turned to see the chief standing in the doorway.

"Jesus," he said again.

"Seems to be a popular word today," said Terry. "Must be because it's Sunday."

Blackbeard gave Terry a look that demanded he show more respect.

Terry ignored it. "What happened to the cops you were going to replace us with?" he said.

The chief continued to stare at Captain Dave. "That was a mistake. You two are the homicide detectives. This is your case. This and the Hilton case."

"What about the mayor?" said Terry.

"The mayor can go to hell. We're the cops, not him. We clear the cases."

The chief looked at Blackbeard. "We clear the cases. Clear these two. Fast."

• • •

"All right then, I'll see you in the morning," said Lizzie, using her hand to shield the phone's mouthpiece while she talked. She had driven into town, to the pay phone by the Waffle House, to make this call. She was wedged with her back against the phone stand, watching the traffic on 98 through her dark sunglasses. She was still shaking, and she was cold despite the hot day.

Music was playing on the other end of the line.

"Sure you don't need more help than what you're asking?" said a voice over the music.

"No," said Lizzie, and clamped her mouth down hard. "This mess is mine. I'll clean it up."

"Might not hurt to have a friend."

"I've made up my mind." She dropped the phone back on its hook, got into her truck, and drove away.

"I CAN'T EAT THIS." Terry shoved the plate of pork barbecue away. "Bring me a box. Maybe I'll eat it at home later."

"I just brung it to you," said the waitress at Sweet Sal's, standing with one hand on her hip. "Now you want a box?"

"Yeah. Sorry. Just not hungry."

"Me, too," said Blackbeard.

"If you'd a wanted it to go, you could a told me." She flounced off while Terry nursed his beer; Blackbeard his sweet tea. Terry felt out of place here in the barbeque joint tonight. Still, they had done everything they could at the scene, and this was where they went when they had nowhere else to go. Quieter than the station house, and they served beer and food here.

Blackbeard looked up. "Two events don't make a pattern, but I don't like the direction this is headed. First we got some kind of mob, or pros, or whatever bringing their fight into our backyard, and now we've got somebody killing our own."

"Getting rougher, too," said Terry. "Ten years in Chicago, I never saw anything like that last one."

"Yeah," Blackbeard looked down at his plate. Both of them were looking down a lot, and not smiling or joking with each other. Except when the door opened or someone made a loud noise. Then their eyes jumped up and their hands went

to their hips. The same pot-bellied good old boys from An-
dalusia in their Margaritaville shirts that had seemed so funny
and friendly a few days ago now looked like slouching monsters in disguise.

"OK, what have we got that sits on the fence between the
outside world and ECB?" said Blackbeard. "Know Carmex
was bringing something down from Chicago, joking about
going to a prayer meeting."

"Know a little more. Know the Sunshine boys were pissed
at the Lord for not providing." Terry told Blackbeard about
the Wednesday morning prayer meeting.

"Huh," said Blackbeard. He took a sip of his tea, his eyes
tracking a man in a suit as the man walked from the bar back
to the restrooms. Blackbeard kept his eyes on the men's room
door after it closed but glanced at Terry with a quick smile.
"Sounds like you're doing police work on your own time."

"Just doing my job, following the gospel of John Christopher."

"Don't spread around my first names. Cops ain't supposed to have first names," said Blackbeard.

"Now who's living the story?" They looked at each other
and smiled again, back to being buddies.

The front door slammed at the same time as the men's
room door opened. Blackbeard and Terry both jumped up,
knocking over their chairs, Terry covering the front door,
Blackbeard covering the men's room. The guy in the suit
paused coming out of the men's room, looking at a quiet
room with two men standing over knocked down chairs with

their hands on their hips and the whole room staring at them and at him.

"Hey, I washed my hands," was all he could say with a look that said he didn't. The room laughed nervously.

He eased around the edge of the room back to the bar, avoiding Blackbeard and Terry. At the door, a tiny woman with two kids bigger than herself shook one of the kids and said, "Don't slam no door. Want folks to think I raised you in a barn?" and led them off to the dining room on the other side.

The waitress slammed two Styrofoam boxes down on their table.

"If'n I'd a known you were in that big a hurry, I'd a brought your food out to the curb." She set their checks on top of the boxes with a flourish. "But don't give me no take-out tip."

She marched away and Blackbeard and Terry looked at the other diners. Most had started back to their meals after the excitement.

"Sorry," said Terry, to nobody in particular. Blackbeard picked up his chair and sat back down without looking anybody in the eye.

"OK," said Terry, scraping his food into the box. "So Carmex was bringing something valuable down to Sunshine, maybe something to do with that big Hole in the Beach deal, maybe not. Somebody in Sunshine decides to collect the money early."

"If you believe it's Sunshine," said Blackbeard, "then you got to believe that they celebrate by beating the crap out of Captain Dave just for the hell of it. Sounds like you're thinking with your ass."

"These are fine Christian people," said Terry. "Those folks can get pretty vicious sometimes."

"Don't let BeaAndra hear you tell that."

"My point exactly. Still, you're right. We sure don't have anything linking the biggest church group in the panhandle to an old, drunk dope-smuggler."

"We do have one connection between the two murders."

"What's that?"

"Hilton. You see that bag of shrimp boil, sitting out on the back of Dave's boat?"

"Yeah."

"Talked to Eric. He said the only prints that came back from the do not disturb sign was Hilton folks, not Carmex, and not the mystery bellhop."

"He say whose prints from the Hilton?"

"Yeah. Just the early maid. Lizzie the singer," said Blackbeard. "So how you reckon the killer brought shrimp boil to Captain Dave's? Think maybe they got into a fight over a recipe?"

Terry took a long breath and looked straight at Blackbeard.

"Don't think the killer brought that shrimp boil."

Blackbeard saw that Terry was serious and leaned in.

"Why do you think that?"

"'Cause I think I saw that bag of shrimp boil Sunday morning, hours after Dave was killed."

They sat there for a few seconds not saying anything.

"I saw it at Lizzie Gaffney's."

Terry saw Blackbeard's eyes glaze over and lose their emotion and knew that he was going into his cop pose with Terry, treating him just like another witness or suspect.

Blackbeard gave a small, controlled nod. "So you're saying Lizzie Gaffney's prints are at the first murder scene, and she left a bag of spices at the second?"

Terry pressed his lips together and stared back. "She didn't kill Captain Dave."

Blackbeard waited.

"I was with her the whole night," said Terry.

Terry saw the darkness rise up in Blackbeard's eyes like a tide.

"We got a suspect at both scenes, fingerprints all over the place, girl we knew was playing us even when she talked to us the first time, and you're taking advantage of Doc's little girl?"

"She's not a little—and I'm not—look, she's not a suspect. Wasn't even a suspect. Shouldn't be a suspect. You know she didn't do this. This is all Sunshine and that outfit."

"You know that?"

Terry looked out the window. "No."

"Then you dagnabbed better stop contaminating our witnesses."

Terry started to say something but couldn't think of anything that would help.

Blackbeard waved a finger across the table.

"I ought to report you to the chief, have you thrown off of the case."

Terry didn't say anything.

"When I accused you of thinking with your ass, I had the wrong part of your anatomy."

Terry still didn't say anything, just sat there trying to sort this out.

Blackbeard looked at him. "Tell me this: you really think that girl is honest?"

Terry thought about the last couple of days and looked out the window. "Yes."

Blackbeard looked at him now with no emotion, just a cop trying to nail down the facts. "You think she's told you the truth about everything?"

Terry thought more. "No."

Blackbeard waited for Terry to say more.

Terry stood up, threw some money on the check, and picked up the Styrofoam box with his food. "I'm going to walk home. See you in the morning."

thirty-three

TERRY DIDN'T WALK HOME to Portside. He went straight to the garage on Sundial, saluted Ron, and pulled the 396 snarling out onto the street.

The wind was swirling a mix of fall night cool, and left-over summer heat. Dark clouds stirred overhead as he passed Mack's and turned down Front Beach toward the tourist end. He realized he was goosing the throttle, making the engine thunder, and backed off. Front Beach Road was a quiet road with mommas and babies wandering aimlessly across it, and teenagers on electric scooters buzzing up and down with their mouths more open than their eyes. No place for the aggressiveness Terry felt tonight.

He thought about heading north, taking 79 out in the woods where he could open the 396 up, let it run while he put the top down and screamed at the night. Maybe keep going to the interstate. Maybe keep going from there.

Maybe. But later. Right now, he saw a woman trying to get a tribe of kids across Front Beach to the McDonald's and having no luck. Every time the traffic turned, a kid would get away and head back toward the beach. Every time she got the kids herded together, traffic picked up. Terry pulled into the condo lot next to the woman, got out and held up traffic until the woman could get across. She thanked him and he nodded and turned back to his car.

"Sonny," he heard her yell at his back, and he turned around. She was holding a wadded-up five-dollar bill. He shook his head but she grabbed his wrist like she had grabbed the youngest boy's wrist to drag him across the street. She shoved the bill in his hand and shook her finger in his face.

"You done a good deed. You got a reward coming."

Then she and the gaggle disappeared behind the glass doors of America's most popular restaurant and Terry was left standing on the sidewalk wondering what he was doing. That's it, he thought, he was just a goddamned Boy Scout traffic cop. He picked his way back across the street and wondered what to do.

Terry pulled in to the drive-through beer store and got a six-pack of Bud. He opened one of the beers and drained it as he drove, his mood getting darker with every block—and not helped with the next beer. He parked in his spot at Portside and thought about going inside. Instead, he took the remains of the six pack and the barbecue and walked over to Hole in the Beach and sat on the sand making empty beer cans and then throwing them down at the beach. Between throws, he picked at the smoked pork.

He turned slowly and took in a long panoramic view from the ocean, back to the unspoiled dunes, all the way around until he was facing the Hole in the Beach property that ran across Front Beach Road all the way to 98. Beyond his view there was nothing but original Florida scrub and a few cinderblock houses that were built years ago. He tried to imagine what it would look like with another condo on the beach side, maybe a souvenir store on the inland side. Wished he could stop it from coming, and knew he couldn't.

Terry wondered exactly what he could do about anything. Where was the line between trying to do the right thing, and doing your job? Maybe he should have arrested the drunk kid from a few days ago, rather than sent him home to Atlanta. Maybe, even now, the kid was getting in trouble, maybe even getting hurt because he hadn't done his job and locked him up. Maybe. Maybe he shouldn't be standing up for a girl just because she seemed like something special.

He stood up after a couple of tries and started to walk home, then looked back at the beach and knew he couldn't walk away like this. Stumbling down to the white sand, he picked up his beer cans and threw them into the trash. He kept at it until the Hole in the Beach was free of his and everyone else's beer cans and trash, and looked shining white and pure in the night.

Terry stumbled halfway across Front Beach and heard tires screech. He looked up to see a minivan stopped a foot in front of his legs. A tired-looking, middle-aged man sat in the driver's seat. Terry waited for the man to curse at him.

Instead, the man smiled and waved Terry across the street, looking out for him. Terry stood on the side of the road, smiled back while pointing at the man and said, "Boy Scout."

thirty-four

A KNOCK SOUNDED on Lizzie's door in the middle of the night and Lizzie knew it was the demons coming for her. She grabbed her shotgun and went to meet them. But when she threw open the door, she found Terry leaning against the front jamb.

"You haven't been honest with me," he said.

She eyed him carefully. "And you haven't been sober with me." Then she opened the door and pulled him toward her. "Let's get you inside."

Terry was a lot bigger than she was, but she half-marched, half-carried him through the house to the kitchen. If someone had been watching, they might have remarked that she looked like an ant with a giant leaf on its back. Lizzie dropped Terry roughly into a wooden chair.

"Told me you were honest and you haven't been honest with me," he said.

"Sounds like a country song," Lizzie said. "'Cept you've got to change 'haven't' to 'ain't.'" She poured a scoop of coffee beans into the grinder, looked at Terry, and added another scoop.

"Have it your way. You still ain't . . ." Terry started.

Lizzie held up her hand for him to be quiet.

He started over. "You ain't . . ."

"Shush," she said.

Terry straightened his backbone and raised his voice. "You ain't . . ."

"I said shut the eff up." She turned on the grinder and the conversation stopped.

When the coffee was brewing, she sat down and looked at Terry. He was red-eyed and glaring at her.

"You were saying?" she said.

"You ain't—haven't—been honest with me."

"I sang you my songs and I showed you my water," she said. "Showed you more, if I recall. Don't know how to be more honest with a man."

"Not that part. The cop part."

She nodded, lips tight. "I never told you a lie. Not you, nor Mister Blackbeard neither."

They sat and stared at each other.

"There's more to being honest than not lying. You didn't tell us everything," said Terry.

"No." She got up and poured a large cup of coffee, brought it back and set it down in front of Terry. Then she motioned for him to drink up. He took a sip.

"Good coffee," he said.

"Good. You need to be awake for this."

He looked at her and took a deep, scalding, jolting swallow. And another. She waited until the cup was empty and got him another.

"None for you?" he said.

"No. Busy day tomorrow, starting early. I have to get some sleep."

"Look," he said. "I've got to have some answers. Last night doesn't change that."

She gave him a look that was a slap.

"This is all about last night, and about nights to come," she said. "Last night was nothing if it wasn't honest. There can't be another night if we're not honest now."

Terry waited.

"You're right. I've not been honest. Haven't been dishonest either, but that's not the same thing as being honest. I've got to set things right. But that don't mean I can tell you everything you need to know. At least not right now."

"Lizzie," he said slowly. "I'm a cop. I've got to have answers."

"And you'll have them. Soon. But I've got to have some time. I did something that wasn't honest, and people have paid a terrible price. I've got to be the one to set it right, today. By the end of the day—maybe the end of tonight—I'll have you answers. Then we can be honest again."

Terry looked into her eyes and tried to divine what that meant. Her eyes were as clear and transparent and open as the comment was opaque and closed. He thought, yet again, that looking into those eyes was like looking down into the Gulf on a clear day: crystal blue-green that showed every detail. But now he realized that when his vision hit the hard sand on the bottom, everything became a mystery.

Lizzie stared back. He was such a big guy, with so much confidence and bluster. But his eyes were little boy eyes, always full of questions, always searching for something. She wanted to give him answers. Wanted to, but couldn't.

"Lizzie," he said, "people are dying."

"I know."

"You know I'm a cop, and you know I'm going to get to the truth."

"I know. You'll have your truth by tonight."

"I have to ask, and I have to have an answer. Lizzie, did you kill either of those men?"

"No."

He thought a long time.

"And if I give you until Tuesday morning, will anybody else die?"

Her mouth grew tight. "That," she said, "will be up to them."

He thought for a moment, then said, "I will do my job."

Lizzie saw that Terry was trying to make up his mind about something. But in the middle of his concentration, the alcohol won out. His eyes rolled up and he crashed down onto the table, breaking the coffee mug and raining black coffee and jagged, clinking shards of pottery from the table to the floor.

Lizzie stood up, suddenly filled with the kind of tiredness she only felt when she knew there were things she had to do before she could sleep. She took a dishrag, picked up Terry's head, and cleaned him and the tabletop with the other hand. Then she took a mop and cleaned up the floor.

After, she squatted down and wedged herself under Terry, got him in a fireman's hold and carried him back to the couch. She found an afghan her momma had knitted years ago, tucked it around him, and stood to look at him. Finally, she kicked off her shoes, climbed under the afghan, put her head on his chest, and cried herself to sleep curled up around him.

• • •

An edge of the sky was turning pink when she woke up and shook him awake.

"C'mon," she said. "You've got to get up and get out of here."

Terry sat up painfully, started to shake his head and then thought better of it.

"Coffee?" he said.

"Get your coffee on the road," she said. "You've got to get out of here." She stood him up and he faltered before he found his footing, but then walked to the door on his own. At the door he turned to face her. He seemed to be confused, not sure what had gone on or what he needed to say.

"I want you to know that I had a nice time," he said, when he couldn't come up with anything but the old lines.

Lizzie opened her mouth and stared at him.

"A nice time?"

He took her surprise the wrong way.

"Yeah. But, I mean, we both need to know that's all this is. I'm not the kind of person to get tied down to anything. That's not my story."

She still hadn't closed her mouth.

"Buddy, we're a long, long way from that speech," she said, putting a hard finger into his chest. "I don't know where we are—if we're anywhere—but it ain't just fun, and it ain't to the point where we can ride off into the sunset together either, or whatever kind of happy ending your playtime books have got."

Terry took this in, not sure what his next line was supposed to be.

"Get your head out of those books, stop living by other men's words, and figure out who you are and what you want to be," she said. "Find out what's yours and what's not. You figure that out and come back here. Then maybe there's a chance for you and me."

She thought about that for a minute.

"Yeah, a chance," she said. "That's what we are: a chance. And that's all."

Then she slammed the door in his face.

LIZZIE SAT ON THE FRONT PORCH, thinking about Terry and watching the sun rise when a long black limo pulled up, crunching the oyster shells in her driveway. She stood up, brushed the dust off her backside and walked over to the back window. The window rolled down with a whine and air conditioning poured out, driven by a heavy rap beat.

"P?" she said. "P-Teet?"

A giant hairless white head poked out of the window and broke into a grin.

"Attitude Baby," he said. "I always liked that nickname, even if you were the only one who ever called me that."

"And I always liked when you called me 'Attitude Baby.'" She put her fingers on top of his head, shoved him back inside, and stuck her head in the window and looked around. "Looks like y'all got everything you need in here, but you're welcome to come in the house and we can talk there."

P-Teet cocked his head and listened for a minute to a voice in the back of the limo.

"Boss Man says we're coming inside."

Lizzie stepped back. The door opened and P-Teet unfolded out of the car. He was a big white guy, close to seven feet tall and heavy for his height, which was why his name as a rapper was P-Teet, pronounced "petite." He stood beside the limo, alone for a minute, and slowly scanned 360 degrees.

When he was satisfied, P-Teet stepped out into the road. Two identical black men got out wearing identical black silk T-shirts and black silk ball caps turned to the side. They stood shoulder to shoulder at the door and smiled. One showed a mouth full of a gold grill, the other with some kind of white metal in his mouth. On a silent cue, they stepped apart for Boss Man to get out.

Boss Man was a small man, as small as P-Teet was big, but the way he carried himself let you know that he was bigger than P-Teet in every way that counted. He stood like a general surveying a battlefield until Lizzie smiled, then he smiled and threw his arms open.

"Lizzie girl," he said when they broke from the hug. "Used to be the best white girl in the music business."

"I still am," she said. "They just don't know it."

"Then let's remind them."

"I'd ask how the best rapper in the world—"

The rapper on the left of Boss Man interrupted Lizzie. "The greatest entertainer," he said, and nodded to the other rapper.

"Of all time." The rapper on Boss Man's right finished.

Lizzie continued. "I forgot. I'd ask how you're doing, but I saw you on MTV yesterday, so I'd say you're doing fine."

"So—so." Boss Man held up his hand and waggled it back and forth. "Holding off the young guns as long as I can." He looked out at the big tree that shadowed half of Lizzie's house. "I haven't seen a live oak that big since I left home."

"I thought you grew up in Compton, and were raised with a Glock for a pacifier," said Lizzie.

Boss Man smiled. "You been reading the publicity stuff. No, I grew up in Louisiana, on a bayou a lot like this. Momma still lives there, in a house like this, a house with a story behind every room." He paused to take a deep breath, getting as much of the waterside air in his lungs as he could. "'Cept Momma's house is the brightest pink you ever saw, and always was. Said she wanted the world to know the kids who lived there were something special."

"Got her wish," said Lizzie.

Boss Man shook his head. "Got it long before I hit the big time. She believed in us long before the world did, will believe in us after the world gets tired and throws us on the trash heap. She's as proud of my sister who teaches troubled kids in the back woods as she is of me. Always will be."

Lizzie nodded. She remembered how proud Daddy had been of her the first time he heard her sing one of her songs there in the garage. And, she remembered he was prouder of her in that moment than he was years later when she handed him her CD and told him she'd hit the big time. Sort of.

"That kind of pride comes out of places like this," said Boss Man. "Grows out of the water and the soil." He smiled. "Think it comes from eating blue crabs. All those crabs they got on the West Coast, stone crabs, whatever. Giant monsters, but they ain't nothing like blue crabs." He looked at

Lizzie and smiled. "Course you ain't got no blue crabs here like we got in Louisiana."

Lizzie said, "We got the best ones here. Remember Josh Turnbow, folk singer out of Baltimore? He was bragging on their Chesapeake Bay crabs, how everybody knew Baltimore crabs were the best in the world—until I brought him here and fed him panhandle crabs and converted him. No. Louisiana's got some good eating, but blues are better here than in Louisiana or Baltimore, or Shangri-La, for that matter."

Boss Man smiled. "Ought to be a song there, somewhere. Wish we had time to take that boat of yours out, spend the day out on the water with God and the fish and the crabs, spend the night picking out crabmeat and drinking beer. But we only got a couple of hours to get our business done here, get back on the plane to a party in Miami I'm supposed to be at tonight."

"Shoot," said Lizzie. "Don't need to spend the day on the water for crabs around here. We can do this." She turned and marched off toward the dock, walking fast and not asking them to follow. Boss Man watched her turn her back on him, something that nobody did. He laughed, and followed.

They filed out on the dock, Lizzie in the lead, followed by Boss Man, the two rappers, and P-Teet bringing up the rear with his head swiveling, watching for danger. Lizzie got to the end and pulled up the crab trap. It was full of scuttling, snapping crabs.

"Good haul. Thank you," she said, talking to the crab god somewhere in the clear blue sky. She looked back at the entourage. "Still, not enough for all of y'all. Boss Man, you think you could send somebody up to the house about a quarter-mile down the road that way, ask the Jenkins' if we could have a couple of dozen from them?"

"Sure. I'll send P-Teet."

"Maybe I should call them first, so they don't have a heart attack," Lizzie said. "Still, it'll give them something to talk about for six months." She looked at the trap. "We've got to get these back to the house." She opened the trap and pulled out a snapping, angry jimmy crab.

"Gimme that," said Boss Man. He took the slimy crab from the back, away from the claws, the way that someone who grew up around the water would do. He turned to the rapper with the gold grill, and the guy pulled back from the slimy thing in the Boss Man's hand.

"Here," said Boss Man. "Thang 1, Thang 2, you going to learn how to carry blue crabs." The rapper called Thang 1 wasn't happy about it, but he held out a hand to Boss Man. "Tempted to just hand it to you," said Boss Man. "Let Mister Crab here dig a couple of holes in your fingers till you learn to hold him right. But I'll do you a favor; show you how to hold him like my momma taught me."

They unloaded the trap and marched back up to the house, Lizzie and Boss Man with their hands full, Thang 1 and Thang 2 with a crab in each hand, held out as far from their bodies as they could get.

They were in the studio an hour later with the Boss Man listening to Lizzie's new songs while he picked out crab meat and drained a Tecate.

"Pretty good," he said, when she finished the song.

"The music or the crabmeat?"

"Music's good. We ought to make some money with that."

"Crab?"

"Crab is manna from heaven."

"Better than Louisiana?" said Lizzie.

"Nothing is ever better than Momma's," said Boss Man. "but it's close."

He wiped bits of crabmeat and Slap Yo Mama seasoning on a paper towel.

"Believe I've heard enough," he said. "What you had, you still got. Our business guys checked out what we talked about, think it makes sense. Still want to do this?"

"Yep." Lizzie reached back behind a couple of boxes and took out the bag from the Hilton. She started to hand it to Boss Man but he waved her to Thang 1. Thang 1 opened the bag and tipped it to show the money inside to the Boss Man.

"Just so we're clear," said Boss Man. "We take this, use part of it to go to Peace and Light and persuade them to release their entire back catalog to each of the original artists for one payment."

"Think you can get them to sell? This isn't enough to buy out the whole back catalog, based on the prices they wanted just for me."

The two Thangs grinned, showing their grills.

Boss Man said, "Girl, half of L.A. still thinks I killed the head of Sony Music for back talking me. Think they going to say no to me?"

"No."

Boss Man said, "This is going to be more than enough. You gonna have change coming back to you on the deal."

"Keep it."

"Keep it?"

"Keep it. It doesn't belong to me."

She put her guitar back in the rack, turned and shut down her electronics.

"You want to make even more money?" she said.

Boss Man smiled a very wide smile.

"Take the leftover money. Open a small studio, right here in ECB. A lot of Nashville singers like to come down here on vacation, and they might not mind having a place to get some work done while they're here. Might make some money on a studio like that."

Boss Man thought about it.

"We could expand our brand," he said. "Right now there's East Coast rap and West Coast rap. We could start our own Third Coast rap, stuff like nobody ever heard before. Pull some of those Nashville folks in, do some crossovers. And you say there's local talent down here?"

"Lot of good musicians down here playing music for the tourists. They would love to play something other than Buffet covers," said Lizzie.

"And, of course," Boss Man smiled at Lizzie. "We get Third Coast's first big star, Lizzie Borden. You got anybody down here for your band?"

"Got a guy in mind. Maybe."

Boss Man looked out the window at the water. "We going to make some money here."

"That's the idea," said Lizzie.

Boss Man nodded. "Sure you don't want to keep any of the money?"

"Doesn't belong to me. I want my music."

"We'll get you that."

They walked out to the limo, and Lizzie leaned on the door. "There's one more thing."

Boss Man's lips tightened and he gave her a look that said there always was.

"Don't spend the money until I call you tomorrow. I've got one more thing to take care of. If you show the money before I call, people will come looking for you. Bad people, even for you. You don't hear from me tomorrow, you take that money and throw it away. You don't want the bad mojo that will follow that money unless I put the mojo back where it belongs."

He looked at Lizzie for a long time without saying anything.

"I reckon if I was to leave P-Teet down here with you to protect my investment, you'd take offense and send him back to me in little bitty pieces," he said.

Lizzie held his look. "You know I wouldn't hurt P-Teet for nothing." A smile flickered on her face and then went out. "But I would send him back to you. I gotta do this myself."

Boss Man looked up at the dark clouds rolling in from the west.

"You got a storm coming, girl. In more ways than one."

TERRY SAT ON HIS UPSTAIRS DECK and watched the sun come up in the East and the storm clouds roll in from the West. His head felt like the storm clouds.

Surprise, he thought. *You drank more than you have in years, drove drunk for the first time in your life, and got two hours sleep on the side of a swamp road when you finally realized you were too drunk to drive. Finally made it home with the sun coming up, and your head hurts. Lucky that's all that hurts.*

He saw Blackbeard's Crown Vic pull into Mack's empty parking lot and thought about going down to join him.

Music from the old Peter Gunn detective show was playing in the bedroom behind him, the heavy bass rhythm that had been the standard for detective shows for fifty years pounding out to him through the open sliding door. Terry looked down at the parking lot that led to Front Beach Road and then to Mack's. He tried to see himself swaggering along the road easy, like a big cat in a cool suit looking for adventure, strutting to the beat of Mancini's bass. Same opening he had followed every day since he'd been here. Except today the big cat felt more like a cartoon character, maybe an R. Crumb drawing from the sixties with the feet impossibly stretched out and a goofy, prideful grin on it's face.

"Screw it," he said to nobody in particular. His head still hurt and he was angry at something. Everything. He didn't know what.

"I don't want any eggs today." He stood up and wondered what to do next. Wondered who he was talking to, as well.

Didn't stop him from talking.

"Just do your job," he said to himself and laughed. That's what he'd do: his job and no more. Blackbeard could eat his breakfast by himself. He would show up at the station later, on time, and not one minute sooner. Do his job, and nothing more.

He went inside and got cleaned up, put on a subdued dark blue suit and looked at himself in the mirror. Yeah, he looked like a guy going to work, maybe a job in a bank. Nothing special. When he looked out the window he found that Blackbeard's car was no longer at Mack's. He went out and locked the front door behind him.

The 396 was parked sideways, taking up the slots for SD6 and SD5. The SD5 owners, Mike and Pat, wouldn't mind since they were in their city home in Huntsville right now. Still, it wasn't a parking job he was proud of. Just glad he hadn't tried to put the car in the narrow garage last night.

Terry cranked up and drove down to 79, then north on 79 to the ECB Police Station. He picked up his mug from his desk and filled it at the coffee pot before he sat down and looked at Blackbeard.

Blackbeard stared at him with no expression for quite some time. Terry sipped his coffee and stared back.

"C'mon," Blackbeard said finally. He pointed at Terry's coffee cup. "You need better than that today."

Blackbeard stood and walked to the door. Terry watched him a minute before he got up to follow. Then he reached back and grabbed his coffee cup, feeling like he would collapse if he got more than three feet away from caffeine.

They got in the Impala and drove without a word to Pier Park. As Blackbeard was parking, Terry started to say something, but Blackbeard stopped him.

"Let's get some coffee into you first." He looked at the empty cup on the dash. "Some decent coffee."

They walked past the pink cinema to Starbucks, and after getting their orders, sat outside at an ironwork table that faced the kiddie rides in the middle of the park. Blackbeard took a sip of his coffee and looked at the ticket stand in front of them.

"I'm going to run this investigation, partner," Blackbeard said. "And run it the right way."

"I know that. Don't need three-dollar coffee to know that."

"Could have said this at the station. But there's not much privacy in the squad room."

Terry nodded.

"So I need to know what you know."

"You already know," said Terry. "Soon as Lizzie became a player, I told you."

"Yeah."

"I still don't buy it," said Terry. He shifted forward, a little more animated as the good caffeine started to kick in. "Lizzie, I mean. This thing's still tied up with Sunshine and that real estate deal. That morning prayer meeting wasn't a coincidence."

Blackbeard shrugged. "We're cops. We follow facts. Those are facts, and we'll follow them. But there's a couple of stray facts hanging around your Miss Lizzie."

Terry thought about the sound of that, his Miss Lizzie, and snorted. Blackbeard smiled.

"Told you she'd be a handful."

"You have no idea."

Blackbeard laughed. "That's the one thing in her favor. These killings are not her style. If Lizzie had a done this she would have used a shotgun, not a .22. When we showed up to investigate, she'd have been sitting there on the bed waiting for us, would have told us, 'I did it, and I'd do it again.'"

Terry smiled. It felt like his face was going to crack, but it didn't. "She'd probably hold up her hand that cute little way that she has, tell us we had to wait to take her to jail until she could write down the song she was writing about how good revenge felt."

"Yeah." Blackbeard looked at Terry. He couldn't see Terry's eyes through his sunglasses, but he could see that the smile stayed plastered on his face while he thought about Lizzie.

"Still don't think she did it," Terry said. "No matter what the facts look like."

Blackbeard looked at the ticket booth. "A cop has to follow the facts. But sometimes the man inside the cop has to take a stand and go with what his heart tells him." He looked at Terry and held his gaze before he continued. "You're a good cop, Terry. A good cop and a good man. Don't get your head swole up over me telling you, but you are. Your instincts are worth following." He stood up. "But right now we're cops, and the facts are down yonder." He pointed beachside, to where the Hilton loomed over the Pier Mall buildings. "We're going to walk down to the Hilton and get some answers from Miss Lizzie." He looked at Terry with the flat, patient stare he used in interrogations.

"Got no problem with that," Terry said, staring back.

They walked down the sidewalk past the restaurants and stores, and across Front Beach to the Hilton, all without saying a word. The Hilton manager took them back to the head of housekeeping and slunk away before she could see him.

"Are you Yolanda?" asked Blackbeard. The woman tapped her nametag with her pencil and went back to filling out some forms without looking up.

"We need to speak to Lizzie Gaffney."

"Ain't here." The woman, old, black, and thin, looked up and past Blackbeard and Terry.

"Hey," she yelled. "Get your butt up and clean up the mess that country singer left after his concert last night. Don't you be sneaking off for a smoke break while I got work for you to do."

Terry thought she was talking to them but he turned to see a woman in a Hilton uniform scurry by behind them. They waited, but Yolanda was back at her forms.

"Do you know where Miss Gaffney is?" Blackbeard said.

"No."

"Did she call in?"

"Yes."

Blackbeard waited until it was clear he wasn't going to get anymore from Yolanda in this lifetime without asking.

"What'd she say?"

Yolanda looked up and Terry saw that she was more tired than angry.

"Said she wasn't coming in. Asked her if she was sick, thought she might want to give me some lame-ass lie, but no, she couldn't even be bothered to lie to me. Just said, 'No, I ain't coming back.'"

She went back to her forms and Blackbeard and Terry stepped outside.

"We're still going to talk to your Miss Lizzie," said Blackbeard. "But before we go way out to the woods chasing her, we're going to stop by Sunshine."

thirty-seven

BLACKBEARD PULLED into the Sunshine Development parking lot and Terry saw a black SUV with the tailgate down, parked crossways by the door. They unclipped their seat belts and walked to the back of the Escalade and looked in.

"Huh," said Blackbeard. "Coming or going?"

The third seat was down and the back was half-filled with packing boxes. Terry reached in and poked the back three boxes.

"Going," he said.

Blackbeard looked at him until he explained. "Only half full. Somebody's packing in a hurry."

"Huh," said Blackbeard. "Maybe."

They walked through the glass doors and stood there watching. The curved wooden receptionist's desk in front of the door was empty, but it was the only thing empty in the building. The floor was littered with papers. Two women dressed in expensive clothes were scooping papers up and feeding them into a big shredder.

A tall young girl with black hair hanging down her back smiled at Terry and he smiled back.

"I don't believe you're dressed for manual labor," he said, still smiling.

She laughed. "Didn't know I'd be housecleaning when I got dressed today. Thought I would smile and answer the phone as usual."

"Sounds like a better plan. Why'd you change your mind?"

"Didn't. He did." She jerked her head to the back office. "He's been a madman all morning, screaming that we've got to get this stuff cleaned up fast."

Terry smiled and started to say something cute, but Blackbeard cut him off.

"Is that Rob Roberts, the president here, back in that office?" said Blackbeard.

"The one and only. Praise Jesus for that."

They walked in on a balding man bent over a file drawer, throwing papers into a pile on the floor. He saw one file folder, pulled it out and dropped it in a box on his desk.

"Emma," he yelled with his head still down. "Get those freaking papers shredded."

He looked up and saw Blackbeard and Terry. Then he turned white under his good Florida tan. He tried to smile but it just looked crooked.

Terry said, "Mr. Roberts, we'd like to ask you some questions." He started to pull his jacket back to show his badge but never got the chance. Roberts looked at the door behind them, saw he couldn't make it, and crashed through a private side door to the outside.

"What the hell?" said Terry.

"I got the front," said Blackbeard.

Terry hit the side door before it bounced shut, paused, and saw Roberts running for the parking lot. Terry slipped on the grass, and Roberts opened up a lead.

Terry rounded the corner as Roberts flung open the driver's door to the Escalade. Blackbeard barreled out the front and got one arm on Roberts, but Roberts slammed the door on Blackbeard's arm viciously once, twice, three times until Blackbeard fell away clutching his arm.

The engine cranked and Terry dove for the open tailgate. He almost had a grip on one of the folded-up seats when the SUV peeled away and he slid out and bounced on the pavement on his rear end.

"C'mon," Blackbeard said, heading to the Impala. As he ran, he held his right arm like a broken wing.

Terry made it into his seat as the car started moving. Blackbeard flipped on the flasher and the siren.

"How's your arm?" said Terry, looking at the useless limb dangling from Blackbeard's right shoulder.

"Been better," said Blackbeard. As they pulled onto 98, he glanced at Terry and grinned. "How's your ass?"

Terry pulled out his cell phone, talked for a minute, and hung up. "I've called for backup. They said Roberts's home is over in Autumn Breeze."

"Looks like where he's headed," said Blackbeard.

The Escalade made a hard right, and papers and boxes sailed out of the back. Blackbeard slowed down, but went on by.

"Let him think he lost us," he said. He flipped off the siren and flasher, made a U-turn and went back into the neighborhood from another street.

"His house is that way," said Terry, pointing down a street.

The Escalade was parked mostly in the driveway. They pulled up as Roberts came out dragging two suitcases, followed by two small, crying children. Blackbeard tapped the siren and pulled in behind the Escalade. Roberts stood and watched them as they got out.

"You're police," he said.

"What the hell'd you think we were?" Terry said.

He looked at Terry. "Well, with your accent, I assumed you were from Chicago and I assumed you," he nodded at Blackbeard, "were reaching for a gun." Roberts relaxed when he realized these were just city employees, no threat to a respected pillar of the community such as himself. He smiled and put out his hand toward Blackbeard.

"Sorry to run out on you like that. I was in a hurry to get home and catch a plane."

Blackbeard glared at him and looked down at his lifeless right arm.

"Oh, that," said Roberts, snatching his hand back. "Sorry if your arm got caught in the door as I was closing it."

"Something like that," said Blackbeard. He stood there now, waiting for Roberts to talk.

"We were just leaving."

Terry snorted.

"Mind telling us where you're going?" said Blackbeard.

"Well," Roberts hesitated. "We have heard the call. America has gotten so wicked that God has turned his back on her, just turned his back. We're going to Australia, where there is still a need for godly men to spread the gospel."

Blackbeard stared at him.

"Or maybe Brazil," said Roberts.

"God hasn't made up his mind?" said Terry.

Roberts straightened up. "I'll not have you blaspheme in front of my children."

Roberts put the suitcases in the back and closed the tailgate.

"I'd like to stay and talk, I surely would. But we have to get to Birmingham to catch a flight."

"The new airport's only ten miles from here," said Terry. "They say you can get anywhere in the world from there. Why not fly out of there?"

"Thought we'd have better connections in Atlanta," said Roberts.

"Or Birmingham," said Terry.

"That too. I'm sorry, but we've really got to be going."

"I'm sorry, too," said Blackbeard. "But I'm going to have to ask you to come down to the station and give us a statement, fill out some paperwork. You know," he glanced at his arm, "explain how my arm got caught."

Roberts kept his smile. "We can do that," he said. "We surely can. I can call my friend the mayor; have my lawyer meet us at the station—if you think that's necessary. Probably won't delay us more than five minutes. Or maybe the mayor will just let my lawyer handle it."

Terry saw Blackbeard's lips tighten. "Yeah, you're probably right."

Blackbeard turned to walk away.

"Oh, Mr. Roberts." Blackbeard turned back when he got to the Impala. "What's going to happen to Sunshine Development with you gone?"

"We've got new management coming in, coming in today, in fact."

Terry looked at him. "From Chicago?"

Roberts nodded, but the smile was gone.

"YOU DRIVE," Blackbeard said to Terry. He was in a bad mood and needed to order somebody around. Terry had made him go to a doctor about his arm. The doctor wanted Blackbeard to go to a hospital, but Blackbeard told the doctor what he thought of hospitals and marched out the door.

It was past lunchtime. Terry couldn't remember when he'd last eaten but they both wanted to get to their next stop.

"I still want to get out to Lizzie's," said Terry.

"Me, too. But, if Sunshine's in a panic over something, and Progress is their competition, I want to talk to Progress."

"Just saying, Lizzie's a priority, too."

"Lizzie didn't nearly break my arm because she thought I was from Chicago. What do we know about this guy?" said Blackbeard, pulling out a printed sheet with a copy of the business card they had found at Captain Dave's.

"The guy at Progress Bank?" said Terry. "I called around while you were pretending to let the doc fix you up. Progress is a small, independent bank, scrambling for real estate deals like everybody else. Rolvaag—that's the name on the card—is the manager. Worked in Atlanta most of his life, then came down here. No record."

"Could be a wild goose chase," said Blackbeard.

"Could be. I used to work with a guy who said, 'do your job; let the facts come out.'"

"Yeah, well, that guy looks like a one-armed old coot right now. I like that other guy's approach, shoot 'em all up with your Captain America ray gun, hope you get the right one in time to go eat dinner."

Terry smiled. "So you want me to go in and shoot this guy so we can get some lunch?"

"Let me talk to him first. He might offer me a free toaster if I open an account."

They stepped into the brace of cold bank lobby air. A couple of tellers faced them, idle since the bank did little consumer business. Off to the left a man stood watching them from his office door. He reminded Terry of Bob Newhart, with an almost bald head and worried raccoon eyes. As soon as Terry made eye contact, the man ducked back into his office.

Blackbeard pulled his notebook out of his pocket and asked one of the tellers about the name on the business card and he pointed to the office the man had disappeared into. They stood in the office doorway, and Blackbeard looked down at his notebook for effect.

"Are you Mr. Roll-wag?" he said. Terry smiled behind him, for the first time today. Blackbeard was going to start off playing the simple country detective, a man too dumb to even know how to pronounce names.

"Rolvaag," the man said, not getting up. Terry thought he seemed irritated and impatient. Blackbeard stood in the door without saying anything.

Rolvaag lost patience first. "What the hell are you here for? I didn't call for the police?"

Terry started to say, "Sometimes we come on our own," without the sir, but he saw a little smile on Blackbeard's face and kept quiet. Blackbeard stayed quiet, and Rolvaag felt compelled to fill the silence.

"You guys work for us, or at least you're supposed to. We make the money, get the jobs and keep this town going. You're supposed to protect us and see that we can do our jobs."

Blackbeard finally spoke. "You think we don't?"

"You got a reputation. Not ECBPD, just you."

Blackbeard turned to Terry and said, "I don't recall introducing ourselves. We could be Abbot and Costello."

He turned back to Rolvaag and smiled. "Mr. Rolvaag," Blackbeard carefully pronounced the name, "this here boy is Detective Costello."

Terry said, "I forget. Am I the dumb one or the smart one?"

"Kind of answers its own question, don't it?"

Rolvaag interrupted. "You're Detective Blackbeard. Used to be Lieutenant Blackbeard, before the chamber of commerce got you busted down for hassling that Hollywood star."

Terry said, "We did our job, sir. And if you'll recall, we closed that case."

"Yeah, well, you could have closed it without embarrassing our guest. He was thinking about making a movie here, until you chased him away."

"Still surprised you recognized us," said Terry, leaving out the sir. "Our picture hasn't been in the paper or anything. Don't recall ever having met you before."

Rolvaag hesitated before he said, "Heard you described at C of C meetings." He stared at Blackbeard. "We have to watch out in our business. Never know who's going to rip you off." He stared hard at Blackbeard, issuing a challenge. "Let me take a wild guess: you were friends with that fisherman who was murdered."

"I knew him," Blackbeard said.

"I bet."

"You talked about being ripped off," said Blackbeard. "You think somebody has something that belongs to you?"

"I know somebody thinks that."

"Then you should call the police," said Blackbeard.

They all stood there for a minute not saying anything. Then Rolvaag retreated—for now—smiled, and tried a businessman approach.

"Well then, what can I help you gentlemen with today?" He went behind his desk, sat down and motioned Blackbeard and Terry to the visitor's chairs. They elected to stand.

"We're collecting some background, sir," said Blackbeard. "Probably nothing significant to do with our cases, but we have to nail down every little detail. You know how that is."

"Yes, sir, indeed I do. Without these little details, none of us would have jobs and we'd have to spend our time fishing all day."

"Yes, sir," said Blackbeard. "Don't sound too bad, some days."

"Until it's time to pay the mortgage," said Rolvaag.

"Yes, sir. Got to pay the bills."

"That's right," said Rolvaag, leaning forward. "Who's your mortgage with, if you don't mind me asking."

Blackbeard said, "Don't have a mortgage. Live in a house originally built by my daddy." Rolvaag's smile seemed to fade. "Don't like to be owing anybody."

"A wise policy," said Rolvaag. "Of course, with the judicious use of borrowing, you can live at a higher level. Come see me, I can make that happen." He paused. "Perhaps we can work out a deal advantageous to us both."

"Thanks. Sometimes, though, when you take something that ain't yours, specially from a bank, there's a cost down the line."

Rolvaag smiled. "Yes. But when you bring it back, the bank can be grateful." The smile grew colder. "And if you try to hang onto it, there can be consequences. Sometimes, even for your intermediaries." He leaned back again. "Hypothetically."

Blackbeard actually smiled. It was gone quickly, but Terry saw it before it left.

"We're trying to get a little background and thought you might be a good place to start. Do you know anything about the piece of beachfront property across from Mack's and Portside? I believe Oasis is in the process of putting together a development deal for it. Wondered if you knew who was financing that, who was bidding on it, that kind of thing."

Terry watched Rolvaag closely while Blackbeard talked. Rolvaag's mouth was still in a smile, but his eyes reacted to a detective asking about that deal.

Rolvaag answered carefully, "My understanding is that the Oasis deal is on hold for the moment, waiting on a piece of financing before Oasis selects a partner."

Terry exploded. "A piece of financing? Maybe that piece of financing is coming from Chicago? Maybe a guy named Carmex? Maybe you and Sunshine were in it together. Lost the 'financing,' and now you've killed a fisherman and left a girl to take the blame."

Rolvaag jumped up. "You know better."

They stood there staring at each other. Blackbeard stepped up beside Terry and pulled a picture of Captain Dave out of his pocket.

"Mr. Rolvaag," Blackbeard said, "the fisherman who was killed. Did you ever see him?"

"Hell, no," said Rolvaag, shaking his head furiously.

Blackbeard stared at Rolvaag and thought. He then reached into his pocket and pulled out Lizzie's picture. "How about this woman?"

Rolvaag shook his head. "You are running a shakedown here," said Rolvaag. "All of you, somehow. All you locals stick together. Dirty cops, dirty old sailors. Probably even cousins."

"That old sailor that you've never seen," said Blackbeard, showing no emotion.

Rolvaag looked at Blackbeard, deciding how to deal with him. "You know what I want. This is going to be your last chance."

Terry said, "Or what? You going to call the chamber of commerce and file a complaint?"

Rolvaag smiled, "Might. Might call somebody else."

Blackbeard reached across his body with his left hand and touched Terry on the sleeve. "I don't believe we need to trouble you anymore, sir."

"Wait," said Terry, "I want to—"

"Later," said Blackbeard. He turned back to Rolvaag with a big, fake smile. "I don't believe we need to trouble a businessman like you anymore." He stood there for several seconds, now with a fake, ugly smile and cold blue eyes before he finished. "Today."

Rolvaag walked around the desk to Blackbeard. "No. I'd like us to finish our business today. One way or the other. Today."

Blackbeard stood there without moving. "And what business would that be, sir?"

"Today."

Blackbeard nodded. "We'll be back, sir."

Blackbeard and Terry turned. The young man who had been sitting at the desk outside Rolvaag's office was now standing right behind Terry, so they were nose to nose when Terry turned around. Terry and Fabbi stood for a moment, facing each other. Terry glared and waited for him to move. Fabbi smiled a fake smile, stepped aside, and motioned for them to come by.

At the door, Terry turned to look back. Fabbi smiled again, this time a cold smile. He raised his hand like a gun, and pointed his finger at Terry.

He twitched his thumb like he was firing the gun, jerked his hand up, and blew the imaginary smoke off his finger.

thirty-nine

IN THE PROGRESS BANK PARKING LOT, Terry had his car door half open when Blackbeard said, "Look at that."

"What?"

"That. Big silver BMW with a hole the size of your head in the fender."

They walked over and stood, staring down at the car.

"What kind of accident you reckon would leave a hole like that?" said Blackbeard.

Terry squatted down and squinted in the hole. He reached his hand in, dug something out and pulled out a little piece of metal, like a big BB.

"Kind of accident that leaves double-ought shotgun pellets."

"Huh." Blackbeard looked back at the bank, staring at his reflection in the mirrored window.

"Put that in an evidence bag, if you would, partner."

"I'll put it in a bag in the car, after we're back in air conditioning."

"No, do it out here. Give the people on the other side of that glass something to talk about." Blackbeard stared at the glass while Terry pulled a little plastic baggie out of his coat pocket, wrote something on the label, and dropped the pellet inside. They walked around to the back of the car and stared at the license plate for a minute before they walked back to the Impala.

"You drive. Let me make some calls," said Blackbeard.

Terry backed the Impala out, drove down a few spots and pulled into another parking spot.

"I want to sit right here in front of Rolvaag's office. Let him see you sitting here making phone calls," said Terry.

BeaAndra answered her phone out of breath. "Just come in from the garden," she said. "Pulling weeds to grow you some squash."

"Don't like squash."

"Don't matter. I read that they's good for you, so you're getting squash. Make up for all the hamburgers and barbeque you eat with that worthless partner of yours."

"Well, good, I reckon. Hey, listen Bea, the other day, that crazy story of yours about chasing Florida Gators fans out of the house, where did you say you shot their car?"

"I told you, in the fender."

"Driver's side or passenger side?"

"Driver's side. Don't you listen to nothing I ever tell you?"

"One of those big black limousine kind of cars?" Blackbeard said.

"No, a fancy silver car. Mercedes or BMW. BMW, now that I think on it. Had that little propeller symbol on the back. Thought about aiming for it as it pulled away."

"And what kind of shot did you have in the gun?"

"Double-ought. You know that's what I keep in my shot-gun."

"Damned, Bea, you ever shoot someone with that, there won't be enough pieces left to bury."

"My husband's a detective. He'll find the pieces."

"That's what I'm afraid of." Blackbeard hung up and dialed another number.

"Chief, this is Blackbeard." He filled the chief in and gave the chief the license number of the BMW.

"Rolvaag," the Chief read the owner's name back to Blackbeard when it came up on his computer screen.

"Huh," said Blackbeard. "Chief, you reckon you can get Rodriques and that boy from Wewa to come over to the Tom Thumb across the street from the bank here, keep an eye on Rolvaag if he goes somewhere? I got some folks I want to go talk to pretty quick."

"Sure." The chief paused and waited for the rest of Blackbeard's call. When it didn't happen, he said, "Detective Blackbeard, usually when you call me directly, there's another part to the conversation. The part where you tell me who you're in trouble with."

Blackbeard exhaled. "Yeah. This time, too. Rolvaag threatened us. Since he's tight with the C of C. I don't know if he's going to call them up and get them to lean on you, or shoot us."

"I vote for shooting," said the chief. He hung up.

"Wait here," said Terry. He got out of the car, walked back inside the bank, and came back a minute later.

"What was that about?" said Blackbeard.

"Went back, stuck my head in Rolvaag's office. Gave him a big smile and said, 'Thank you very much for your help, sir.'"

Blackbeard smiled at Terry. "You might turn into a good cop yet, letting the guy know with a big smile that you're coming for him."

"Maybe that's my story," said Terry. "The Smiling Detective."

"Oh, Christ," said Blackbeard.

Terry turned right on 98 from Ashburn and pulled away, watching the traffic coming from the east. He didn't see Lizzie's pickup coming from the west.

FABBI AND ROLVAAG STOOD at the window watching Blackbeard and Terry pull away.

"Want me to follow them?" said Fabbi.

Rolvaag thought about it. "No. I'll call them later, after the bank is closed, tell them I got something for them. Make sure you've got that little pop gun of yours when they come." He saw Blackbeard and Terry pull onto 98. "If we get to Oasis tonight with the money, we still might salvage that deal and keep your daddy from cleaning house here."

He then watched an old pickup truck pull into the same spot Blackbeard and Terry had pulled out of.

A crazy-looking girl got out, slammed the truck door, and marched into the bank like she was going to war. The first thing Rolvaag noticed was the mohawk in a shade of red never produced by human genes. The second was her general scrawniness. He thought of that detective Blackbeard, and that whole scurvy-looking class of human water rats that infested the Florida Panhandle. He wished the bank still kept a security guard, but a development bank mostly held paperwork and computer bits. Not much a casual thief could put in a bag and run off with.

Swamp girl burst through the doors, put her hands on her hips and looked around until she decided Rolvaag was the man in charge. She shot one finger out at him.

"You," she said. In a voice like a hurricane, she sang at him, "You took my joy. I want it back," and marched into his office, dragging Rolvaag by his sleeve.

"I want my money back," she said when she turned him loose.

So. That's all this was, thought Rolvaag. Just a damned redneck who wanted to take her thirty-seven dollars and forty-two cents out of the bank and go blow it all at Walmart. Didn't want to stand in line at the teller windows, just tell the bank manager to hustle it up for her.

"Mabel?" Rolvaag leaned out his door to the first teller he saw. "Can you help this young lady?"

Mabel got up and started to come around the counter.

Rolvaag turned to Lizzie and smiled the warm friendly smile he practiced for customers and publicity photos for the bank. The smile that was supposed to say, "I am here to be your friend and help you," to the customer even though Rolvaag was always thinking, "Get the hell out of my life and leave me alone" when he smiled it.

The redhead seemed to catch both meanings and smiled back with her own fixed smile.

Without breaking the smile, she said, "My ten thousand dollars that was given to you last Friday by Captain Dave."

Rolvaag lost his smile and slammed the door in Mabel's face. He then opened the door, apologized to Mabel, and closed the door more politely. When he went around to his side of the desk he sat down in the big leather chair; it made him feel powerful and in charge.

"I don't have your ten thousand. No one gave me ten thousand." Now Rolvaag smiled his big predator smile, the one that said, "I'm going to eat you alive, little girl."

Lizzie smiled her own smile, the one that said, "I'm going to gut you like a fish, old man."

"You took my joy. I want it back."

The girl leaned over the desk. She was actually pretty, now that Rolvaag was no longer distracted by the mohawk. Good, he thought. Pretty, in his mind, meant vulnerable.

"You don't understand, missy. The bank doesn't have your money. We take the money people give us and put it into other people's houses. Your money's in your neighbor's house, and the Jenkins's house, and the Martini's house. You can't just come in here and take your money."

Rolvaag smiled to himself now. He'd always wanted to use that line from *It's a Wonderful Life*; had even used it on himself when he took this job. Felt proud, back then, to be serving the community. Oh well. Then he remembered to add, for this one. "If we had your ten thousand dollars in the first place. If you were the one who gave me the money. If you were the rightful owner."

"My money isn't in the homes of a bunch of hard-working little men and kindly old grannies." She swept Rolvaag's golf trophy to the floor and sat down on the desk. "It's in another condo tearing up another beach. It's in another big store being built across the street from a little store, a little store owned by a little man who spent his life helping folks around here, a little man who is now going to lose his livelihood because he can't compete with the big Chinese store you're building. No, you don't use that money to build up our home here. You use it to tear it apart and make rich men in Atlanta and New York City richer."

Lizzie paused but didn't smile anymore. "Besides, the man who give you the money is dead," she said.

Rolvaag paused a second too long before he put on a look of fake sympathy. "I'm sorry to hear that he—I mean I'm sorry to hear that anyone has passed on."

"His life didn't belong to you. I want my money back."

Rolvaag was tired of playing nice. "You don't understand the waters you've gotten yourself into here, missy. There are sharks here. Give me the rest of the money, and I'll tell the sharks to leave you alone."

"Don't insult sharks, mister," Lizzie said. "I know sharks. You're not even close."

She brushed past him and marched out the door without looking back. Rolvaag stood in the doorway and watched her go. When she pushed open the door to the bank, Rolvaag stepped into Fabbi's cubicle.

"That one you follow," he said. "She knows where the money is, maybe has it herself."

Fabbi put down his book. "I thought the cops had the money."

"I don't know who's got the money now. But she knows something. Find out where she goes and where she lives, then come back here."

Fabbi stood up.

"But don't kill her," Rolvaag said. Fabbi smirked back at him. "At least, don't kill her unless you have the money in your hands first."

Rolvaag followed Fabbi out the door. He stood in the parking lot watching as Fabbi pulled out of the west entrance to the bank, one car behind the old pickup truck.

• • •

Lizzie was singing in the pickup truck with her shotgun on the seat beside her as she rolled down 98. She was happy and proud and in charge of her life again. Even the dark storm clouds couldn't take away the joy she felt.

"Reckon I got your attention now," she sang out loud. It was a good first line. The rest would come to her as she went along.

forty-one

TERRY CHANGED LANES to get around the slow traffic on 98.

"So Progress thinks they've lost something, too," he said. He thought about running code, putting on the flasher and siren to get to Oasis in a hurry.

"And they blame us," said Blackbeard.

"No," said Terry. "They blame you. Or BeaAndra. Although it doesn't sound like they'll be back there again."

"Still," said Blackbeard. "You never know." He pulled out his phone.

"Bea?" He said after a minute. "Remember those two boys that broke into the house? Think I know who they are. I want you to come down to the station and see if you can identify them."

Bea said something Terry couldn't decipher.

"Yes, now," said Blackbeard. "Well, in a little bit. We got one more thing to do, then we'll pick them up and bring them down to the station. Want you to be there when we get there."

While he couldn't make out the words, the tone of Bea's voice that Terry could hear didn't sound good. Eventually Blackbeard said, "Yes, I know Bea. I owe you one for this."

Blackbeard hung up. "That ought to get her down to the station. Keep her safe for a little while at least," he said.

"You afraid they might come back and hurt her?"

"Afraid they might come back and she'd kill them, and we'd have to arrest a loved one."

Terry thought about that and nodded. "OK," he said. "So Carmex was bringing something from Chicago. Sunrise expected to get it, and didn't. Now we know Progress is mad because they didn't get it either."

"Hard to believe Carmex was bringing it to both of them," said Blackbeard.

"Maybe he wasn't," said Terry. "Maybe Progress tried to take it. Something went wrong; nobody got it."

"And they blame us?"

"Crooks think everybody's as crooked as they are. Especially cops. That's the way these wise guys from Chicago think."

"That's 'cause the cops up there are crooked," said Blackbeard.

Terry didn't answer.

Blackbeard realized what he had said. "Some of them," he said.

Terry pulled into the lot across from the Oasis offices. The sky was blood-red from the setting sun and the gathering storm.

Terry looked out the window. "Seem to be a lot of lies going around on this case."

Blackbeard reached across himself to open the door with his left hand. "Let's go hear some more."

They went past the waterslide and wound their way around to Chop Raines's office. They didn't bother with the receptionist this time, just walked into his office. Raines looked up, irritated, then saw the look on Terry's face.

"I believe we're done for the day," he said to a young man in a khaki suit.

"But, Mr. Raines—"

"Tomorrow."

The man gathered up some papers from Raines's desk and went out the door.

"Sherise," he called out. "You can take off, too."

The receptionist left her papers where they were and was out the door before the words finished echoing.

"Here for a progress report?" Raines smiled at Blackbeard.

"You making progress?" said Terry.

"Cute," said Raines, still looking at Blackbeard.

Terry said, "We want more background on Hole in the Beach."

"Why? You afraid it's going to block your view from Portside?" Raines smiled at Terry. "Are you surprised I know where you live? SD6, isn't it? Maybe we'll rip those damned decrepit Portside townhouses down next and put up a modern mall."

"We're not the planning board. We're the police," said Terry. "We save lives, not grubby deals."

"Well, you can stop worrying about saving the Hole in the Beach deal." Raines went to a big couch and sat down. "It was supposed to be awarded last Friday. Sunshine Development pulled out, claimed there was some kind of unnamed 'Act of God.' You know them. Everything's always a 'Blessing of the Lord' or 'God's Will' to them. They play as rough as anybody when it comes to business, but they smile and quote scripture while they do it."

"We heard there's new management coming in from Chicago," said Terry.

Raines eyes widened and he said, "Huh."

"Thought there were two bidders," said Blackbeard.

Raines shrugged. "Progress? So far, all they've come up with are excuses. At their request, we extended closing for bids until tomorrow. But I ain't heard nothing from them all day. Left them a message: I don't hear from them by the end of the day today, we're folding. Owner of Oasis wants to give the land to that camp, so kids from around the world can sit around and sing Kumbaya and make the world a warm and fuzzy place."

Raines shrugged and held up his hands to show that he thought that was a stupid waste of perfectly exploitable land. "Anyway, owner's accountant tells him he can make almost as much money that way with the tax break as he can by developing. Progress and Sunshine both threatened him, but so far he's laughing. Says he's too old to care what they threaten him with. So, if Progress doesn't come through today," he looked at his watch, taking care to show off the expensive

Rolex in the process, "and it looks like today's almost over, then the owner will get to play hero, preserving an undeveloped stretch of beach and saving the world for future generations."

"Unless Progress walks in with something like a big bag of money," said Terry.

"Unless Progress lives up to our mutually agreed upon commitment." Raines smiled. "Honor is important in our business."

Terry looked at Blackbeard and nodded, and they went back to their car. As the air conditioning in the Impala was coming on, Blackbeard looked out the window and said, "Look a here."

Another black Impala pulled up next to theirs, and the window rolled down. Detective Rodriques smiled at Blackbeard from the other car.

"Thought Chief told you to do some honest work for a change," said Blackbeard.

"Honest work is fishing. Or shrimping. No, Chief told us to tail some friend of yours out of the Progress Bank."

Blackbeard turned to look at Terry.

"This ain't Progress Bank," said Blackbeard, back to Rodriques.

Rodriques pointed. "That's his car." Blackbeard and Terry looked where he was pointing and saw a silver BMW with a hole blown out of one fender.

"Just got here. He went in just before you came out."

forty-two

LIZZIE GOT THE CALL from the Andersons up the road while she was out on the boat. She answered it on her new cell phone

"Yes?" she said.

"A white Mustang with one man in it just went by on the way to your house. Nobody we recognize. Think that could be the fellow you want us to watch for?"

"Could be. There might be more coming, too."

"You need anything from us? John'll be glad to come help you."

"No, thanks. Appreciate your watching out for me." She hung up and wrapped the blanket tighter around her shoulders and huddled back deeper into the cabin of the boat. It was way past dark now and the first edge of the storm was coming in with bursts of rain followed by brief clearings. She watched the Mustang pull up to her house and then slowly ease past. Lizzie had two fishing lines in the water and no lights turned on, fishing while she waited. From here in the mouth of the creek, she knew from experience, she could see the lit-up house but no one on land could see her darkened boat.

The Mustang came back slowly, the growling Ford engine held to idle to keep the noise down. The Mustang found a break in the pines opposite her house and carefully backed in until only the nose stuck out. Once the lights were off, even she had trouble seeing it.

One of her lines jerked. She reeled it in quiet and slow, easing the foot-long fish with the pink belly out of the water flipping and gasping. Snapper. Good eating, but not tonight.

"Thank the Mustang boy, fishie. Swim another day." She leaned over the side of the boat until she had the fish completely under water to prevent a splash before she let it go. She never took her eyes off the nose of the car. By feel, she reeled the line in, latched the hook onto the reel, and pushed the rod into the clips inside the work area of the boat. She took a chance and shot a quick glance at the cockpit. The shotgun was still clipped there, five feet from her hand, a bag of shells hanging next to it.

Lizzie pulled in the other line and secured it, sat back down on the boards, and pulled the blanket back over her before the rain started again. The boy in the Mustang was patient. He had been there a couple of minutes now, watching without moving. That was fine. Lizzie was patient, too.

She reached into the cloth bag beside her, cloth so it wouldn't rustle. Pulled out a few dark coffee beans, put them in her mouth, and chewed. It was quieter and more reliable than coffee for staying awake. Besides, the awful taste soured her face and attitude, and told her brain not to expect anything pleasant for a while. It was a trick she'd found as a teenager, when a song wouldn't finish writing itself in her head, and she would feel sorry for herself and want to stop working and go to sleep. A few bitter, grainy coffee beans were usually enough to tell her brain that there would be no rest until the job was done.

There. She saw a light flicker, then go out. Lizzie smiled. Mustang boy hadn't thought to turn off the dome light before he got out. If he could make one mistake, he would make more.

She watched him come across the lawn in silence, eyes focused on the windows of the house, looking for any sign of life. He held something in his hand that could be a gun.

The boy went to the big window in the front of the house, and crouched down below the sill. Then he eased his head up until he could see in the window. After a minute he stood up, confident that no one was in the room in front of him. He stared into the room for a long time.

Shouldn't be that hard, idjit, thought Lizzie. I left every light on in the whole blessed house. Left the doors unlocked, too, but then I always leave the doors unlocked. Maybe I should have put up a sign, nobody home, come on in. She thought of something from her one college psych class: the many defects in the criminal brain. *Got that right.*

She recognized the boy now, remembered him sitting outside Rolvaag's office reading a book. That confirmed she had guessed right: the bank guy had killed Captain Dave, had probably killed the guy in the hotel, and would come for the money. Nothing wrong with her brain.

The boy moved around the house, window to window, taking his time on each one until he came to one at the back, hidden from the road but clear to Lizzie from the water. He raised up whatever was in his hand and smashed the window.

Lizzie stood up before she realized what she was doing. *Asshole.* I leave the doors open for you, and you still have to tear up my window. She looked back to make sure the shotgun was still there. It looked like it was straining at the clips, ready to get loose.

Through the windows, she saw the boy moving room to room, looking in the obvious places first, not disturbing too much. Good enough. She could put up with that, wait him out until he went back to report the money wasn't there. Then she would report, too. She'd find Detective Blackbeard and tell him what had happened here tonight. It would be enough to point him in the direction of the bank, get both cases solved, get revenge for Captain Dave, and stop the crooks from looking for the money. She needed to tell Blackbeard, not Terry, as she wasn't sure where things stood with Terry after last night. His loss. *Men are all stupid*, she thought.

There was a crash, and a drawer from her dresser came crashing out the window, a drawer from the dresser that had been carved by her great-great-great grandmother while she sat home and waited for her husband to come home from that stupid war over the slaves they didn't even have. Lizzie could fix windows. She hoped she could fix the dresser.

She next saw the boy pull down the wardrobe with her mother's clothes, the clothes Daddy never could throw out, so she hadn't either. She looked at the pile of cotton on the floor, mostly faded and patched. Just clothes, she told herself.

She saw one dress, a church dress. Lizzie's mom had worn that dress to the last one of Lizzie's shows her mother ever saw. She remembered her mother had stood out like a sore thumb among the drunks in torn jeans and dirty T-shirts. Lizzie had been embarrassed. Embarrassed, and proud.

She felt tears coming and pushed her fists into her eyes to hold them back. It didn't do any good. She wasn't a crier, hated crying, but these were the first tears she had ever cried for her mother or her father. The tears came for a long time, and she floated in the water that was her home while water finally poured out of her like rain pouring out of the heavens.

She didn't know how long she had been crying, but when she was done she felt clear, like the sky after a Florida thunderstorm. She looked back at the house. The door to her garage studio was open and Mustang boy was coming out with a guitar in each hand. He smashed the sound box of one of them open, looked inside and found nothing. He decided to get creative and stood with his legs spread wide, holding the other guitar like he was playing it. He waved one arm in a wide circle, like Pete Townsend and the Who had forty years ago. Then he opened his mouth in a silent scream, smashed the guitar and stood there with his arms in the air like he thought he was some kind of a rock idol.

This was too much. He had destroyed her memories and guitars, and now he had insulted rock and roll. She pulled up the anchor and silently sculled the boat back to the dock.

forty-three

ROLVAAG SAT IN HIS CAR a long time, sitting in the Oasis parking garage but dreaming he was back in Atlanta. This wasn't the retirement he wanted. What was he thinking anyway when he came down here? He was a pale-skinned Swede from Minnesota whose father had moved the family to Atlanta when he was a teenager. Rolvaag had no business retiring to Florida and pretending to be a beach bum. And he sure had no business pretending to be a gangster trying to bribe a crook with money from a mob in Vegas. Even worse, the money actually came from a mob in Chicago. He couldn't even keep his mobs straight.

Where had his life gone? The bank he worked for in Atlanta had prided itself on its integrity, even gave him a gold watch with that word engraved on the back when he retired. Like most parents, he had taught his children the story about George Washington and the cherry tree and the importance of honesty (even though, like most parents, he had known the story was a lie even as he fed it to his kids.) Where had it all gone?

A black Impala pulled out of a slot a few rows over, and he wondered if it was that cop Blackbeard and his partner. He looked as they slid by him and saw, no, it was two other guys in suits. Probably flunkies for Oasis going home late to their wives and children, home to the kind of normal life Rolvaag wished he had again.

But he didn't. He pushed the car door open and stepped out onto the concrete. There was a noise and he jumped. A couple in their twenties were leaning against a concrete pillar, the girl giggling with her hair back and the guy telling her lies to impress her. Rolvaag looked at his watch and realized that it was quite late in the afternoon, late enough for the first round of happy hour partygoers to be coming back from the bars farther down Front Beach. Late enough for him to be tired and ready to get this over and done.

He walked up to Raines's office on the lobby level. The receptionist had already left, but Raines was on the couch in his office, drinking a rum and coke and watching a West Coast football game on the big TV. He looked up when Rolvaag walked in.

Raines smiled. "Already counted you out."

"No. We're in."

"Like I said. Already called the Calypso downstairs, told them I'd be down at halftime to watch the game in the bar. Decided to watch the first half here, else I'd have been gone."

"You said we had until tomorrow morning."

"If you ain't done tonight, you won't have anything by tomorrow morning."

"We will. I'll stake my career on it." *Staking a lot more than that*, he thought.

"Well," said Raines. "Tell you what. Why don't I call Calypso back, get them to send some food up here. We can sit and watch the game, go over your proposal one more time."

Rolvaag looked at his watch. Fabbi was already out at the girl's house by himself. He didn't trust Fabbi by himself anymore. But, you never turn down the chance to sell the customer.

"Sure," he said.

Raines got up and went to the bar. "Beer?" he said. "Rum and coke?"

"Beer. Tuborg, if you've got it." He thought about it and decided he needed more. "No, make that a rum and coke." Rolvaag thought again about how much he wished he were back in Atlanta. "Actually, just rum."

• • •

The game had turned into a runaway, the food was finished, and they were going over the financing one final time. Rolvaag looked at the copy of the Progress proposal on the coffee table in front of him, the page splattered with blackened seasonings and coleslaw. He looked at his plate next to the proposal and wondered how he had managed to get any food on the proposal. The blackened snapper was good, very good, but one bite was all he could eat. After that, he'd just shoved food around on his plate every time Raines took a bite, trying to stay in sync with his customer. But Rolvaag's stomach felt full, and even that one bite of snapper felt like it wanted to swim upstream. He picked up his glass and sent more rum down to drown it.

"So we will set you up a line of credit here during construction," he said to Raines, pointing at the line on the page.

"And to reduce the load on the bank," said Raines, "you hire me as a consultant to oversee the line of credit."

"Sure," Rolvaag said. "It'll be done for our convenience, strictly a legal and aboveboard business expense."

"Strictly business as usual. And I get paid a percentage of the amount used from the line of credit." Raines was talking with his mouth full. He didn't seem to be having any trouble eating his gumbo.

"Yes, sir," said Rolvaag. He wasn't real sure what he was saying yes to anymore. He was past the point where he had turned control over to the rum and had to trust that the rum knew what it was talking about.

"Sweet," said Raines. He stood up and took his glass and Rolvaag's back to the bar. "We've killed the rum, son. Mind if we switch to Jack?" He looked at Rolvaag and saw Rolvaag was smiling vacantly.

Rolvaag felt he needed to say something, so he said, "Yes, sir," again, not sure what question he was answering.

Raines filled both their glasses and brought them back.

"Look, the owner's starting to fall in love with this idea of donating the land to that center for kids."

"Aw," said Rolvaag. "We're going to help the little children."

"Not if I can help it. The owner may make money either way, but I only make money if we put up a condo."

Rolvaag said, "Yes, sir," again.

"But I can't hold him off any longer. You sure you're going to get the money now, bring it to me first thing in the morning?"

"Yes, sir."

Raines stood up and Rolvaag realized he should stand up, too. Raines clinked his glass against Rolvaag's and said, "To the morning."

"Yes, sir," said Rolvaag. It felt better to talk like a businessman again and not a thug. But then Raines grabbed his sleeve. Raines was still smiling his good old boy smile, but there was a look of desperation in his eyes.

"One more thing I got to have," he said. "Protection. Sunshine has boys coming in from Chicago, boys who want this deal no matter what. They can bring a lot of pain. I know Progress has some connections like that, too. You got somebody to cover me?"

"Yeah," said Rolvaag. "Got a guy from Vegas." He almost said, probably got a lot more guys coming from Vegas, too. But he wasn't drunk enough to say that, even to himself.

Raines nodded and Rolvaag suddenly realized that Raines was a lot more sober than he was.

"Now go get me my money," Raines said.

• • •

Terry nudged Blackbeard awake. It was late, and they had started taking shifts—one sleeping and the other watching for Rolvaag. Blackbeard opened his eyes and they watched Rolvaag make a more-or-less straight walk from the stairs to his BMW. He dropped his keys twice, laughed about it, but finally got in, started the car and pulled out of his slot.

"Jesus," said Terry, watching Rolvaag slowly weave around the lot. "Hope he gets out of here in one piece. No help to us at all if we have to spend the night writing him up for a DUI or an accident."

Rolvaag finally found the exit. Terry started the Impala, and they pulled out onto Front Beach, Rolvaag weaving at a cautious twenty miles an hour and Blackbeard and Terry following.

forty-four

LIZZIE WAS QUIET as she unclipped the shotgun and held it under her poncho. She looped the cloth bag of shells over her shoulder and slipped onto the deck.

The boy was back inside the garage now, so Lizzie moved fast to the oleander bush in the middle of the yard while he was out of sight. She crouched and waited for him. He came back out with a bass guitar and a Fender Strat and Lizzie had to stop herself from yelling at him. He stopped under the overhang over the garage door, too wimpy to even get wet while he did his dirty work.

He had his back to her, holding the Strat and going, "bo-ing, boing, boing." *Jesus Christ, the boy can't even play a decent air guitar.* She took a deep breath and ran on tiptoe until she was behind him. She shoved the shotgun into the small of his back.

"Know this tune, rock star?" she said.

He froze in mid "boing." *Thank God. At least I've found the mute button.*

"You know what that is you're holding in your hands?" she said.

"Guitar?"

"Guitar? That is a Fender Stratocaster. You know who played a Stratocaster?"

"You?"

"Jimi Hendrix."

"You mean the old guy?" said the boy. "One who played 'All Along the Witchtower?'"

Lizzie felt her finger tighten on the trigger and she almost blew a hole in the boy then and there.

But, she eased up. A shotgun blast would go through the boy and kill her guitar. "OK," she said, "We're going to step back into the studio real slow, put these guitars back where they belong."

She reached into the belt in the middle of the boy's back and pulled out his handgun.

"A .22?" she said. "Ain't good for killing nothing more than ten feet away." She thought a minute. "This what you killed that man in the Hilton with?"

The boy shrugged. He didn't want to either argue or deny. He didn't seem afraid of Lizzie either. That meant his brain was working on a way to get loose. She reached over with her left hand and found a bungee cord. It would have to do until she got to the boat. She hooked one end to his leather belt and pulled his left hand back and wrapped the cord around it. She moved the shotgun up to the base of his neck to give her left hand more room to work. She reached across, looped the cord around his right arm and pulled the arm back to his left hand. Wrapped the cord around both hands until it was tight. She hooked the other end onto his belt and gave it a twang like he was a big guitar.

"Now, walk down to the dock," she said.

"That where the money is?" The boy said. He was getting more confident. Lizzie knew she'd have to do something about that. She kept him moving until they got to the boat.

"Only money here is seven hundred and forty-six dollars in Grandpa's old cigar box in the kitchen. You ain't stole that from me, have you?"

"You know what I mean," he said.

Lizzie leaned forward and put her mouth right against his ear.

"I do," she whispered. "Now get." She marched him onto the dock, put her foot against his backside and shoved him over the side and into the boat. Lightning flashed and showed him lying still in a puddle. She watched him and knew that if he wasn't squirming and fighting, he was thinking of a way to get away.

"Stand up," she said. He struggled to get to his feet and stood facing her with the rain running down into his eyes. She looked in the hate in those eyes and saw that he was thinking of more than getting away. *Good*, she thought. *Get mad, get stupid.*

She prodded him back to the transom.

"Sit down there on the back of the boat. Good. Now turn around until your toes are dangling in the water, like you was a little kid having fun on your daddy's boat."

Once he was facing backward, she pulled a coil of rope up from the deck and tied one end to a cleat opposite the boy. She tied the other end to one of his hands, moved his hands to the front and tied them both together.

"Let you keep your hands in the front, so you can hold on to that cleat there, make sure you don't fall overboard," she said. "Not accidental, no how."

She stepped back and untied the line holding the boat to the dock, cranked the engine and pulled away. As they cleared the mouth of the creek into West Bay, she called back.

"Comfortable back there?"

"Money on the boat?" he said.

"Nope." She goosed the throttle, which made the boy grab the cleat to stay aboard.

Lizzie motored into the bay, away from lights and the channel that led to the Inland Waterway, and cut the power so the boat idled along on its own. She went back and stood behind and to the side of the boy.

"OK, let's talk. We'll try it friendly-like at first, just you and me conversing and me telling you what's true and you telling me what's true. Tell it all, I'll give you to the police in one piece."

The boy snorted.

"All right, I'll go first. I took the money from the Hilton. Now this is the part where you say you killed the man at the Hilton."

"Never been to the Hilton," the boy said, staring out at the water.

"Wrong answer." Lizzie put her boot into the small of the boy's back and shoved him into the black water. When he was halfway back aboard, she goosed the throttle until he lost his grip and fell behind. When the rope tightened she slammed the throttle forward and looked at her watch. She looked back at the big rooster tail of water flying up from the boy being towed at the end of the rope. Then she looked back at her watch and pulled the throttle back to idle, picked up a boathook and went back to the transom.

The rope was heavy but Lizzie kept pulling until the boy was back at the boat.

"Want to talk, or play in the water some more?"

"Give me my money, and we'll talk."

"Your money? Well, we've got a problem there. I don't have the money anymore. I made what you might call a charitable contribution."

The boy was holding on and getting his breath back. "Then we got nothing to talk about."

"Suit yourself," she said. "That was one minute. This time, we're going for two minutes."

She pointed at a sea of brown grass waving in the storm. "See that? That what they call 'sawgrass.' Try to walk through it, it'll cut you to shreds. Course, once you get to bleeding like that, then the alligators come for you."

She pushed him away with the hook.

"Two minutes," she said as he tried to splash back.

The rooster tail behind the boat glowed like a waterspout in the storm. After a minute or so, she dragged the boy into the edge of the sawgrass and heard him scream. She pulled him back in again, and he said something uncomplimentary about her parents.

"Oh, what a mouth on you. I don't believe I'll ever write a song with those kind of lyrics. Look." She smiled down at him. "I'm a nice person. What's your name?"

"Fabbi."

"Fabbi? What kind of name is that? Well, Mister Fabbi, I'm gonna let you rest here a minute and catch your breath."

She stood up and looked toward the bridge in the distance.

"Oh, is that a gator over yonder?" she said.

"That won't scare me. Gators are mostly harmless, and they don't like to come out in open water like this," he said.

"That's a fact," said Lizzie. "That's what they told my brother, right after he lost an arm to a gator, swimming out here in the bay. They said, 'gators don't hang out in the bay, mostly.' Mostly. Now I'm not so sure about that 'harmless' part. I think that's just what the chamber of commerce likes to say to keep from scaring folks away. I don't know a family around here that hasn't lost somebody."

She pointed, "Oh look, that is a gator. You can see his eyes glowing. So you're all right. Long as you can see his eyes, it means his mouth is closed. My brother says he still wakes up dreaming of that moment when the gator opened his mouth and his eyes disappeared behind his snout and my brother knew he was in trouble."

She picked up the hook and pushed him away.

"Three minutes," she said as she pushed the throttle.

The boy was starting to look worn when she pulled him in. He was gasping for air and fidgeting at the waterline of the boat.

"All right," he said. "What do you want to talk about?"

"Start with the Hilton."

"I killed Keeper. Was supposed to take the money, but I forgot."

"You forgot two million dollars? Remembered to kill a man, but forgot to take the money?"

"In fairness, my boss wasn't very clear."

"Your boss that Rolvaag fellow?"

"Yeah. Well, he thinks he's my boss. Not much longer."

"All right, but that ain't the murder I'm mad about. What happened with Captain Dave?"

"Not my fault. I just wanted him to talk—like we're talking." The boy paused and grunted, and Lizzie could see he was doing something under the boat.

"What's going on down there?"

The boy was quiet for a moment but kept doing whatever it was he was doing. "Cramps," he finally said. "My hand's cramping from all this. Trying to work it out."

"Well, finish talking to me and you can get out of the water and into a nice dry cell. How the hell was Captain Dave not your fault?"

"Old goat died on me. I was just trying to persuade him."

"Same kind of persuasion you're going to try on me," said Lizzie, "if I give you the chance."

The boy pushed away from the boat. "You don't have to give me anything," he said. "I take what I want." He ducked under the water.

Lizzie started pulling the line to get him back to finish their conversation, but the line stayed limp and finally the frayed end of the line came out of the water.

"Son of a bitch," said Lizzie. She looked at the line and realized that between the sawgrass and the barnacles on the boat, the rope had been sawed apart.

"You can't trust some folks," she said as she saw his head pop up a hundred yards away.

She pulled up the shotgun and sighted, then put it down. *Let him go. Got what I want.* Mister Blackbeard can pick him up when he comes out of the water. I got a house to clean up.

• • •

Marie the Canadian came out on the deck and found Paul sitting, wrapped in a blanket watching the bay through his binoculars.

"Can't sleep, honey?" She put her hands on his neck and massaged it slowly.

"No, I just like it out here," he said. "Something about a storm on the water. The air tastes good. The sky and the water put on a beautiful show. It's the same thing for me every fall when we come down here: for the first week or so, I can't get enough of this place. Afraid I'm going to miss something. Want to eat twelve meals a day just so I can get to all the good restaurants. Want to stop and talk to everybody to hear the stories."

Marie said, "Maybe in a few years we can come down here full-time, when Marianne gets out of college."

"Maybe."

Marie sat down in the big Adirondack chair next to him and picked up her knitting.

"Anything happening tonight?"

"Not much. Lizzie's teaching some boy to water ski. He's not very good."

forty-five

ROLVAAG'S CAR ROLLED through the stop sign at Front Beach and 79. Blackbeard and Terry followed.

"Think we ought to give him a ticket?" said Terry. "My guess is he's so drunk we could probably hold him in jail longer on the DUI than we can if we get him for murder."

Blackbeard smiled. They passed the gas stations and Waffle House on 98 and trailed Rolvaag north to the bay.

"Not much down this road," said Terry.

"My house," said Blackbeard. "Airport." He paused and waited for Terry to add something. When he didn't, Blackbeard said, "Your Miss Lizzie's house."

"Yeah." Terry wondered if Blackbeard was suggesting Lizzie was working with Rolvaag or threatened by Rolvaag.

They passed a side street into the woods and Rolvaag kept going.

"Missed your house," said Terry. "Probably a good thing for us. BeaAndra might have hit us while she was shooting at him."

Blackbeard grunted and said, "Bea hits what she aims for."

"Like I said, she might have hit us."

Terry looked out at the pine forest on either side of the road and said, "There's a whole lot of nothing up this road."

Blackbeard gave him a look.

"Whole lot of nothing from a banker's viewpoint," Terry corrected himself. "Home of watermen, salt marsh . . ."

"God's country," said Blackbeard.

"Yeah," said Terry. "But the point is, he's got to be going to Lizzie's. Only thing out here, for him. What if he thinks she's got the money?"

Blackbeard nodded. "The missing piece. Sunshine and Progress are both mad because someone has their money. Lizzie was around the hotel at the time. Makes as much sense as thinking we've got the money—if there is any money."

Terry was looking straight ahead at Rolvaag in the rain and his jaw was getting tight.

"And what if Lizzie has got the money? What if she's in on this?" Terry said.

"You don't know that."

"But she might be."

"No. You don't know that. Listen to me, partner. Whatever you think Lizzie might have done, do you think she might have killed those two men?"

Rolvaag slid sideways in the rain and Terry backed off to give him more room. He could see that Rolvaag didn't have his wipers on, was driving blind in the storm.

"No," Terry said when Rolvaag got control again.

"Then you don't know if Lizzie has the money. You bring that girl into this and she'll never get out. So don't even think that way."

"Yeah," said Terry. "If Rolvaag's heading her way, Lizzie may have somebody who's already killed two people coming for her. May not get out of that unless we get there in time."

Rolvaag took up most of the road, riding the center line and barely moving over for cars in the other lane. They came to the turn to Lizzie's house. Rolvaag slowed and Terry tensed.

Just before the turn, Rolvaag swung wide into the oncoming lane before making the right turn onto Lizzie's road. A Toyota coming the other way bailed out of the road and into the ditch.

"Jesus," said Terry. Rolvaag disappeared down the road to Lizzie's, probably didn't even know what he had caused. Terry turned his head and watched the Toyota drop down into the ditch and try to climb up the other side before rolling back down into the ditch upside down. Blackbeard flicked on the flasher and reached for the radio mic.

"Dispatch, we have a traffic accident with possible injuries on Highway 79 approximately four miles north of Highway 98. Request Bay County deputies and EMTs respond."

There was a squeal of static and then a female voice. "Acknowledge. Injuries?"

"Unknown."

Terry cursed under his breath as he whipped the Impala around and pulled off the road beside the Toyota. Before the Impala had stopped, Terry was out and running for the Toyota.

A Hispanic child stood next to the car. He was maybe six years old, not crying or screaming, just dazed. Terry grabbed the child's shoulders.

"Are you all right?" Terry asked. The child didn't respond. Terry tried Spanish. "*Esta bien?*"

The child nodded. Terry pointed to the Impala. "*Ir alli.*"

The child climbed up the muddy ditch. Blackbeard held the back door open, and the child crawled in and curled up on the seat.

"Anyone hurt in here?" Terry called into the Toyota.

A woman in the back seat said something in Spanish, and Terry had to sort out the words. My husband, he realized. The woman handed out another child to Terry and crawled out herself. Terry pointed to the Impala and she climbed up the ditch and into the Impala with her children.

Terry stuck his head in the upside down front window. A young Hispanic man hung upside down, trying to get the seat belt loose with one hand. His other hand was steadying a jagged piece of wood that was stuck in his shoulder. Blood was pouring out.

"No," said Terry, stopping the man from unclipping the seat belt.

"Rest. Let me do that." Terry put pressure around the stake to stop it from bleeding, and to keep it from coming out before the EMTs got there. He tried to translate his words to Spanish, but the man said, "I speak English."

Blackbeard came up, stuck his head in the back window and looked around. "Nobody else," he said.

"Tell me where it hurts," Terry said to the driver.

"Shoulder. Maybe chest also, but I think that is just the seat belt."

Blackbeard pulled out his cell phone and called in the updated information. Terry heard a siren coming from the West Bay fire station. It was five minutes before the first car, a Bay County deputy, arrived.

"Blackie," said the deputy as he got out of the car smiling at Blackbeard. "What brings the famous detective out to the county?"

Blackbeard reached out with his good arm and drug the deputy to the Toyota. Pulled him down and pressed the deputy's hand on the driver's chest, freeing Terry.

"We're taking your car," Blackbeard said to the deputy. "Look after the family in mine."

The deputy started to yell something but he saw the look on Terry's bloodstained face and closed his mouth.

LIZZIE BROUGHT THE EMPTY BOAT to the dock just in time to see the silver BMW slide to a stop in the mud in front of her house. She thought about waiting to see what would happen next, but decided she was tired of waiting.

She yanked the shotgun out of its clip and headed up the hill to the house in the pouring rain, too angry for stealth. As she got closer to the car, she saw a figure slumped over the steering wheel. She grabbed the door and yanked it open. The driver straightened up and smiled at her.

"You!" she said. "What the hell's wrong with you?"

"Business," Rolvaag said, though it came out more like "bizdiz."

"Humph," said Lizzie. She had the shotgun an inch from his midsection but he didn't seem to care.

He stuck out his hands through the door opening with the palms up and she stepped back to give him room.

"Put it there," he said.

"Excuse me?"

"My money," he said, smiling like a banker about to close a deal and go to lunch with the rotary club.

"Your money?"

"Fabbi came to get it from you."

Lizzie thought a minute and then she smiled, too. "So you want the payoff Fabbi got?"

"Oh yeah."

She stepped back and gestured with the shotgun. "Come on out, Mr. Shark, and we'll get you your payoff."

Rolvaag pulled himself out and stood there in the mud.

"It's raining," he said.

"It's just water," said Lizzie. "Wash away the shit storm you started."

She nudged him with the shotgun and he stumbled down to the dock with Lizzie cursing and shoving behind him.

"Get in," said Lizzie, pointing at the boat.

"I don't think that's a good idea. My stomach's a little touchy."

"Yeah, well, I'm the only one here whose brain is working well enough to have ideas right now. So get in."

It took a little doing, but Rolvaag climbed aboard and sat down on the deck. Lizzie got in and opened one of the side lockers and pulled out a long, steel fishing leader. Wrapping it around Rolvaag's hands and snapping it on the rope at the stern of the boat, she said, "I'm not going to let you get away like I did your friend Fabbi."

Rolvaag looked at his hands and looked at her. "He's no friend of mine. He kills people, you know. He was supposed to come here to learn how to be a banker. Instead, he decided he wanted to be a thug."

Lizzie untied the line to the dock and pushed the boat away.

"There's a difference?" she said.

"Of course," Rolvaag sat up straighter and tried to look offended. "Bankers belong to the chamber of commerce."

"Clears that up." Lizzie put the boat in gear and headed back to the bay.

Lizzie fell into enjoying the storm on the water and didn't notice what was happening in the back.

"Jesus, Mary, and the saints," she said when she turned around.

Rolvaag looked up with a little-boy smile. "I got sick a little."

"A little?" she sighed. No point in being mad at a child. Right now, Rolvaag was a child. She opened a locker and pulled out an old cotton mop and a five-gallon bucket.

"Clean up your own mess. Dump it over and the rain will take care of the rest."

After a few minutes he smiled up at her from a sort-of clean deck. "See?" he said.

Lizzie started the engine again. "I can't put you out here where you've just dumped all that filth."

Rolvaag's eyes opened up. "You can't put me out anywhere. This is water. I can't swim."

Lizzie glared at him as the boat idled along the edge of the channel. "Why the hell would someone who can't swim live at the beach?"

"I don't know. I want to go back to Atlanta."

"OK, but first, tell me about the money and about Captain Dave."

"No."

Lizzie smiled her biggest smile for him. "Back at the bank, you told me you were a shark." She put her foot in his stomach and shoved Rolvaag into the water. "My crab babies love shark meat."

He hit with a big splash and thrashed furiously until he got a grip on the back of the boat.

"It's cold," he said.

"Not much better up here. Tell me what I want to know, and I'll let you sit down in the cabin and dry off."

Rolvaag said, "I got to know. Did you steal my money?"

Lizzie was outraged. "I've never stolen anything in my life," she said. She took the boat hook and pushed him away from the boat. Then she popped him on the head with the hook for emphasis. "I took out the trash. That's all I did. Like now."

She went back to the cabin and eased the throttle forward. Over the growl of the engine and the drumbeat of the rain, she heard him crying. She idled the throttle, looked back at him and sighed.

"If I tell you what you want to know," Rolvaag said, "will you let me back into the boat?"

TERRY SAW THE PIECES OF GUITAR in Lizzie's yard and knew she was in trouble. He was out and running for the house before Blackbeard could maneuver his arm out of the patrol car. Blackbeard caught up to him at the front door.

"Terr, be careful," he said. "This is a crime scene."

"No. This is a crime in progress." Terry pointed at the guitars, broken and lying out in the rain. "No way Lizzie would put up with this. No way. Not unless she can't stop it."

He pulled his gun and pointed it up at the dark sky, listening for anything. Blackbeard listened too.

"Don't get any blood on anything," Blackbeard said. "I don't want to have to explain why blood from a traffic accident showed up at a crime scene."

"Careful, my ass."

Terry picked his way through the garage and into the house. He went to the left, through the added-on rooms of the old house, and motioned Blackbeard through the kitchen and living areas to the right.

This was my fault, he thought. *Lizzie tried to warn me something was going on, told me she needed me, and I should have been here. I wasn't.*

Before long he heard Blackbeard say, "Clear" from the front of the house. He reached the back of the house without finding anyone and said, "Clear" himself. He met Blackbeard back at the door to the garage, but kept his gun out and pointed at the ceiling.

"No one here," Terry said, and added to himself, "including Lizzie."

"Huh," said Blackbeard. He jerked his chin at the guitars on the walls. "Why you reckon they broke those guitars and left these?"

"Got interrupted?" said Terry. "Found what they were looking for?"

"Maybe."

They walked out onto the old driveway and stood under the overhang in front of her studio. Terry saw something in the brush and motioned toward it. Blackbeard saw it, too, and moved off to Terry's right to cover Terry while he checked it out.

Terry moved in a crouch, but he moved fast. He got to Fabbi's Mustang and rose up to look inside, then bent down to look under the car.

"Clear," he called back to Blackbeard. He was starting to come down from his initial adrenaline rush but he was still on edge, struggling to stay cool.

Blackbeard walked over.

"Thought I saw a car that looked like this parked at the bank today."

"Could have been that young guy that tried to stare us down," said Terry.

"Could have been a little old lady using the ATM," said Blackbeard.

"You figure this Mustang came here looking for an ATM?"

"No."

Terry looked around the corner of the brush where the driveway curved down to the dock.

"Maybe not an ATM, but a banker." He pointed at the silver BMW parked sideways in the drive.

Blackbeard motioned to the dock.

"Boat's gone," said Terry.

"Let's check out the boathouse."

The door to the boathouse was locked, so they went around to the one window. Blackbeard took out his Maglite and shined it in and around the inside.

"Nothing appears to be disturbed in there. Either they didn't need to get in there, or they got interrupted first. You know enough to know if anything's missing?"

"No," said Terry. "Never been inside." He thought about something. "Wonder if Lizzie had a gun?"

Blackbeard laughed. It was a nervous laugh, but still a laugh. "How long you lived on the panhandle? Course she's got a gun. You didn't see a gun safe or closet when you was out here?"

"No."

"Think I know." Blackbeard led the way back to the house, into the main bedroom.

"All these old Florida houses are different, but they usually have a few things the same. Keep the guns in the bedroom locked up to keep the kids out of them. Make it easy to get to them fast, too, if you had to." The room had two closets. He opened one, which had a pile of clothes all over the floor.

"Someone made a mess searching this one," Blackbeard said.

"Uh, no. That's just Lizzie," said Terry.

Blackbeard went to the other. "Bingo," he said.

In the other closet was a glass cabinet. The door was open and there was an empty set of pegs at the top.

"Took the shotgun, left the deer rifle and the handgun," Blackbeard said.

"That's a good sign," said Terry. "Shotgun seems like Lizzie's style. Someone stealing things would have taken them all."

"Yeah," said Blackbeard, "maybe."

They walked back to the yard.

"Two cars and a truck come in but nobody here. Boat's gone," said Blackbeard.

"We need to get out on the water," said Terry.

Blackbeard holstered his gun and pulled out his phone. "I'll call the Bay County sheriff and the water patrol guys."

Terry jogged for the Bay County car. "Call for backup while we're on the road. I know a faster way."

forty-eight

MARIE PUT DOWN HER KNITTING and turned to Paul.

"I'm going back to bed and leave you to your spying."

"Not spying," said Paul. "Just enjoying the view."

"Anything happening now?"

"Not much. The fellow Lizzie was teaching to water ski seems to have given up and decided to go for a swim instead." Paul put down the binoculars and looked at Marie. "You don't suppose they had a fight or something do you?"

She shrugged. Even in the dark, after all these years, he could feel the gesture without seeing it.

"I don't know," she said. "You know young people these days."

"No," he said. "I don't."

He picked up the binoculars.

"Boy seems to be swimming for the creek," he said. "Hope he doesn't scare Speed Bump."

"Nothing scares Speed Bump, Paul. He's an alligator, even if you do think he's your pet."

"We're friends."

"He's an alligator. I wish you would stop feeding him. He's going to lose all fear of people. He already recognizes you when you go down there, opens his mouth soon as he sees you and waits for you to throw food in."

"Yeah, he's one smart gator."

"He's going to be one smart gator with your arm up his gullet if you aren't careful."

"Naw, he wouldn't hurt a fly." Paul put his binoculars down on the little table between them and stood up.

"Coming?" Marie said.

"Yeah. Figure there's not much more to see out here." He paused and said, "Might be more to see in the bedroom."

Marie gave him a smile he could see in the darkness. "Might be," she said.

• • •

Fabbi was closing on the shore in long easy strokes. He was into the rhythm of the swim and thinking about what he was going to do to the bitch when he got back to her. Get some payback for her dragging him behind her boat before he got away. He got to the mouth of the creek and stopped, treading water while he looked for a good place to come out.

Up on the hill, the lights blinked out on a house that sat by itself. He saw a small beach down from the house and decided to come in there, go up to the house and steal a car—and maybe some dry clothes. Do what he had to do to make sure there were no witnesses.

A log floated in the creek between him and the beach. Fabbi started to move around the log, doing the breaststroke now so he could keep his head up and watch. The log shifted and he stopped, treading water for a better look. The log had two red eyes on the end closest to him, and Fabbi suddenly realized it wasn't just a log.

Fabbi thought about what Lizzie had told him about alligators and blood. He imagined a long plume of blood reaching through the water from his cuts to the gator's nose, calling. He remembered the one alligator wrestling show he had seen when he first came down here, the wrangler using a mannequin and a trained gator to show how the gator would thrash his victim back and forth until it was dead. The trainer said the gator would dive down into the water and shove the dead body into some tree roots for safe keeping until the gator was ready to come back and feed days later. It had seemed like cheap hokum at the time and he had laughed at the tourist kids who acted scared. He wasn't laughing now.

He rose up as far as he could, so he could see better. In the darkness, the giant mouth opened and Fabbi watched the glowing red eyes disappear. He panicked and splashed wildly to the other shore. It was overgrown and swampy, but at least it was away from the gator. He smiled as he reached a small mangrove and grabbed at it. Then he pulled his head up into the thicket, safely away from the gator.

The two water moccasins who were curled up in the mangrove branches were just getting friendly with each other when the monster stuck its head right up into their nest. So of course they defended their home. They struck the head and neck of the monster over and over until they had filled his head with venom.

Poison flooded Fabbi's brain before he could react. Fabbi disappeared below the water without a sound, and Speed Bump swam away.

TERRY SLID THE CRUISER TO A STOP in the oyster shell parking lot of the restaurant under the Intracoastal Waterway Bridge, jumped out, and ran to a tin-roofed cabin on the edge of the lot.

"Jason," he yelled as he banged on the door. He kept banging until the door opened and Jason stuck his head out.

"Terry, what the hell's the matter with—"

Terry grabbed him by the arm.

"I've got to have your airboat. Now. Give me the keys."

Jason looked at Terry. "All right, I can see you're in trouble." He stepped back out of the door and picked up a ripped pair of fishing shorts from the floor.

Terry turned his head away from the sight of Jason's bare butt. "Jesus, Jason, I don't need you dressed for church, I just need the keys."

Jason pulled on a pair of old running shoes and grabbed the keys from a hook by the door.

"You ain't driving when you're wound up like this. I'll take you where you need to go."

"We ain't got time to argue."

Jason set off at a dogtrot toward the little shack beside the restaurant. An airboat with three rows of bench seats and swamp thang painted on the side was tied up at the dock next to the shack. Jason jumped aboard and pointed to the lines. Terry untied the bow line and threw it in the boat, and Blackbeard, who had followed them, did the same with the stern.

The big propeller at the back of the boat was spinning when they jumped aboard. As the engine caught with a roar, Terry yelled to Jason.

"Can't let you stay, Jason. Police business. You might get hurt."

"You'll kill yourself on this thing, Terry. You got a license, but you don't know how to drive this thing in a storm. Wind will turn this thing every way but loose."

"Don't care. Police business."

Jason looked at Blackbeard hoping for a reprieve, but Blackbeard nodded support for Terry. Jason climbed off.

Terry cranked the throttle. The boat jumped from the dock in a cloud of spray and Blackbeard fell to the deck.

"Easy," yelled Jason. He yelled some more, but they were out of earshot by then.

Blackbeard picked himself up and braced himself on a seat.

"You told me you knew how to drive this thing," he said.

"I do," said Terry. But the boat got away from him and went skittering sideways for a second before he got it back under control. "Just not very well. Especially when I can't see. Especially in a storm."

"Might have mentioned that," said Blackbeard.

"Look in that locker," said Terry. He tried to point and almost lost the boat again. "The one on your right."

"Starboard," said Blackbeard.

"Yeah, that one. Jason keeps an old pair of binoculars in there so tourists can look through them. It makes the gators seem bigger."

Blackbeard took the glasses out and started scanning the horizon.

"Going to be hard to find them until the light comes up," he said.

"That might be too late."

Terry turned the boat and they skittered sideways out into the bay on a line toward Lizzie's house.

A sudden flash of lightening lit up the entire bay like a high contrast photograph. Blackbeard pointed.

"Head that way," he said. "Thought I saw something."

Terry turned the boat. The wind caught it and turned it back and he had to do a three sixty to get back on course.

"There," said Blackbeard.

"I don't see anything."

"Phosphorescence," said Blackbeard, pointing. "Glowing trail left by boats in the water when they stir up little water creatures. Follow that path. Quiet down that dadgum noise back there, too, so we can hear something."

Terry dialed the motor back, but it wasn't much quieter. They followed the path until Blackbeard picked up Lizzie's boat.

"They're running without lights," said Blackbeard. "I see two people, one with hair sticking up, standing in the boat. The other's just climbing aboard over the transom."

"There were two cars back at Lizzie's. Where's the other guy?"

"Don't see him. Look, idle that thing down; get it as quiet as you can. We don't need to get any closer to them than we have to be right now." Blackbeard kept scanning.

"All right," Terry said.

"Quiet as you can, bring this thing in a big circle that a way. We'll try to come in from downwind, keep our noise down as much as we can. It's starting to get a little lighter now, might be able to see what we're into before we approach."

Terry eased the stick over and gave the motor a little gas until they were moving off to the side of Lizzie.

"OK, hold up here, partner," said Blackbeard. Terry idled the motor and gave it just enough gas to hold it steady against the wind.

"Still can't tell much," said Blackbeard. "Don't want to risk too much noise." He looked back. Terry was peeling off his orange life jacket.

fifty

ROLVAAG CLIMBED OUT OF THE WATER, and the girl grabbed his arm and snatched him aboard like he was an empty crab trap.

"Oh, thank you, thank you," he said as she handed him an old blanket.

"You really are pathetic, you know it?" she said.

He didn't care. He was cold and the blanket was warm and he wasn't going back into that water again.

"What do you want to know?" he said.

"Captain Dave."

"That was Fabbi. I told him to find out where the old guy had the money, not to kill him. Fabbi's turned into a freak. All he knows how to do is kill people and read French."

"He knows how to swim," said Lizzie, scanning the water for signs of Fabbi. The sky was starting to pink and the clouds were starting to break.

Rolvaag said, "Alive?"

"Last I saw. Look, you keep talking or I'll put you back in the water and you can ask him yourself."

"I can't believe you got the drop on him. He's tricky."

"Not any more. He was sober; made him a little harder to catch than you. But not much. If my crabs were as easy to catch as you two I could quit my jobs and just sell crabmeat."

"Yeah, well," Rolvaag said. Time was starting to sober him up. Time, helped maybe by emptying his stomach and being dunked in cold water. He also realized that Lizzie wasn't taking the drunk old man seriously. The shotgun was just resting loosely in her lap, not even pointing at him anymore.

"Yeah, well, yourself," she said. "Tell me about the money and the Hilton, or go swimming again."

"Screw-up number one," said Rolvaag, assessing Lizzie for an opportunity. "Fabbi was supposed to kill the guy and take the money so we could use it to get the deal to develop the Oasis beach property. But he forgot. Or didn't understand. Like I said, Fabbi's only good for two things, and helping me isn't one of them."

"Let me get this straight," said Lizzie. "You knew that guy was coming in with money?"

"Yeah. The Sunshine boys are bad about talking. They think God will protect them no matter what; think anything they do can't be wrong because they go to church."

"So all this," said Lizzie, "was just so a group of rich assholes could turn another stretch of beach into concrete and steel?"

"And jobs and money. Everybody wants jobs and money."

Lizzie looked out at the water. "I've got a job at the Hilton that I hate. I had a bag of money that drove me crazy until I got rid of it. I'll take the water and the sand and the sun and the music and the things that belong to me."

Rolvaag saw her look at the water and smile. Smiling, but looking at the water away from him. He gathered his legs under him.

The storm was dying down and they both heard the motor from the airboat a hundred yards away. Lizzie stood up and looked for the boat, and Rolvaag lunged for her and grabbed the shotgun. Instinctively, Lizzie put a foot in his stomach and pushed back but he turned the gun and hit her in the face with it. The gun came free and Lizzie fell against the cabin.

"Don't move," he said. "We're going to pick up the money at your house. I can still make a payment and get out of this."

"I'm not going to tell you where the money is, because you won't believe me."

"Up to you. I can find the money by myself. Find the money, and tell the police that Fabbi killed you. Your choice."

"I can't tell you where the money is because the money is gone."

He raised the shotgun and sighted down the barrel at Lizzie. "Then so are you."

fifty-one

AS ROLVAAG CLIMBED OUT OF THE WATER, Terry pulled his pants off and was down to his shorts.

"What are you doing?" Blackbeard was talking to Terry but his eyes were still on Lizzie's boat.

"Swim for it. If I can get on board without them hearing me, I might be able to help Lizzie."

"Don't look like she needs your help none." Blackbeard pointed at Lizzie's boat. Rolvaag had just climbed out of the water. Lizzie was standing over him with a shotgun in her hands and they were talking.

"Yeah," Terry smiled. "Looks like she doesn't need me."

Terry climbed back in the pilot's seat and sat there in his underwear as the airboat closed in. They both watched the body language in Lizzie's boat. Rolvaag was waving his hands. Occasionally, Lizzie would dip the shotgun, telling him to keep talking.

When the lull came in the storm, both Lizzie and Rolvaag heard them, and looked over. Blackbeard and Terry both saw Rolvaag take the gun and point it back at Lizzie.

"Christ," said Blackbeard.

Terry slammed the throttle and the airboat leaped forward, gathered speed, and flew across the tops of the waves with a roar. Terry stood almost naked and still bloody. He saw the shotgun come up on the guy's shoulder, saw him sight down the barrel and knew what was coming next.

He jerked the stick and the airboat spun with a roar, sliding into Lizzie's boat propeller-first. At the last minute, Rolvaag looked up at the propeller bearing down at him and screamed as the wash from the airboat blew him, Lizzie and the shotgun into a heap in the bottom of the boat.

Terry leaped into Lizzie's boat and wrestled the shotgun out of the pile. Then he backed away and pointed the gun at Rolvaag. He stood there tall and beaming at Lizzie with his best aw-shucks-ma'am-ain't-nothing-no-other-red-blooded-American-hero-wouldn't-have-done grin.

Lizzie grinned back for one second before she said, "I'd have taken the shotgun from him myself and fed it to him."

• • •

Rolvaag recognized the cops that had come to the bank today. Or yesterday, by now. He thought of something and looked at Blackbeard, who was standing in the airboat.

"Thank God you're here, officer," he said. "This woman just confessed to robbing and killing that poor fellow at the Hilton. Killed her own friend Captain Dave once he found out."

"Yeah," said Terry. "Like I believe this woman wants anything that isn't hers."

Lizzie smiled. But Rolvaag smiled, too.

"You may not believe it," he said, and his expression turned hard. "But I know some judges in Bay County that will."

Terry frowned. "You sit in the back where I can keep an eye on you." Rolvaag sat on the transom facing them, still tied to the rope.

"No," said Terry. "Turn around. I don't want you staring at us while we talk."

Rolvaag stared out at the water and smirked. Fabbi was gone. He could still come out of this all right.

"Talk, hell," said Lizzie. She put her foot into Rolvag's back and sent him into the water, stomped back to the cabin and threw the throttles open. Rolvaag bounced along from wave to wave behind them at the end of the rope.

Terry looked back at Rolvaag thrashing in the water. Blackbeard was still on the airboat. Blackbeard grabbed the stick and figured out how to drive well enough to catch up with Rolvaag, running alongside him. Terry wondered if Blackbeard was trying to see if Rolvaag was safe, or if he was trying to scare him. He walked over to Lizzie, who was at the wheel.

"Lizzie Gaffney," he whispered, just loud enough for her to hear. "As an agent of the law, I order you to stop this boat and help that poor man who fell overboard. As soon as it is safe and practicable, of course."

She looked back at him and beamed. He put his arm around her. Terry looked back and watched for a minute. Rolvaag didn't seem to be fighting quite as hard.

"Might want to bring him in and ask him how he's doing now."

Lizzie throttled back to idle and they went back to the transom. Terry handed the shotgun to Lizzie.

Terry started pulling the rope in and Blackbeard brought the airboat up beside them. Terry looked at Blackbeard and wondered if this fell under Blackbeard's definition of doing your job.

"Let's see how this plays out," said Blackbeard, holding on to Lizzie's boat to keep the two boats together.

Terry pulled Rolvaag out and set him back on the transom. Rolvaag was coughing water, but he was healthy enough to complain.

"She could have killed me," he gasped. "You're police officers. You've got to stop this."

Blackbeard looked at him with no expression. "I'm not a game warden. Never interfered with someone doing some honest shark fishing."

"Honest fishing?" said Rolvaag.

"Look at that," said Blackbeard, "talking bait."

"Besides," said Terry, picking up a rag and drying Rolvaag's head a little too roughly, "looked to me like you fell off, and this fine citizen saved you."

"He's right," said Blackbeard. "Look a there. Shark fin. She hadn't pulled you out when she did, you'd be reverse sushi."

"I don't see a fin," said Rolvaag.

"I do," said Terry, "Over there. Looks big, like a twenty-footer maybe. They don't get in the bay often, but when they do they get hungry fast."

Lizzie said, "Naw, that's just a ten-footer. See, the twenties, they get you, they bite you in half, it's over fast. Little ten-footer, they might chew on you all day."

"Course, we'd pull you out if that happened," said Terry.

"What was left of you anyway," said Lizzie.

"I don't see anything," said Rolvaag.

"Must be salt water in your eyes," said Terry. "Let me get it out so you can see." He rubbed the dirty rag hard into Rolvaag's eyes and Rolvaag yelled.

"Sorry," said Terry. He grinned at Rolvaag and shoved him like he was putting him back in the water. Rolvaag jumped and Terry laughed.

Blackbeard leaned over. "Like I said, I ain't going to interfere with a little fishing. Particularly shark fishing with the right bait. Mr. Rolvaag, my wife said you yelled, 'Florida Power' while you and your friend tried to assault her. Notice that Florida State Seminole flag in the front yard? There's a reason why some of us root for a team named after a tribe that people used to call murdering savages. It's because they fought for what was theirs before the rich pale outsiders got here."

"Lizzie," said Terry, "why don't you go back to the controls and get ready." He grabbed both of Rolvaag's shoulders solidly. Blackbeard pushed the airboat away.

"Wait," said Rolvaag. He paused and Terry let the moment hang in the air. "Fabbi did the murders. Fabbi's dad gave the orders. That ought to count for something."

"Might," said Blackbeard. "Depends on what you tell us."

Rolvaag told it all, after Blackbeard read him his rights. He got to the end and looked up at Blackbeard and said, "What happens to me now?"

"My guess, still some jail time," said Blackbeard. "And I arrest you for the murder of Jonathan Jefferson Carmex."

Rolvaag's face fell.

"Not to mention the assault on my wife," said Blackbeard.

Rolvaag looked shocked. "Isn't the victim of the assault usually the one with all the cuts, bruises and damage?"

"Not if they assault my wife."

Terry looked at Lizzie and said, "Florida women."

Lizzie grinned back and stood up. "Let's get that flying boat of yours in tow and go home."

Terry jumped over and got a line from the bow of the airboat, jumped back, and tied it off on a cleat on the stern of Lizzie's boat. Lizzie pushed the throttle forward and they headed back on a slow cruise.

The sun was coming up behind them and the smooth water looked like shimmering orange glass. The hum of the engine was the only sound they could hear. Terry put his arm around Lizzie and she smiled up at him.

When Terry looked back at Rolvaag sitting next to Blackbeard, he looked like a miserable pile of wet laundry. He pulled his arm away and sat down across from Blackbeard and Rolvaag.

"You still haven't told us much about the boys in Vegas," he said to Rolvaag.

Rolvaag snorted. "If I tell you what I know about them, they'll kill me, even in jail."

Lizzie looked back and said, "Might kill you anyway, once the story gets out that you're the ones who killed that man and took the money. They're going to be coming after you and nobody else."

Rolvaag looked shocked. "I didn't take the money. You took the money."

"Ain't the story we're going to tell. The bad mojo for that money is all yours now." She looked at Blackbeard and Terry, and they nodded.

Terry smiled at Rolvaag. "Course there might be a way for you to get out of this, find some place far away and start over clean. Give us enough information and they might put you in a relocation program somewhere."

Rolvaag brightened. "Like Atlanta?"

Blackbeard snorted. "Probably more like some little nowhere town in the middle of the desert, nothing to do but go to work in a little store every day, come home and watch TV. No money, no fancy chamber of commerce dinners, no bigwigs."

Rolvaag smiled at the thought. "Sounds like paradise. I'll talk." Then he paused and said, "Hey, but who's got the money?"

"Not me," said Blackbeard.

"Not me," said Terry.

Lizzie turned back from the wheel with a big smile. "And not me."

Rolvaag looked back and forth between the three of them. "Honest?" he said.

"Honest," they said in unison.

Blackbeard just looked at Lizzie and said, "Guess we'll never know." He paused. "For sure."

Lizzie grinned at Terry.

"I guess the money just disappeared into the economy," she said.

Blackbeard said, "Chamber of commerce ought to give someone a medal."

THE BOEING 737 BANKED TO THE LEFT and Terry looked out the window and saw Emerald Coast Beach laid out below him like a long fishhook. For a moment, he felt like someone had shifted the plane just for him, presenting him with a picture he should learn from. He saw that the arrogant man-made condos were now shrunk to the size of children's toys, all of them revealed to be fragile playthings kneeling before the vast and beautiful ocean they owed their existence to. He actually felt like a fragile creature himself, hung between the ocean and the sky like one of Lizzie's crabs that miraculously hung in the water.

ECB was quiet again these days. Rolvaag was in jail, Fabbi was gone, the Hole in the Beach was now filled with kids from all over the world learning to live together, and the chamber of commerce was once again all smiles. But there were storm clouds that only Terry saw. Storms coming in from the Chicago to the north and Vegas to the west. Sunshine and Progress both had new managers, hard men who scared even the C of C. There would be trouble, and soon.

He looked at Lizzie, who sat in the seat between him and the window. Her face was framed by the view of the place she loved. She was asleep, her face calm, looking like the beautiful child she really was. They were flying to L.A. for her first comeback concert. Her new CD was out, and was climbing the charts thanks to Third Coast Productions.

Terry had a guitar solo on one of the singles, and he was going to play with her band on the first big concert out west, maybe join her later for some others. Some people at the EC-BPD thought this was his chance to leave and be some kind of rock and roll hero.

Maybe. Maybe someday, but not now. The jet banked again and the gods of the sky gave Terry a different picture to consider. He looked past Lizzie down to the West End of ECB and saw his home in Portside. It was his home, and he would be the defender of it all against all the storms coming. The defender of it all, for now.

The plane banked a third time and gave him a view of Lizzie against a clear blue sky. He thought again how she looked like a little girl, a little girl who would always be under his skin, always be a part of him, and he wondered about their future, about what they really had.

A chance. Not some fairy-tale romance spun from sugar that would blow away in the first high wind, and not just come-and-go in the night. A chance. The best thing two human beings ever had.

The plane held Lizzie framed against the sky and he wondered what else the gods of the sky were trying to tell him. He looked at her face and saw the sunburn and the fine lines the old crowd in L.A. had never seen on her before. They would never know how she had earned them, or what they meant.

He wondered how her old fans would accept the changes, and then he smiled. They would love them. The wrinkles and the sunburn were honest.

Turn the page

for a bonus chapter

from Michael Guillebeau's
next book

THINGS TO DO WHEN YOU'D RATHER BE DEAD

one

SOMETIMES IT FEELS like you're drawn by a Looney Tunes cartoonist on a bad day.

Picture this: a second-grade classroom full of tiny human beings, each with ten times the frenetic energy packed in one-quarter of the size of the full-grown models. Running and bouncing for no reason other than that they can.

I sat at the front of the class, three-hundred-fifty pounds of obsolete cop teetering on a second-grader's chair; the wood creaking and moaning, threatening to go at any moment. The buttons on my too-small blue uniform threatening to join in, too.

Looney Tunes.

But I sat here, again, today, in front of a class of rug rats not much bigger than my hands, praying my chair won't break, or my buttons won't fly off like cartoon bullets, and the kids won't all run screaming for the door.

It didn't seem to bother the spiky-haired little girl hugging my leg as far as her arms could reach around it.

"He's my huggy bear," she said.

The teacher was a mournful-faced middle-aged woman. Probably sad-faced because of the way the years had pulled her body down until she looked like a pyramid on top of tiny scurrying feet. Or maybe because someone had shoved it all into a purple mu-mu like some kind of a bad cosmic joke.

Looney Tunes, on a bad day. But here she was, too.

I reached down to pat the girl on the head and the teacher pulled the girl away, "Jessi, today your huggy bear is a cop—police officer." The girl gave me a finger wave and a farewell smile.

I tried to return the smile. My smiles never come out right.

"Please don't make that face around the children," said Ms. Purple Tent.

Even the last woman who ever loved me had described my face as looking like an old-school prize fighter who had just lost a bad fight, and was sad about it. And that was a hundred pounds and several chins ago.

I did my best to look serious and presentable. I put on a blank face and sat completely still and completely expressionless with just my eyes flitting back and forth as I searched the little faces.

Purple Tent rapped a ruler on her desk and the faces all got quiet. Her mouth had the tight lines of someone who fought a losing battle every day to impose authority amid the rampant anarchy of the world. "OK, everybody, let's get quiet for—I'm sorry, what was your name?"

"Officer Joe. What's yours?"

I was trying to be friendly. The class giggled anyway.

The teacher had those angry lines again. "My name is Ms. Capulet. You need to give the class your proper rank and—"

"Just Officer Joe."

A huff. "Very well. Officer Joe." She turned back to the mob-in-training. "Class!"

There was silence again.

"Officer Joe has been sent here to tell you why you shouldn't do drugs."

She hissed at me. "As if we need this kind of fascist government crap in the second grade."

Out loud, she said. "They're all yours. I assume you have a presentation."

"I do." I started to stand up. Decided there was too much risk of winding up with a chair leg up my ass so I carefully and slowly reached over and picked up the spiral-bound poster boards our community outreach people had given me.

Jessi giggled. "You're funny." The class laughed with her.

"I try to please." More giggles.

I flipped to the first page. "This is Henry. He ate some drugs that the bad man there, named Alphonse, gave him, and now Henry doesn't feel good."

Ms. Capulet said, "Alphonse looks very dark-skinned. It's important to tell the children that the bad man could be any color."

Here in Birmingham, Alabama, most of the faces were what the white teacher politely called "dark-skinned." So was mine. But I didn't want to fight. Or digress.

"He certainly could. In fact, he could be a man or a woman, young or old, even a neighbor or a teacher."

The tent had sat down but now it stood up. "What's that supposed to mean?"

"Nothing. Just—look, I'm agreeing with you. I try to be honest with kids."

She snorted. "Go on."

I tried. Jessi waved her hand furiously. I felt like thanking her for the interruption, but I just nodded.

"Henry looks sick, like I look after my mom gives me medicine. Are drugs like medicine?"

"No. Well, yes, but not good medicine."

A boy slouched in the front jerked his chin at me, seven-year-old with teenaged attitude. "Medicine tastes bad. I won't take drugs if they taste bad."

I didn't want to lie.

"Well, sometimes people make them taste like candy."

"I like candy." He hesitated. "But they make you feel bad like Henry?"

I paused. "Well, yeah, eventually." I sighed. "But sometimes they make you feel good at first."

This wasn't going the way community affairs planned. It rarely did.

"Maybe," I said, "we should put off talking about drugs for right now. Let's talk about Henry being safe. If Alphonse tries to talk to you, what should you do?"

Tough Kid tilted his head to one side. "I'm going to ask him for drugs, if they taste like candy."

Ms. Capulet gave a harsh laugh, "Good work, Officer Joe." She turned to the boy. "Trey, you should tell your teacher if a strange man tries to talk to you."

I looked at Trey and tried to hold his eyes. "No. You should tell a police officer. Like me."

She said, "Teacher."

I said, "Cop."

She opened her mouth, but Jessi got the last word in. "What if Alphonse tries to grab me?"

I thought about what I would have told my own daughter. "Kick him in the balls as hard as you can and run away."

The class all giggled and Ms. Capulet rapped the table with her ruler. "Enough. I think we're going to lunch now."

Jessi said, "The bell hasn't rung. I want to talk to Huggy Bear."

"We're going to lunch early. Line up out in the hall and wait for me."

While the kids were filing out, I stood up as carefully as I could. I towered over Ms. Capulet and she seemed to take affront at my size and stepped into my space.

"Some job."

"Believe it or not, I'm trying."

She softened, a little. "The kids seem to love you, though."

"Younger ones, anyway," I said. "Older ones get suspicious of the uniform. I try to catch them before they reach that point. While I'm still a big huggy bear."

"Yeah. Kids are naïve and will trust anyone."
She waited for an argument and didn't get one.
"You really think kids should go to the police first,
tell on their parents and teachers? Beat people up
if they need to?"

"Yes."

"You really think the police can always help?"

"No."

She put her hands on her hips. "You can't teach
them self-defense yet. I don't think giving every
second grader an AK-47 or teaching them to kick
people in the balls will help."

"Kids are getting hurt every day. So-called
grownups aren't taking it seriously enough. AK-47s
might not be a bad idea."

She said, "You're not the one who has to super-
vise recess."

I laughed and looked at her to see if she thought
it was funny. Hard to tell.

She reached up and poked her finger into my
shoulder. "That's a detective rank, pretty high to be
doing community relations. Is this just a day of vol-
unteer work for you? Acting like you know
something about kids?"

"No."

"This is your full-time assignment? Basically a
clown in a cop suit?"

I thought about it. "Yes."

"Quite a comedown, wouldn't you say?"

"Probably."

"You weren't always called 'Officer Joe.'"

"No." She was waiting for more. "Detective Third Markowitz. Hard for kids to say."

"Hard for adults to believe."

"Yeah. People don't expect a guy who looks like a bad version of Sonny Liston to be named Markowitz. Blame my parents." It dawned on me that the name wasn't what she doubted. "Yeah, I know I don't look like a detective. Anymore." I wanted to change the subject entirely. "You know your police ranks."

"My dad was on the job. Brothers, too. We don't get many detectives in here for school officers."

"No." I didn't elaborate even when she waited. Finally, she won and I spoke first. "You seem to be older than the suspicious teenagers I talk to in the high schools. Not sure why you're so suspicious."

"Like I said, my father and brothers were and are cops. I know how you guys think."

We were both silent for a minute.

She broke first this time. "And, when I said the young kids love you, I'm not sure that's all good.

You do seem to take an unusual amount of interest in kids."

    I thought about it a long time.

    "Yes."

    I picked up my props and walked out the door.

Acknowledgements

ANYTHING WORTH YOUR TIME is a labor of love. And I've got to thank all of the wonderful people who loved Lizzie's book from my germ of an idea into what it is today.

John and Marian Conover are the first ones to love Lizzie enough to argue fiercely about every word of the book, starting with the first sentence. Marian won, and the book is better for it.

Then Kim Weldon Chambers, Cheryl Rydbom, Shawn Pethel and Bob Mecoy added comments and perspectives.

Lisa Wysocki, the world's greatest editor and equestrian, corrected mistake after mistake of mine tirelessly.

Donna Cunningham of Beaux Arts took my amateur concepts and created a cover whose beauty honors the name of her company, and my book. Thank you so much for revision after revision.

And Pat Leary Guillebeau always brings more love, to everything from beginning to end, than anyone else I've ever known.

I love you all for treating our baby with such love. Honestly.

.

about the author

MICHAEL GUILLEBEAU is the author of five novels and two short story anthologies. His last book, *MAD Librarian*, won the 2017 Foreword Reviews Indie Award for Humor. Guillebeau has published over twenty-five short stories, including three in *Ellery Queen's Mystery Magazine*. He lives in Madison, Alabama and Panama City Beach, Florida.